## LOCKER ROOM LUST

She'd known the moment Stryke looked her way, she was in deep-ass trouble. She should have left the locker room the moment she'd entered, but the possibility of seeing him up close swayed her heart to stay.

Stryke was a total *man-bite*, so delectable a woman could nibble on him all night long. Years ago, she'd nibbled, nuzzled, sucked…and fallen in love.

Love was not in the air now.

"Remove the costume." His deep, rough tone sliced through her thoughts and resonated low in her belly. His dark look indicated that if she didn't move fast, he'd rip the costume off her body.

So be it. If the man could stand before her in his boxers, she might as well strip down to her sports bra and panties….

# Kate Angell

# Strike Zone

LOVE SPELL     NEW YORK CITY

*To Chris J. Matarese, Strike Zone's for you.*
*To fans of Little League to Major League,*
*there's no better game in town.*

LOVE SPELL®

April 2008

Published by

Dorchester Publishing Co., Inc.
200 Madison Avenue
New York, NY 10016

ISBN 10: 0-505-52708-1
ISBN 13: 978-0-505-52708-0

The name "Love Spell" and its logo are trademarks of Dorchester Publishing Co., Inc.

Printed in the United States of America.

10 9 8 7 6 5 4 3 2 1

Visit us on the web at www.dorchesterpub.com.

## ACKNOWLEDGMENTS

To my editor, Alicia Condon—always appreciated.

Jean Lorenz, Angel's godmother.

Allie Mackay, author and close friend. Love your books!

Debbie and Ted Roome—thanks for being there.

Leigh Wilde, a lady of indomitable spirit.

# Strike Zone

# WELCOME TO
# JAMES RIVER STADIUM

## HOME OF THE RICHMOND ROGUES

### Starting Lineup

| 25 | RF | Cody McMillan |
| 18 | C | Chase Tallan |
| 11 | 3B | Jesse Bellisaro |
| 21 | CF | Risk Kincaid |
| 7 | SS | Zen Driscoll |
| 15 | 1B | Rhaden Dunn |
| 46 | LF | Kason Rhodes |
| 1 | 2B | James Lawless |
| 53 | P | Brek Stryker |

# PROLOGUE

*La Grave, France*

Skill.
  Speed and stamina.
  Guts.
  *Freedom.*
  Taylor Hannah delivered the skiing experience of a lifetime. Three extreme skiers had hit the slopes at dawn, following the region's biggest snowstorm. In the lead, she guided them down a mountain that ate people alive.
  A major adrenaline high kept her body aerodynamic as she blistered steep faces at warp speed. Only those who'd carved the slopes since birth dared La Grave. The majority of the adventure addicts and adrenaline junkies on the the mountain were male.
  As the sun's glare burned off the crackled glacier walls, the group traversed crevasses and rappelled into rocky couloirs piled with fresh powder. Off piste, there was no ski patrol or avalanche control. No boundaries. At their backs, the mountain of La Meije loomed like the grim reaper, waiting for nature's law to bring a man down.
  Far below, the forest line flashed into view. Beyond

that were the shadowed stone cottages of the twelfth-century French village.

Four hours had passed in the blink of an eye. Taylor sensed more than saw the weariness that overtook her group toward the end of the run. Even the strongest and most coordinated skier faced fatigue. Fatigue that would steal his focus.

The rush would soon wear off and their bodies would fold into chairs before the hotel fireplace. Mulled wine would warm their spirits. The Hotel L'Edelweiss would feed their hunger with a four-course spread that included fondue and tartiflette, a potato gratin with cheese, onion, and bacon.

Nearing the base, she shifted her skis perpendicular, snowplowing to a stop. Her pulse racing, her breath harsh puffs on the frosted air, she plunged her ski poles into the snow and pulled off her orange-lensed goggles. Her ski cap came next. She shook out her short blond hair.

Wind burned her sunscreened cheeks. Her lips were now chapped. Her body had grown overly warm beneath the layered ski gear. She pulled off a glove and unzipped her bright blue jacket, then released the bindings on her skis. The three men surrounding her did the same.

The skiers withdrew bottled water and PowerBars from their hydration packs. Taylor went with a handful of cherry jelly beans, her favorite snack.

"Total kamikaze." Blake Carter, a world-class snowboarder who'd taken to his skis, slapped his buddies on the back. "Free riding all the way, man."

Taylor grinned. The graduate students had challenged the elements and lived to tell about it.

"Freakin' insane. My life flashed before my eyes when we sidestepped down that rock rib." Matt Everett fought to catch his breath. "Lady, you're amazing."

She was her mother's daughter. Liv Hannah, a onetime Olympic gold medalist in downhill, had put Taylor on skis within days of her first steps. Over the years, Taylor had skied the world.

Her father, an Ironman triathlete, had groomed her in warmer climates. An outdoorsman of reknowned perseverance and strength, Stephan had competed in countless competitions. From Florida to California to Hawaii, he'd swum, biked, and run to the finish line. He believed in winning. And he had always pushed himself hard.

Now, at thirty-three, Taylor, along with her younger sister, Eve, faced the challenge of running Thrill Seekers, following their parents' untimely demise in a plane crash over the Amazon.

While Eve scheduled the tours from their Richmond office, Taylor guided daredevils and adventurers to off-map locales, just as her parents had done. She seldom returned to Virginia.

"Same time tomorrow?" Jason Cain nudged Taylor with his elbow. She blinked, returning to the moment. The young man's anticipation surprised her. Jitters had claimed him when he'd stepped from the *téléphérique*— nerves that could affect even the most seasoned skiers.

La Meije had a vertical drop of seven thousand feet, one of the steepest terrains in Europe. Taylor hadn't been certain whether Jason had the guts to make it downhill or if he'd return to the base on the aerial tramway.

When his buddies had called him "Snow Bunny," she'd stepped between the men. Goading Jason would serve no purpose. Fear was his enemy. The man would have to be in sync with the mountain to survive.

After several deep breaths and a long moment of silence, Jason had crossed himself twice, then pushed off with the rest of them.

He'd immediately hit cookies—clusters of rocks poking out of the snow—and managed to keep his legs. After the initial rough spot, he'd held his own. He'd hucked—thrown himself off cliffs—and caught big air along with Carter and Everett. He'd also produced the biggest bomb hole when he'd landed.

At the end of the day, there were no cuts, bruises, or blisters. No broken bones. Soreness came with the sport. All in all, it had been a good run.

"Grab dinner, a steam, and a massage," she instructed the men. "Get a solid eight hours' sleep. I'll meet you in the hotel lobby at seven sharp."

"See you, Fearless." Jason Cain winked, then trudged off with his buddies.

*Fearless* . . . The nickname stopped her heart. Another man, in another lifetime, had called her Fearless. No one had since. Sentiment and sadness claimed her so suddenly she massaged her chest, the memory of Brek Stryker a deep, dull ache.

"Mademoiselle Hannah." A man from the hotel staff approached her. He handed her a Federal Express mailer. "This just came for you. Urgent."

Taylor took the envelope and smiled her appreciation. L'Edelweiss valued the business Thrill Seekers brought to the hotel. The staff showed her every consideration. The return address was her sister's.

She propped her skis against a long bench where visitors could sit and view the dangerous, yet picturesque La Meije. Then quickly she ripped open the mailer.

Inside, she found a photocopy of an engagement announcement torn from the *Virginia Banner*. With each word, ice infused her bones beneath her layered ski gear. She shivered uncontrollably.

*Hilary Louise Talbott and Brek Stryker are pleased to announce their engagement. The bride-to-be is the daughter of Mayor Wayne and Alice Talbott and a graduate of Brown University in Providence, Rhode Island. Hilary is employed with the investment firm of Talbott and Myers. Brek is the son of Derek and Jayne Stryker and a graduate of the University of Virginia, Charlottesville, Virginia, and is a professional baseball player with the Richmond Rogues.*

Taylor's legs gave out and she dropped onto the bench. *Fearless.* She'd thought of Brek mere moments ago, and news of the man had followed right after.

News she'd rather not have read.

Stryke was getting married.

The man who had proposed to her three years ago was marrying someone else. Which he had every right to do. Taylor had left him at the altar.

She'd always thought she'd have time to go home and heal their shattered relationship. Brek had been the only man she'd ever loved, yet settling down had scared the hell out of her. He'd wanted marriage within months of the plane crash that took her parents' lives. He'd gone all concerned and protective, telling her to lean on him.

Taylor never leaned—on anyone at any time. She'd been taught by her parents to be strong. Independent. She'd needed her own space. Had needed time to grieve in her own way.

Everything that went into planning their wedding constricted her. Whether choosing the size of the church or going for the alterations on her satin and lace gown, she felt her life was no longer her own.

Without meaning to, Stryke had smothered her. Stable

and sane, he'd nearly killed her with his understanding and his need to make everything better.

Thrill Seekers had kept her alive.

She took up where her parents had left off. Throughout the engagement, she continued to guide adrenaline junkies on the most dangerous adventures imaginable. She pushed the envelope, seeking out the remote and undiscovered.

On her wedding day, she'd done the unthinkable. The church had been booked and decorated for a one-o'clock ceremony. At high noon, Taylor had hopped a plane for the World Paragliding Championships in New South Wales.

She'd never forgiven herself for leaving Brek at the altar. She should have handled things differently.

She was long overdue in offering an apology.

Perhaps the time was now.

Before he married another woman.

# CHAPTER ONE

"Rally Ball's checking you out, Stryke." Right fielder Psycho McMillan snapped his towel toward the corner of the locker room, where the Richmond Rogues' mascot peered over the low partition separating them from the trainers' tables. "Charlie Bradley wants you bad," Psycho teased, referring to the man who performed as Rally.

Brek Stryker slowly turned. Psycho's comments were as crazy as the man himself. Yet there was no hiding for the giant fuzz ball, nor any discreet peeking. The costume stuck out among the players, a big white baseball with red stitching. Leg- and armholes showcased long red-and-blue-striped sleeves and matching tights. The team mascot dipped and bobbed, drawing attention to itself.

Showered and shaved, relief pitcher Sloan McCaffrey toweled off his chest. "Charlie's not himself today."

"Definitely not himself." Third baseman Romeo Bellisaro stepped into a pair of knife-creased khakis. "Man's lost weight. His tights are baggy."

"He grunts like a girl." Psycho slipped on a black T-shirt scripted with *Nude 'Tude*. The man preferred to be naked.

Stryke stared at his teammates. "Bullshit."

"No joke," Sloan returned. "Charlie was all over the

baseline today, tipping and tripping like he was drunk."

"Man doesn't drink." Stryke knew that for a fact. Bradley was a seasoned mascot and a good friend.

"Does he wear nail polish? Perfume?" asked Sloan.

Stryke shook his head. "Never happen."

Sloan lowered his voice and nodded toward their mascot. "You're the team captain. Walk by Rally. Red nails and do-me perfume."

Stryke didn't have time for such nonsense. He had dinner plans with his fiancée and her parents. Punctuality was part of the program. He didn't need to be held up by a team prank.

Bare chested, his black silk boxers low on his hips, he sauntered toward Rally Ball. The mascot froze, then began to back up—slowly at first, then much more quickly. Ten steps, and Rally bumped and bounced off a wall and banged into Stryke's chest.

They both grew still as the red stitching pressed his pecs. A too-close-for-comfort brush between men. Stryke nudged the mascot back. Annoyance filled his growl. "What the hell, Charlie?"

Wiggle. Wiggle. Rally Ball squirmed, once again rubbing Stryke with fuzz and stitching. The mascot's roundness now grazed his abdomen and groin.

*Whoa, buddy. Way too familiar.*

Stryke grabbed the mascot's arms. Slender, toned arms, not burly, like those of Charlie Bradley.

He looked down at the fuzz ball's hands. Claw-a-man's-back red tipped the nails on clenched fingers. Confused, he pulled back and openly stared at the mascot's red-and-blue tights.

Baggy tights, all wrinkled at the knees and pooling at the ankles. The blue Converse high-tops looked big and clumsy, like clown shoes.

There was no scent of sweat on Charlie today. Only a heady sensual fragrance, all sunshine and warm-the-sheets sexy: Amber Nude, a scent he recognized from long ago. The cologne had once seduced and driven him crazy on the neck of . . .

His jaw locked, and his gaze narrowed on the eye slits of the costume. Wide, uncertain, sea green eyes replaced the brown of Bradley's.

*Taylor Hannah.*

Stryke's heart slammed and his body tightened. He swore he'd have a crippling charley horse or a full-blown coronary. Three years had passed since she'd left him at the altar. Instead of an ivory lace gown, she now faced him in a fuzz ball costume.

He shook his head disbelievingly. "No way in hell."

He was a man who used his body competitively, but he couldn't move a muscle. Time lengthened as he stood stunned and rigid. Not until Psycho yelled, "Need help?" did Stryke's breath hiss through his teeth, releasing him to take action.

"I'm fine," he shouted over his shoulder as he grabbed Taylor by the elbow, more roughly than he'd intended. He half walked, half dragged her down the hallway to the mascot lounge.

Once inside, he slammed the door so hard the glass shook. He jerked down the shade and turned the lock. Before him now, Taylor stood stiffly, her arms crooked over her rounded sides, her legs braced.

"Damn, woman, this has to be the stupidest stunt ever," he snarled. "What are you doing here? And why are you dressed as Rally?"

Taylor had to agree with Brek Stryker—this was a stupid stunt. She hadn't rallied well. The costume was big, bulky, and sauna hot. Despite her flexibility and coordination, she'd spent more time weaving and wobbling than rousing the fans. Had it not been for a bat boy coming to her rescue, she'd have rolled into the Rogues' dugout.

At game's end, she'd gotten caught in the players' exit. She'd staggered down the steps, struggled along the tunnel, then stumbled through the set of double doors that led to the locker room. The room was deep and wide and modern.

Rally Ball had *roll*. Before she'd found a hiding place, she'd wobbled around and gotten an eyeful.

Broad shoulders.

Bare chests.

Six-packs.

Tattoos.

Athletic supporters.

And penises. So many penises.

While Taylor embraced life and all its experiences, her pulse rioted and her entire body blushed. From behind the low partition, she'd witnessed men in all states of undress. All handsome as hell and comfortable in their skin.

She wasn't a prude. She did, however, know better than to invade an entire team's privacy. She'd shut her eyes.

Eventually, the scents of soap and aftershave replaced that of sweaty male bodies. She'd peered through the eye slits and noticed that most of the Rogues now wore boxers or briefs. A few let freedom ring. All around her the men discussed their evening plans. She knew many of the older players from the time she'd dated Stryke: Risk Kincaid, Zen Driscoll, and the Bat Pack—Psycho, Romeo, and Chaser, who played catcher. The younger players she recognized from the occasional sports magazine and televised game.

Locating Brek had been easy. At six-foot-four and testosterone driven, he was the embodiment of baseball. A pitcher like him came along only every twenty, maybe thirty years. Few batters laid wood on his blazing fastball and sharp slider. He'd won the Cy Young Award five times, as well as seven Gold Gloves.

He had a strong presence both on and off the field, maintaining a variety of business, charity, and personal interests in the community.

Rogues fans loved him. Bred and born in Richmond, he was one of their own. Once, he'd belonged to her.

An unexpected sigh had escaped as she'd taken him in, from his cropped brown hair to the bold line of his eyebrows. Sun lines slashed near his eyes. His cheeks were lean, his chin formidable.

She'd stared openly at his athletic build, from the breadth of his shoulders to his size-fourteen feet. The shadowed shift of his sex between his thighs flirted with her as he'd toweled off and tugged on his boxers.

The man was generously sized.

He looked hot in his Rogues uniform. Hotter still in silk boxers. She'd wondered if he remained ticklish just below his ribs. If he would still get hard if she blew softly on his belly.

It had taken Psycho's snap of the towel and a nod in her direction for Taylor to blink. She'd known the moment Stryke looked her way that she was in deep-ass trouble. She should have left the locker room the moment she'd entered, but the possibility of seeing him up close had swayed her heart to stay.

Stryke was a total man-bite, so delectable a woman could nibble on him all night long. Years ago she'd nibbled, nuzzled, sucked . . . and fallen in love.

Love was not in the air now.

"Remove the costume." His deep, rough tone sliced through her thoughts and resonated low in her belly. His dark look indicated that if she didn't move fast, he'd rip the costume off her body.

So be it. If the man could stand before her in his boxers, she might as well strip down to her sports bra and panties. Charlie Bradley had warned her when she'd rented the costume to wear next to nothing inside Rally. In no more than Barely There underwear, she'd still perspired profusely. She swore she'd lost five pounds.

So much for her best-laid plans. The silence was getting on her nerves. Sweat dripped off her brow and onto her eyelids. Her eyes burned and would soon be bloodshot.

She toed off the high-tops, then went to work on the long stretch of zipper that ran beneath her left armpit, down and over the curve of her hip. A zipper that soon stuck below her breast.

Frustrated and all thumbs, she twisted, strained, and swore beneath her breath as the metal teeth bit and bruised her skin. It had been so much easier getting into the costume than it was getting out.

"Little help here," she finally requested.

Stryke bent toward her. "Raise your arm."

Up went her arm and down came his hand. His knuckles brushed the soft underside of her breast as he prodded and pulled on the zipper. Her nipple puckered and her heart pounded so hard and fast, her chest hurt. The slide of the metal teeth soon bared her to him. She caught the shift of his jaw, the narrowing of his eyes as he stood back and watched her peel off the costume down to her black bra and matching boy shorts.

She felt like a stripper. The slide of the red-and-blue sleeves down her arms, followed by the unrolling of the baggy tights, held his slate blue gaze. As did the big bruise on her inner thigh and the ACE bandage that wrapped her left knee. She'd taken a tumble on the slopes her last day on La Meije. Her mind had been on Stryke and not the sharp dogleg that made the mountain treacherous.

Now, beneath a flickering overhead light, they both stood in their underwear. The situation was as familiar as it was strange, because both their lives had changed. She was seeking his forgiveness, and he looked far from forgiving.

Nudging the costume aside with her foot, she curled her bare toes against the white-tiled floor. She waited for Stryke to meet her gaze.

He finally looked up. His expression was stone cold.

She shivered. Long gone was any hint of a smile, any ounce of warmth. The man was closed to her.

The moment stretched, thinned, finally broke when he demanded, "Where's Charlie Bradley?"

"I have no idea." Which was the truth. "I offered him three hundred dollars to rent Rally for the weekend. He mumbled something about overdue child support and a trip to Norfolk."

"You *rented* Rally?"

Crossing her arms over her chest, she went on the offensive. "You have a problem with that?"

Confusion creased his brow. "Why would you pull such a stunt?"

*Because I heard you were getting married and wanted to see you one last time as a single man.* "I seek thrills."

He snorted. "Tell me something I don't know."

He deserved an explanation. "I arranged to have a cab bring me here and entered the stadium through the gate near the bullpen. Security let me pass with a flash of Charlie's identification badge. The guards believed I was their veteran mascot. The taxi driver was going to pick me up after the game. I'd planned to sneak out of the park without anyone noticing. Winding up in the locker room was a fluke."

"What brought you to Richmond?" He'd drawn a line between them, and she was trespassing in his town.

She had the perfect excuse. "Addie's birthday. My grandmother turns eighty next weekend. Eve and I are throwing her a party."

"After the party?"

"Desert hiking across the Sahara."

"Pack sunscreen."

She'd be less exposed then than she was now. "Any chance I could borrow a pair of your sweats?" she asked. "I hadn't planned to get caught, nor to face you. I was going to wear the costume home, not strip down to my underwear in the mascot lounge."

Brek Stryker ran one hand down his face. He and Taylor stood in an uncomfortable and compromising position. Even though the door was locked, the trainers and maintenance men had keys. Someone could walk in at any time. He was an engaged man. Being caught nearly naked with a previous fiancée would trigger gossip he didn't need. He wanted Taylor gone.

He took in her tousled blond bangs, sea green eyes, and kissable lips. Years ago, he'd never missed an opportunity to make love to her mouth.

He wondered if she still tasted like the cherry jelly beans she'd always carried in her pocket.

Shaking off the thought, he said, "I'll see what I have in my locker."

Tension hummed through his body and echoed in his ears as he left the lounge. His muscles remained so tight, he felt like the Tin Man.

He found the locker room empty, his teammates long gone. He had fifty minutes to cut Taylor from his life and connect with his fiancée.

Hilary Louise had been on his mind when Psycho snapped his towel and nodded toward Rally. She was a soft-spoken woman, sweet and unassuming, and always available when he called.

Employed by her uncle, Hilary dealt in stocks and bonds and investment portfolios. Outside of work, she gardened and dabbled in pastels. She'd never once proved a distraction to him.

That he valued most. She made no demands on his life. Hilary didn't follow baseball, yet she understood his need to succeed. This was the year he could surpass several major-league records held by his father, Derek, who'd once pitched professionally for the Ottawa Raptors.

Sportscasters were eating up the father-son statistics. With each start, they pulled out the record book, ready to write his name one line above his old man's.

Stryke needed every ounce of concentration.

It was time to best his father. And Derek would be cheering him on loudest of anyone in the stands.

Facing Taylor had resurrected old times and bad memories. His first glimpse of her had hit so fast, he hadn't had time to brace himself. She'd gutted him once again. He hated the fact that her thrill seeking affected him so strongly. He'd be counting down the days to her North African departure.

Lifting a white T-shirt and pair of gray sweatpants from his locker, he returned to the mascot lounge. He tossed her his clothes.

"Shower and dress," he said flatly.

"And you'll show me the door?"

He nodded. "I'll be in the locker room when you've finished."

"Maybe then we can talk."

*Talk? No way in hell.* "I've nothing to say to you, Taylor."

"I owe you an explanation."

"You're three years too late."

She looked as if she were about to argue the point, but instead remained silent—for which he was grateful. There wasn't a reason she could give that would set things right between them. Not after all this time.

His life with her was over.

From the corner of his eye, he watched her walk to the mascot shower. Her banged-up body surprised him. He'd caught the bruises and ACE bandage on her knee. He'd tamped down his concern. She could take care of herself.

Taylor shut the door, and his breath rushed out. It took little imagination on his part to visualize her movements. He'd watched her undress countless times when they'd lived together. At that very moment, she'd be unfastening her bra. She had a slow, sexy way of slipping the straps off her shoulders that allowed her breasts to fall freely from the cups. She'd raise her arms over her head and stretch out her spine until it cracked, then draw down her boy shorts.

In the stillness, he was certain he'd heard her panties drop.

He felt his dick harden in memory of her sleek and sinewy body. Taylor Hannah was as kick-ass as she was feminine. She'd always embraced shower sex with eucalyptus gel, steam, and pink-skinned slickness. She'd remained hot even after the water ran cold.

His curse colored the air. Disgusted with himself,

Stryke left her to the warm spray and walked stiff-legged to his locker. He needed time and whatever distance he could manufacture between them to clear his head.

Time was not on his side. Taylor came to him quickly. She scuffed across the locker room in the mascot's too-large sneakers, her body lost in his clothes. His XXL T-shirt hung to her knees. She'd cuffed his sweatpants three times over her calves.

As if time had stood still and she belonged in his life, she dropped down on the bench and watched him dress.

Ignoring his glare, she focused on his groin. "I always loved your tat."

His tattoo from his rookie year, small, yet representative of his pitching career. Taylor had modeled for the drawing. Beneath a miniskirt, a pair of shapely legs spread over home plate, a baseball thrown and centered between her thighs. *Strike Zone* was scripted between her red stilettos.

His tattoo had lasted longer than their relationship.

He nodded toward the double doors. "Feel free to leave." She'd left him once; she could do so again. He didn't need an audience while he dressed.

"Yeah . . . I could." But she didn't move.

He tugged on a pair of black cargo pants, then reached for a cream-colored polo. Then he slipped on leather loafers, without socks.

Still, she sat, her gaze on him. He noticed the wariness in her eyes and the weariness etched on her features. She suddenly looked tired.

He'd never seen her less than supercharged.

"Point me to a phone and I'll call another cab," she finally requested. "My ride's long gone. I'll need a loan to get me home." She patted her thighs. "I didn't bring a purse to the park. I'll pay you back when I return your T-shirt and sweats."

"Keep the clothes." Their reunion was over. "There's no need to repay me. I'd prefer our paths didn't cross a second time."

"But they will, Stryke," she told him straight out. "One more time. I'm Rally again tomorrow."

His stomach clutched. "Not going to happen."

"It will happen. Charlie's out of town and the Rogues need a mascot. I've got Rally down now. I can control the roll. I'll have better balance next time."

"You're *not* going back on the field."

"Who's going to stop me?"

It was an open challenge. During their time together, she'd issued so many. Challenges he'd won more often than lost, but he hadn't been engaged to another woman then.

Stryke didn't want Taylor parading as Rally. He was scheduled to start against the Raptors. A glimpse of her wobbling like a Weeble would prove too damn distracting from the mound.

He jammed his hands in his pockets, broadening his stance, and went for intimidating. "I'll tell management that Charlie's sick."

She wasn't afraid of him. "I'll phone Guy Powers and offer to replace him."

She had him by the balls—and knew how to squeeze. They were both aware that the team owner adored her. Powers admired bold, beautiful, free-spirited women— women like his first wife, Corbin, whom he'd divorced when the competition between them as rival team owners separated them as widely as the American and National Leagues.

Corbin refused to sell the Louisville Colonels. And Powers lived and breathed the Rogues. Ultimately, baseball meant more to them than their wedding vows.

Powers had sympathized with Stryke when Taylor had left him at the altar. But he also said he understood Taylor's feelings.

Stryke didn't share Powers's empathy.

Taylor Hannah had ditched him before one thousand guests. Her departure had cut him sharp and deep, and he'd nearly bled out. He'd canceled the reception, then cashed in their honeymoon package to Parrot Cay for half its value.

His good buddies, center fielder Risk Kincaid and shortstop Zen Driscoll, along with their wives, Jacy and Stevie, had helped him pack up and post every gift. It had taken three weeks, six days, and two hours to clear the wedding presents from his living room and foyer.

Taylor had fractured his ego.

She'd made him look a fool in front of his friends.

Worst of all, she'd broken his heart.

He'd never let her near him again.

Nor would he put Guy Powers between them. He had too much respect for the man to involve him in their dispute.

Fixing Taylor with a stern look, he warned, "Go ahead and play Rally. However, if you so much as wobble within a foot of my peripheral vision, I'll have security haul your ass—"

She flashed her palm. "I get the picture."

He unclipped his cell phone from a side pocket on his cargo pants and tossed it to her. "Make your call."

She dialed the cab company from memory. By the end of the conversation, she was frowning. "My taxi won't arrive for thirty to forty minutes."

"I don't have time to wait."

"I can wait by myself."

Dusk cast shadows over the stadium and empty parking

lot. No matter how anxious he was to send Taylor on her way, he couldn't leave her alone. It wasn't safe.

"I'll give you a ride," he finally decided.

"Harley or McLaren?"

"I now drive an SUV."

"A family man's car."

He saw it in her eyes then; she knew he was engaged. He'd figured the news would reach her eventually. But he had no intention of discussing his present engagement with his ex-fiancée. "Let's go. I'm late for my dinner date."

"No reason to keep the lady waiting."

"No reason at all."

He followed Taylor through the double doors, separated from her by silence and their years apart. He cut a glance to the woman by his side. Dressed in his T-shirt and sweatpants, she appeared to belong to him—which rode his last nerve.

Once seated in his Cadillac Escalade, he asked, "Where to?"

"Thrill Seekers."

"On John Adams Parkway?"

She shook her head. "The business moved last week. We're in the same historical landmark building as Jacy's Java."

His jaw worked. The coffee shop was his first stop in the morning and oftentimes his last one at night. Years ago, he and Taylor had been Jacy's best customers. He'd continued the coffee tradition long after she'd gone.

For two years and four months, he'd ordered an Americana, then sat and read the newspaper. Each new arrival had drawn his gaze. He'd continued to hope Taylor would breeze through the door, as in need of her caffeine fix as she would be of him.

He'd waited and waited.

She'd never shown.

Now, with Thrill Seekers in the same building, chances were good he'd run into her at least once during her stay. Taylor liked her coffee.

That did not please him. At all. He'd hardened his heart against this woman. She could buy her own iced lattes and raspberry scones. Game face on for the next seven days. Taylor would never hit another home run off him. The lady had struck out.

# CHAPTER TWO

The sun baked the sidewalk outside Jacy's Java. An unusually warm spring day had brought out tank tops, shorts, and sandals. Taylor Hannah knew she'd be perspiring freely in the mascot costume later that afternoon. She needed to figure out a way to stay cool.

She stopped short outside the coffee shop and debated going inside. Brek Stryker's SUV was parked at the curb. She didn't know whether he was alone or with his fiancée. She preferred not to face him before her first cup of coffee, especially as he'd given her no more than a curt nod when he'd dropped her off at Thrill Seekers the previous evening. His indifference cut deep.

With one hand on the elongated brass door handle, Taylor inhaled deeply. The strong scent of coffee and freshly baked goods drew customers like a beckoning finger. The enormous picture window revealed a crowd inside. Some customers sat while others stood. All were enjoying their favorite blend.

Inching the door open, she slid in behind the last person in line, a big, bald man in a business suit. He completely dwarfed her. If she stayed in his shadow, no one would notice she was there.

Ever so discreetly, she looked around the gourmet café,

absorbing the ambience. In her absence, Jacy had gone retro—wildly so. The shop pulsed with her eclectic tastes. Geometric shapes, pop art, and psychedelic paintings, along with an enormous atomic sunburst wall clock, decorated bright orange walls—walls that awakened the coffee crowd as quickly as a double espresso.

Mushroom chairs in funky gray velour, olive green Lucite seats on casters, and white vinyl swan chairs with high backs and wide armrests were tucked into boomerang-style Formica tables and pulled up to solid wooden cubes.

Plexiglas terrariums sat on every tabletop. Vintage metal newspaper racks stood on the floor with a collection of papers and glossy magazines. Subdued lighting from chrome hanging lamps with frosted white bulbs created a feeling of intimacy. Lava lamps at the ordering station drew customers' smiles.

Taylor's gaze darted to the darker corners. She needed to locate Stryke before he noticed her, then fly beneath his radar.

She found him at a triangular table, alone, all game-day casual in a white knit shirt and blue jeans; he was reading the newspaper. Six of his teammates were gathered nearby, seated around a 1950s-style diner table with a shiny grooved aluminum edge. Taylor recognized Risk Kincaid, Zen Driscoll, Psycho McMillan, and Cooper Smith—men who set the standard for fair play and athleticism.

The unwritten rule—never disturb a starter on his day to pitch—was upheld here. The men honored Brek's privacy and need for mental preparation. They left him to his paper.

Since no one other than Stryke knew she was in town, she could order her iced hazelnut latte and scone and hit the door without being noticed. She crowded up against the man ahead of her, who cut her an annoyed look. Taylor willed the line to move a little faster.

If anything, the line slowed. After a second furtive glance at Brek, she breathed easier. He was still buried in the news. She'd seen no sign of Jacy Kincaid.

She had almost reached the ordering station when Jacy pushed through the kitchen doors and spotted her. *"Taylor Hannah?"* Her voice carried from the cappuccino machine across the coffee shop. "You're home!"

Taylor winced. Her cover was blown big-time.

So much for keeping a low profile.

She looked at Stryke and saw him square his shoulders and clench his jaw. When he located her in line, he held her gaze for ten long seconds before returning to the comics. She'd been openly dismissed. He'd chosen Garfield over her.

Taylor nearly folded. Her breath rasped out, and she locked her knees so they wouldn't buckle. Jacy Kincaid's warm welcome soothed her ragged nerves. They hugged like two lost sisters, finding each other after three long years.

Jacy would always be Jacy, with her metallic blue hair, dangling red earrings, and generous smile. She was as eclectic as her coffee shop in her burgundy velvet jacket and tuxedo-yoke blouse. She'd stuffed the hem of her pink corduroys into knee-high brown leather slouch boots with studded cuffs. The lady made her own fashion statement.

Jacy immediately tugged Taylor out of line and customer earshot. "When did you get home? How long can you stay? Have coffee with me?" Her words tripped over one another.

Taylor couldn't help smiling. She and Jacy had grown

close during Taylor's engagement to Stryke. Jacy had been one of few who'd remained her friend following the wedding fiasco. They'd exchanged letters and phone calls over the years.

"I arrived in Richmond two days ago. I'm here through next weekend. We'll have coffee later this week," Taylor assured her. "Just not today."

Jacy nodded toward the corner of the shop. "Have you seen Stryke? Spoken to him?"

Confession was good for the soul. She lowered her voice. "He caught me playing Rally Ball at yesterday's game. I'd wanted to see him one more time before he got married, and hoped to go unnoticed. Unfortunately, I was discovered. Stryke had me stripping off the costume in the mascot lounge, down to my bra and panties—an unsettling way to face off with the man I left at the altar."

Jacy covered her mouth and choked back a laugh. "Talk about tense moments."

"He's engaged. He had no time for me."

Jacy looked at her intently. "Can't really blame him, can you?"

"The blame was all mine," Taylor admitted. Her stomach twisted on her next request. "Tell me about Hilary Louise Talbott."

"A need to know?"

"A want to know."

Jacy understood. "Hilary has brown hair and eyes, and is petite and curvy," she began slowly. "She's heavily involved in her father's mayoral campaign. I don't believe she works out or is the least bit athletic. She's quiet, analytical, and a homebody. She teaches Sunday school, loves kids. She'd never take the road less traveled. She's quite dedicated to Stryke. She defers to him on all decisions. Hilary is sweet and—"

"Predictable." Taylor's breath hissed through her teeth. "Hilary and I are complete opposites."

Jacy nodded. "Pretty much so."

"Is Hilary"—she could barely get the words out—"the love of his life?"

Her friend shrugged. "There are many kinds of love. You and Stryke sparked so much heat, I'd fan myself. With Hilary, there's a softer warmth. She's kind and comfortable and—"

"Reliable. She won't leave him at the altar," Taylor finished for her.

"He doesn't deserve to be left a second time," Jacy stated. "Stryke's a good man."

"Too good for me." Taylor sighed. "I should be happy for him."

"But you're not." Jacy read her well. "You have regrets and need closure."

"It's hard to wrap up loose ends when Stryke wishes me gone."

Jacy looked toward the players, then linked arms with Taylor. "Hmm, perhaps he's not as indifferent as he might seem. There's more than one Rogue checking you out. Stryke's given you as many slanted glances as Sloan McCaffrey has direct ones. Come meet Sloan. He's the new reliever. He's cocky and conceited, and would do himself if he was able."

Taylor resisted. "I'll meet Sloan some other day."

"Make it today," Jacy insisted. "Risk," she called to her husband. "May we join you?"

Taylor stiffened. Never one to be embarrassed, she now blushed. She didn't want attention drawn to herself. And Risk's obvious uncertainty did little to reassure her. The Rogues were as close as a fraternity. She'd screwed over one of their own. There was no love for her from the team. Nor forgiveness after three years.

A man hot for his wife and still eager to please her, Risk waved them over. Taylor knew that if anyone other than Jacy had requested they join the group, Taylor would've been turned away.

"Iced hazelnut latte?" Jacy asked.

"And a raspberry scone," she added. "The only two constants in my life."

Once Jacy served both coffee and scone on ivory china, the two women crossed to the table of players. Jacy placed a reassuring hand on Taylor's shoulder, squeezing lightly. Introductions followed. "Risk, Zen, Psycho, and Cooper Smith you already know. You've yet to meet relief pitcher Sloan McCaffrey and first baseman Rhaden Dunn. This is Taylor Hannah, a close friend. She's in town for a week. Play nice, guys."

*Nice* came in sideways glances, quick sips of coffee, and a rolling of shoulders. Casting a glance at Brek, Risk added one chair to the table—a chair meant for Jacy. Taylor stood off to the side.

At an unexpected call from one of her employees, Jacy returned to the front counter, which left Taylor alone with the six Rogues. Six *reserved* Rogues. Though not outwardly rude, Risk, Zen, Psycho, and Coop nodded hello, but didn't extend an invitation to sit. Sloan and Rhaden took their cue from the veterans and stared her down.

Despite the fact that she'd tackled the Alaskan Iditarod and rafted the Brahmaputra River in India, these men posed an even bigger challenge. She was an outsider with no way in. Their loyalty lay with Stryke. She'd once hurt their starting pitcher. No one trusted her now.

She brushed invisible lint from her white poet's shirt

and shifted her stance. Twice. The unnerving silence told her all she needed to know. So much for relaxing with her iced coffee and scone. It was time to go.

She'd taken one step toward the door when the sudden snap of a newspaper page cut the tension at the table. The sound came from Brek Stryker as he flipped from comics to sports. The snap seemed to be a message to his teammates. Its effect on the players was immediate.

They made nice to her.

"Gotten naked lately?" asked Psycho, wearing a black T-shirt scripted with *Born to be Nude*. He claimed a chrome-backed chair from a nearby table and crammed it between himself and Sloan McCaffrey.

Shaken by the turn of events, Taylor was slow to reply. "You're the nudist," she finally managed. "You show enough skin for ten men."

Psycho grinned and patted the red vinyl seat beside him. "Park it, Fearless." He dared to call her by her nickname—a nickname given to her by Brek Stryker.

She sucked in her breath and squeezed into the narrow space, protective of—

"Watch her knee." Stryke's warning rose over her shoulder as he stood, coffee mug in hand. Edging by their table, he strolled toward the counter for a refill.

Psycho tracked Stryke, then turned back to Taylor, narrow eyed. He was obviously contemplating how their team captain knew she had a bad knee. The ACE bandage wasn't visible beneath her mocha linen slacks. Ignoring the pain, she hadn't been limping.

Psycho was usually so blunt, he made people blink. But he respected Stryke, and for the first time in his life he didn't raise questions. Taylor appreciated his discretion. Easing back, Psycho gave her plenty of room to maneuver.

She collapsed into the chair and attempted to sort out

what had just happened. For whatever reason, Stryke had come to her rescue. His acceptance had been signaled by the snap of the newspaper. He'd allowed her to have coffee with his teammates. He'd also protected her knee.

She met his gaze as he sauntered back toward her. What a difference a few minutes could make. His return expression was hard, all steely eyed and lockjawed, as if his moment of concern were a major lapse in judgment. One he now regretted.

She hid her disappointment by turning a smile on Sloan McCaffrey. Sloan took it as a come-on and shifted his chair closer, so the chrome legs of both overlapped.

"You single?" he immediately asked.

McCaffrey wasn't aware of her history with Stryke. Apparently locker room gossip had died before he'd joined the team.

She broke off a piece of her scone and took a small bite. "Most certainly am."

"Interested in more than coffee?" he asked, openly making a move on her in front of his teammates. He was all Rogue, assuming she'd go weak in the knees to date him.

Sloan was younger than she by several years; his life experience didn't equal her own. Taylor sought maturity.

Psycho immediately put Sloan in his place. "The lady's a thrill seeker. She's fearless. Taylor doesn't flirt with men, only with danger. Danger that would make you piss your pants."

Sloan wasn't the least bit put off by Psycho. He leaned his elbows on the table, his shoulder brushing Taylor's own. "Extreme sports are a turn-on. I'm looking for an adrenaline addiction. The lady looks like a total free fall."

"Book a trip at Thrill Seekers, two doors down," suggested Zen "Einstein" Driscoll. A tall, lean man, he was known for his intensity, intelligence, and skill as a shortstop. "Taylor's the best guide around."

"I'll stop in sometime," Sloan said, probably expecting her to hold her breath until he showed. "Maybe book a trip for the off-season."

If he did come to Thrill Seekers, looking for more than an outdoor adventure, Taylor would set her sister, Eve, on him. Eve knew who was showboating and who was serious, and her sarcasm shriveled a man's danglers.

Taylor sensed that Sloan wasn't a bad guy. He just came on too strong. She had the ability to read people quickly; she had to in her business. A person showed his true colors within seconds of facing down a mountain or running with the bulls in Pamplona. She knew when to push a man forward or pull him back from disaster.

McCaffrey was a diamond in the rough. His white T-shirt had yellowed around the collar, and he needed a shave. He was the type of man who didn't stick around long enough for a woman to add bleach to his wash nor Downy to the rinse cycle. Softness wasn't a part of his life.

When he fell for a woman, he'd fall hard.

Taylor wasn't about to encourage his attention.

She handed the conversation over to Psycho, allowing the players to talk statistics and upcoming games.

Thirty minutes passed quickly. She sensed more than saw Stryke's gaze on her. His occasional glance was nerveracking. Jacy eventually rejoined the group. The discussion shifted to wives and children. Jacy admitted she and Risk were working on a family. *Work* drew Risk's grin. Taylor foresaw beautiful babies in their future.

Seconds later, when Psycho gestured with his left hand, Taylor caught the flash of his gold wedding band. The wild man had gotten married.

Poking Psycho in the ribs, she wished him well. "Congratulations. Who's the lady?"

"I married my restoration designer, Keely Douglas." Heat flashed in his eyes as he spoke of his woman. "I took on a deteriorating Colonial, two orphaned Newfoundlands, and the spirit of Col. William Lowell. Keely pulled our lives together."

"Romeo and Chaser have also married," Jacy told her. "Last year Romeo backed into sports reporter Emerson Kent on Media Day during a team brawl. After a rough start, she found him newsworthy, and he stopped running from the press. Chaser married his longtime neighbor, Jen Reid."

Taylor hadn't met either Keely or Emerson, but she knew Jen. The woman had a dancer's body and a positive outlook. She'd prove a stable force in Chaser's life.

Life had moved forward for these men. They'd found women to love. Everyone seemed so damn happy.

Everyone but her.

The scrape of a chair turned the players' attention to Stryke. He stood now, tall and imposing as he folded his newspaper, then pushed in his chair.

Sloan McCaffrey broke the silence rule. He made the mistake of drawing the starting pitcher into their conversation. "Maybe I could talk Stryke into ice climbing this winter. Inside his locker he has half a picture of his climb in the Canadian Rockies."

*Half a picture?* Taylor's heart slowed, then sank. Brek Stryker had cut her out of a scene once snatched from the gods who guarded improbable ascents. At three thousand feet, their guide had snapped photographs over his shoulder, amazing pictures of her and Stryke against a vertical sweep of ice and gray sky.

It had been an exhilarating climb—a climb that could

have damaged his pitching arm, perhaps ended his career. Yet Stryke had taken up the challenge—for her. They'd faced nature at its rawest. At the end of the day they'd both been half-frozen. It had taken a bottle of brandy, a roaring fire in their bedroom at the lodge, as well as skin-on-skin friction for them to thaw out.

They'd produced friction four times that night.

A duplicate of the picture taken that day remained in her scrapbook, along with countless other photographs of them hang gliding, kite surfing, and deep-sea diving.

Stryke loved sand and sunshine. No man looked better in a pair of Hawaiian-print swim trunks, mirrored sunglasses, and a dark tan. Women worshiped him in a wet suit.

Now, as he passed the players' table, Stryke slowed. He looked from Taylor to Sloan and gave a self-deprecating shake of his head. "You enjoy the climb," he told the reliever. "I've done Thrill Seekers. Once was more than enough." And he kept on walking.

The finality of his statement shook her. She turned slightly, watching until he'd reached the door, a man with an athletic stride and a definite purpose: to get as far away from her as was humanly possible.

She'd disrupted his morning coffee, as well as his mental preparation for the game. When they'd been together, she'd practiced silence on days he'd started. She'd left him to his world of visualizing pitches and the batters he would face.

Next time she saw his SUV parked at Jacy's Java, she'd return to Thrill Seekers and brew her own pot of coffee. Or better yet, send Eve for the iced latte.

Newspapers touted 2008 as Stryke's year to break records and secure his place in Cooperstown's National Baseball Hall of Fame.

The man deserved to win games and be honored for his achievements. No major-league pitcher had his rifle-arm precision. Brek set the standard for fastballs.

Taylor wouldn't interfere with his goals.

Stryke was on his way to becoming a legend.

Three hours later, Brek Stryker was throwing shit. Bottom of the third, and his pitches were wild, so high and wide, the Ottawa batters counted four balls and took their walk.

Catcher Chase Tallan had trotted to the mound to help clear Stryke's head of all distractions. Stryke blamed Taylor Hannah for his inability to focus. He'd let her get to him once again.

She'd thrown him off his game.

He was about to self-destruct.

He wished he could rewind time, delete the twenty minutes he'd spent with her in the mascot lounge prior to the game.

He'd made a major mistake in playing Good Samaritan, an act he couldn't take back. He'd gone and offered Taylor six ProSeries ice wraps. The compression packs would keep her body cool inside the costume.

She'd stood and stared at him in her white tank top and black short-shorts, her sea green gaze wide and startlingly soft. She'd nodded her appreciation, then proceeded to Velcro the wraps over her pulse points.

Stryke had avoided touching her until the very last wrap that wound behind her knee. The Velcro had stuck to her ACE bandage. Unable to reach the back of the strap, she'd asked for his help. He'd hunkered down, dipped his head, and avoided a direct visual of her crotch. Amber Nude had seduced him, the fragrance drawing him closer to her body. He'd resisted, fought her scent and nearness as he'd quickly adjusted the ProSeries pack.

Taylor had shifted against the cold. Her stance had widened just enough for his thumb to graze her inner thigh—a thigh he'd stroked and kissed a thousand times on his way to her sweet spot.

Feeling and not thinking, he'd stretched his thumb higher, skimming the skin at the hem of her short-shorts . . . sinfully soft skin that seemed to invite his touch.

Her lips had parted.

His jaw had set.

They'd both gone still as stone.

He'd wished the moment back. He'd have sold his soul not to have touched her. But he had.

Shooting to his feet, he'd fled from the mascot lounge. The ice wraps would protect her from heat exhaustion. She could finish dressing on her own.

The mascot's appearance on the third-base line coincided with Stryke's walk from the bullpen to the mound. The fans loved Rally. It didn't matter if the fuzz ball tripped, dipped, or couldn't walk a straight line; the crowd applauded Rally's efforts.

Stryke willed the mascot beyond his peripheral vision. Rally finally rolled out of sight yet remained on his mind.

Now, with two batters on base, the catcher signaled for a fastball.

Brek dipped his head, wound up, delivered.

"*Strike!*" was called by the home-plate umpire.

He exhaled sharply. It was about damn time. He was back in the game—a game that went to the bottom of the fifth before loud hisses from the stands echoed in the dugout. Seated alone at the far end of the bench, Stryke hadn't a clue as to what was causing disfavor with the fans.

The top of the Rogues' order was ready to bat. Psycho McMillan stood in the batter's box. Romeo Bellisaro was on deck. The Rogues led the game, four to two. The crowd should be cheering, not booing.

He cut Risk Kincaid a look. The center fielder shrugged, got to his feet, and joined his teammates at the dugout railing.

"Roll left; lead with your right." Psycho cupped his hands over his mouth and shouted, "Punch him in the beak."

*A fight?* The scuffle sounded nearby. Water bottles and soda cans now flew from the lower deck. Play was called as the batboys and groundskeepers dashed to clean up the debris.

His concentration broken, Stryke stood up and moved to the dugout steps to get a better look. It didn't take long for him to locate the commotion. Before God and eighty thousand fans, the Raptors' mascot circled Rally, taunting, poking, and pushing the fuzz ball.

"Rappy's been picking on Rally from the first pitch," Chase Tallan informed Stryke. "The bird's got a wild feather up its ass."

"Thought Charlie was an amateur boxer." Risk's words hit Stryke full in the gut. "The man's slapping like a girl."

*Slapping like a girl.* Just beyond third base, Rappy—an enormous bird with a hooked beak and a wide wingspan—swooped in on Rally Ball. The Raptor wing-slapped Rally. Rally belly-bounced the bird.

Rally's roundness limited the mascot's motion. Rappy danced around Rally, making the fuzz ball look bad. Sticking out an enormous plastic foot, Rappy tripped Rally. Rally wobbled, then went down, landing on its back.

Rappy kicked the downed mascot with its long yellow

bird toes. Rally rolled from side to side, but couldn't gather the momentum to rise.

Stryke saw red and his control snapped.

He needed to get to Taylor.

Elbowing through his teammates, he hit the third-base line with a speed denied most pitchers. The Raptor saw him coming. Rappy gave a bring-it-on wiggle of its feathered fingertips. Stryke had the urge to pluck the bird.

He would have, had Risk Kincaid not had his back.

"Easy, man; Charlie can take care of himself," Risk shouted over the roar of the crowd.

"Not Charlie, *Taylor*," Stryke corrected.

"Fearless?" Kincaid spiked a brow. "What the—"

Rappy took that moment to poke Risk in the nose with a wing tip.

Kincaid took care of Beaky Boy.

And Stryke went down on one knee beside Taylor. Cameras clicked in a blinding flash, an irreversible Kodak moment. He and Rally would soon be plastered all over the sports section of the *Virginia Banner*, possibly even syndicated. He preferred being photographed on the mound, not hunkered down beside an arm-flailing, spitting-mad mascot.

"Damn, Taylor, you're not keeping a low profile," he gritted out. "This isn't a sixth-grade playground. Get a grip."

"Rappy started it," she hissed through the mouth slit. "The bird dissed you. He's all trash talk and profanity. He tripped me and I went down." Her eyes flashed and her fists clenched. "I didn't get in one good punch."

Stryke grew still. However juvenile, the bird had bad-mouthed him and this seriously irate woman had jumped to his defense. Dressed as a baseball, she'd taken on a feathered mascot twice her size. She'd lost the battle, landed on her butt, and would be bruised tomorrow.

All because Rappy had called Stryke names.

He shook his head and asked, "You hurt?"

"The Raptor tripped me, and my knee gave out. Did you see his gigantic plastic feet? My only defense was these oversize high-tops. Every time I tried to kick Rappy, I'd roll backward."

This could happen only to Taylor. "Can you stand?"

"I think so."

Stryke rose, then pulled her to her feet.

Her knee turned in, unable to hold her weight.

He curved his arm around the fuzz ball and held her upright. He then called to the trainer. Jon Jamison crossed the field.

"Sprained knee," Stryke told him.

Jamison nodded. "Let's get you to the locker room, Charlie."

Stryke and Taylor exchanged a look through the eye slits. Neither one corrected the trainer. The man was in for a little surprise. Painted toenails and shaved legs would be his first clues that Charlie wasn't quite Charlie today.

Stryke brushed dirt off the fuzz ball's rounded ass. Additional camera flashes blinded him with the reminder that he was touching a mascot that fans assumed was Charlie Bradley. His hand dropped before he dusted baseline chalk off Taylor's thigh.

Supported by Jamison, Rally hopped off the field. The Rogues' mascot got a standing ovation—a first in mascot history.

"How's Taylor?" Risk Kincaid came to stand beside him.

"She'll live. Her pride took as much of a tumble as the costume."

"I've seen mascots taunt, but never go at it. Rappy must have really pissed her off."

"Apparently he did." Stryke had no desire to discuss the fight in detail. It was too personal. He tipped back his baseball cap and looked at his friend. "Thanks, man."

Clubhouse buddies and close friends, he and Kincaid had been staunch allies over the years. Together they watched as a security guard ejected the Raptor from the game. At the gate, Rappy flipped Stryke the bird.

Shortly thereafter, Risk turned toward the dugout. "The grounds crew has restored order. Let's get back to work."

The two men jogged toward the dugout.

Following three consecutive Rogues strikeouts, Brek returned to the mound. Top of the sixth. He threw his ass off: fast windups, and quicker releases.

When the batter looked for a fastball, Brek threw a splinter. He pitched up and in, crowding the batter with curveballs.

Expletives rose from the batter's box with each swing and miss. Bats were thrown and dirt kicked as Brek retired the heart of the Raptors order.

He brought his team up to six to two before reliever Sloan McCaffrey took the hill following the seventh-inning stretch. Brek then headed for the trainer's table to have his shoulder iced—and to check on Taylor.

A red-faced Jon Jamison awaited him. "Jock hawk?" he guessed, questioning Brek about the woman inside the mascot costume.

Stryke shook his head. Taylor was the last woman to prey on players. "The lady replaced Charlie for the day," was all he offered. "How's her knee?"

"Swollen," Jamison returned. "Looks like torn ligaments. She refused an X-ray."

Stryke removed his jersey and undershirt and allowed the trainer to work on his shoulder. Once iced, he accepted a shoulder brace for added support. He then headed toward the mascot lounge.

He found Taylor all cushy and comfy in Charlie's favorite overstuffed chair. She'd showered and changed into a vintage Orange Crush T-shirt and cutoff jeans. Her leg rested on the ottoman. Her knee was wrapped in cold compression packs. Her gaze was focused on the television mounted on the wall.

She cut him a glance. "McCaffrey's throwing decent heat."

"He's our strongest reliever."

She placed her hands on the armrest and pushed up, then winced. "Game's almost over. I was just about to sneak out the players' exit."

"You have a ride?"

She nodded. "I've called Eve. By the time I reach the side gate, she'll have arrived."

"Need help?"

"I'll manage. The trainer lent me crutches, which I'll have Risk return. I won't be back to the locker room. Nor the ballpark. Our paths won't cross again, Stryke. I promise."

"Works for me." It worked so well his throat closed and his insides felt squeezed by a fist.

She looked at him then, long and hard. Her expression was a little sad as she eased to her feet. He handed her the crutches. Their fingertips brushed, light and quick, yet charged with sensation. "Have a super season," she said softly. "And a happy marriage. I wish you well."

Annoyance pricked, and his jaw set. He had every right

to happiness, yet for some reason her good wishes rubbed salt in his old wounds.

He swung the door wide and she hobbled past. Her Amber Nude seduced him one last time. The fragrance drew forth memories of cool satin sheets and red-hot sex.

Memories that needed to die.

He propped one shoulder against the jamb and watched her slowly traverse the tunnel to the side exit. The dip of her head and the slump of her shoulders registered defeat.

He'd never seen her move so slowly.

She was dragging her feet, not wanting to leave.

A part of him wanted to go after her, to shake her and demand the reason she'd left him three years ago. While momentarily soft in the heart, he wasn't soft in the head. Logic backed him up, turned him toward the future. He was engaged, about to settle down.

His fiancée expected him at a campaign fund-raiser for her father, the mayor, at seven. It was an election year. Stryke's donation and endorsement would go a long way toward ensuring that the incumbent remained in office.

He'd stand by Hilary Louise, help her work the room. Her shyness charmed constituents.

It was small-talk-and-tuxedo time.

# CHAPTER THREE

Brek Stryker sat at a linen-covered table in the ball-room of the Old Dominion Country Club and tried to focus on two conversations at once. To his right, City Councilwoman Marian Morris wanted his opinion on an upcoming tax hike for road improvements. On his left, the mayor's secretary, Lucille Thayer, questioned the need for a sixth school board member. She felt five opinions prevented the possibility of a stalemate.

Across the room, he caught Wayne Talbott patting Hilary on the head like a child before sending her back to Stryke. Hilary was a grown woman, yet her father treated her as if she were twelve.

Brek watched her weave through the crowd. She looked soft and sophisticated in her gray suit. Her engagement ring was her only jewelry. Her honest eyes, shy smile, and unaffected innocence collected more votes for her father than any political slogan. She had a disarming sweetness that charmed supporters into donating heavily to the mayoral fund.

Her sincerity had drawn Stryke the moment he'd met her. She'd been at campaign headquarters when he'd dropped off his first donation. The incumbent backed the Boys and Girls Clubs of Richmond, an organization Stryke strongly supported.

Hilary had asked him several questions, then listened intently as he'd spoken about the importance of keeping kids off the street, of giving kids hope. Stryke volunteered at several of the clubs. He'd seen incredible promise and potential in the young athletes, many of whom faced insurmountable odds.

At the conclusion of their conversation, he'd asked Hilary to dinner. She'd blushed, smiled, and accepted. Her shyness had endeared her to him.

They'd gotten along well. There were no arguments or disagreements, merely a smooth coming together of minds—but not of bodies. Six months of dating, and they'd yet to have sex. The last time he'd tried to round second base, she'd gone all mannequin on him.

Stryke didn't mind going slow. Hilary wanted time to know him fully before sharing his bed. He could live with that.

Her nose powdered and her lipstick reapplied, she returned to their table. In her wake came Stuart Tate, a small man, short on hair. As the mayor's campaign manager, Tate was a name-dropper and walked in Wayne Talbott's shadow. He'd latched onto Hilary, and she was too nice to shake him loose.

Stryke didn't feel the same compulsion. Tate was a weasel. Stryke didn't trust a man who couldn't talk sports. Tate went blank when discussions turned to team standings, record setting, and salary caps.

He and Tate had nothing in common—except Hilary. The man drew his importance from the people he met. Hilary was introducing him to Richmond's elite. There were enough millionaires in the ballroom to found a bank, and Tate hoped to grow rich by association.

Marian Morris rose, relinquishing her chair to Hilary. She slid in beside Brek. Tate didn't think twice about stealing someone's seat. He dropped down between Hilary and a portly man Stryke recognized as a prominent local contractor. The man looked ready to reconstruct Tate's face.

Brek glanced at Hilary. "Reaping enough votes for your dad?"

All flushed and fluttery, Hilary tried to catch her breath. "I'm not good at small talk," she confessed. "I understand my father's political platform, but it's difficult to discuss in depth."

"You're his secret weapon." Stryke knew this to be true. Throughout the campaign, he'd watched Talbott use his daughter to soften his own directness. Constituents were drawn to Hilary. She posed no threat, only offered reassurance that her father was the best man for the job.

Stuart Tate leaned around Hilary and looked pointedly at Stryke. "You working the jock vote?" he asked.

*The jock vote?* "Sorry, I don't discuss politics in the locker room," he replied. He'd never apply pressure to any player to back a candidate—not even the father of his fiancée.

Over the past month, Brek had contributed heavily. He'd written three fat checks, all with five zeroes. He'd yet to see enough flyers, buttons, or banners to justify his donations. A flicker of concern had him wondering how the money was being spent.

Twice a week, Wayne Talbott's face popped up on the tube during the late-late shows. The campaign commercials lasted all of fifteen seconds. They were so brief, the man barely had time to state his name and the fact that he was running for reelection. Talbott's opponent, Scott Beatty, took sixty-second spots, laying out his platform and making promises in short but efficient sound bites.

Stryke had attended five fund-raisers thus far. Expenses had been spared on the meals, all child-portioned. He hadn't expected to be fattened up, but he'd walked away hungry. He always grabbed a sandwich at Jacy's Java on his way home.

He now pressed his hand to Hilary's thigh, then lowered his voice. "We'll talk a fourth donation when I have you alone."

*Will the donation go up as I work down your body?*

His breath hissed through his teeth as Taylor's—not Hilary's—voice whispered in his ear, all sexy and sultry and teasing.

"You look tense," Hilary said, concerned. "I'd thought you'd be relaxed after your win today."

He stretched out his legs beneath the table. "The team played well. We're starting the season strong."

"The late-afternoon addition of the *Virginia Banner* pictured you and Rally Ball on the lower half of the front page," Stuart Tate put in. For a man who blanked on sports, he was suddenly animated. "The article mentioned that the mascot took a beating."

Those words would tick Taylor off. She held her own in most situations. He'd never known her to fall until today, when she'd been unfairly tripped by the plastic-toed Raptor.

"Rappy tripped Rally." Stryke found himself defending Taylor. "The Raptor was twice the fuzz ball's size."

"The bird was a bully," Hilary added sympathetically.

"You"—Tate pointed to Stryke—"came to Charlie Bradley's rescue. One photograph showed your arm around Rally; another had you brushing off his backside. Very chummy, wouldn't you say?"

*Chummy? Shit.* "Charlie hurt his knee." Stryke kept

the focus on Charlie and not Taylor. "I helped support his weight until the trainer took over."

"Looked pretty intimate," Tate persisted, "the pitcher coming to the mascot's rescue. The reporter called you 'sympathetic.'"

Stryke's testicles drew tight. A picture was worth a thousand words. He didn't appreciate Tate's suggestion that he and Charlie were more than friends. Worse yet, he hated explaining himself to a table of strangers.

He would have let the subject drop had Hilary not gone wide-eyed with surprise. He sucked it up, assured her, "I've known Charlie for six seasons. He's divorced, but still loves his ex-wife. They're going through couples therapy. There's reconciliation in their future."

"If Charlie doesn't get back with his wife, he always has you." Tate grinned, a perverse twist to his lips. "A man of . . . comfort."

Stryke stared at Tate. The man had insinuated that Stryke was a switch-hitter. Everyone at the table now looked at him questioningly. They wondered if he did men. Though he wasn't homophobic, Stryke was attracted to women, not men. Always had been, always would be. For whatever reason, Tate wanted Stryke to look bad in Hilary's eyes. Stryke didn't appreciate Tate's smear campaign. He wanted to kick Tate's ass for raising doubt about his sexuality before his fiancée and Richmond's finest.

For a brief moment, he thought about telling all those seated that it was Taylor Hannah, not Charlie Bradley, who'd performed as Rally Ball that afternoon. He decided not to drag Taylor into the mix. An ex-fiancée's antics were best kept secret.

Stryke looked at the four remaining men seated at his table: a contractor, a bodybuilder who now owned a chain of gyms, a community leader and owner of several Harley-Davidson franchises, and a retired high school basketball coach. All were men with athletic pasts and more muscle in their necks than Tate had in his entire body.

Game face on, Stryke turned to Tate. "Guess you've never played sports, Stu. Otherwise you'd know Rally's an integral part of the Rogues organization. We consider Charlie one of the team. No matter the circumstance, the players protect their own. Today I defended Rally."

Color flooded Tate's cheeks. He shifted uncomfortably on his chair and had nothing further to say.

Vindicated, Stryke moved the conversation away from baseball. He asked Hilary about the next fund-raiser. She went on to discuss her father's plans to back a homeless shelter in south Richmond.

Her burgeoning excitement drew interest from nearby tables. Grocery magnate Earl Stone promised to supply day-old bakery goods and produce to feed the less fortunate. Contractor Bud Davidson's offer to set up a job pool for out-of-work men had Hilary so ecstatic she couldn't eat her dessert. Stryke ate two slices of the sliver-thin pecan pie.

At the end of the night, Hilary was all smiles and gratitude. She initiated their good-night kiss in the parking lot beneath a quarter moon, a kiss so featherlight, Stryke wondered if it had really happened

Her reticence kept him at arm's length. Since they'd met, all his pent-up sexual energy had gone into pitching. He'd started the season strong.

Their lack of sex hadn't bothered him until Taylor's return to Richmond. Not every couple came together as he and Taylor once had. They'd experienced once-in-a-lifetime sex. A mere glance or light touch, and their attraction unbuttoned blouses and unzipped jeans. Landing in bed was as natural as breathing.

No matter how hard he fought against it, Taylor pulled his thoughts to puckered nipples and erections. He hated the fact that he now stirred and stiffened, scaring Hilary with his increasing size.

To her credit, Hilary didn't jump out of her skin, or scream. She merely patted his chest and eased back a step.

"I'm sorry, Brek." Her voice sounded soft and sad and much more serious than the situation warranted. "I just . . . can't. Not tonight."

*I want you every night for the rest of my life,* Taylor's voice came to him again, breathy and hot and sexually needy.

In the stillness of the parking lot, Amber Nude invaded his senses, and the image of them together played through his mind in Technicolor: a blend of tongues, hot kisses, and athletically honed bodies, naked and sweat-slick, frantically twisting until they locked in the raw climb to orgasm.

The scratch of her nails on his back, the sprint of her heartbeat as she closed in on climax—

*"Brek?"* Hilary called him back to the present where he belonged. She twisted her engagement ring, looking embarrassed and uneasy. "Are you all right? Your nostrils flared and your breath hitched. You . . . shuddered."

Once again, Taylor had ambushed him when he wasn't looking. Disgust hit him like a cold shower. "I'm fine," he assured her. "I want you, Hilary, and when the time is right, we'll be good together."

"I-I hope so." He'd never seen her so nervous. A deep crease split her brow, and her lips pursed.

Stryke wanted her to relax. "How are the wedding plans coming along?" he asked.

"I've hired a wedding planner," she informed him. "We need to set a wedding date."

"Any day but July third." Bad memories surrounded the day Taylor had left him at the altar.

"How about a spring wedding?"

"This spring?" It was already mid-April.

"Next spring."

"You want to wait a year?" This surprised him.

"I need plenty of time to plan."

"A big wedding?" His worst nightmare.

"If my father is reelected, his position as mayor will require that he give me away before family, friends, and government officials. Daddy has gubernatorial ambitions."

Stryke refused to allow their wedding to become a political circus. "We'll work on the guest list together."

Hilary didn't argue. She never did. Acceptance was ingrained in her. She did, however, seem distracted. Stryke chalked it up to tiredness and too many fund-raisers.

They parted shortly thereafter. With a peck to his cheek, she returned to the country club. The moist imprint of her kiss had dried by the time he'd fastened his seat belt.

Setting the SUV in reverse, he glanced in the rearview mirror, making sure Hilary reached the country club safely. He narrowed his eyes as Stuart Tate emerged from the shadows near the front door. The bold little man placed his palm on Hilary's spine, then rubbed her back before guiding her inside. Their heads dipped close, their noses nearly touching. All pretty intimate, in Stryke's opinion.

He waited for his jealousy to spike, yet only a flicker of irritation rose over Stu's familiarity—which Hilary didn't resist. He'd have to ask Hilary about Tate when they next spoke.

His SUV on automatic pilot, he drove directly to Jacy's Java. A decaf and a cranberry turkey wrap would satisfy his late-night hunger. He parked his vehicle across the street from the front door, then checked out the customers before he entered.

He was glad he had. Curled up on white vinyl swan chairs near the large picture window, Taylor Hannah and Jacy Kincaid were enjoying late-evening coffee, relaxed in each other's company.

The dark interior of the Escalade gave him a private moment to observe Taylor without witnesses. Her animation and wild hand gestures had Jacy bent over with laughter.

A toss of her hair, followed by a wide smile, reminded Stryke of the first time he'd seen her. The harder he fought the memory, the more it crowded his mind. He pressed his fingertips against his eyelids, then slid them higher against his scalp, pushing against the start of a headache. The pressure built and broke as he was swept back to a time he'd rather forget. . . .

It was March 10, 1999, Ladies' Day at James River Stadium. The Rogues were playing the Chicago Cubs. Stryke had stepped off the mound and was headed for the dugout when the first baseman jogged past.

" 'Got Balls?' " Shaffer Stone had chuckled. "Check out field level, row B. Sweet baby."

Stryke hated distractions, yet he did a quick scan of row B, and was immediately glad he had. A dozen hot women were sharing bags of peanuts and popcorn, and toasting one another with soda and beer.

*Got Balls?* was easy to locate. The words were printed on a peach T-shirt worn by a knockout blonde with a sunburned nose. She'd glanced his way as he was checking her out. Attraction shot hot and electric straight to his

49

soul. She'd held his gaze until he'd ducked into the dugout.

While the Rogues worked through the middle of their rotation, Stryke snagged two new baseballs and a black marker and wrote his private cell phone number on each. His fellow teammates did this often. A sexy fan was frequently issued an invitation to party.

Until that moment, Stryke had never shared his private number with any woman in the stands. The blonde became an exception to his rule. He'd sent a batboy on his behalf.

He'd gone on to pitch three more innings. The blonde brought out the best in him. He'd shown off, striking out nine of nine consecutive batters. The crowd was on its feet, applauding him. Even the blonde stood, looking excited and happy and clapping her ass off.

On his final return to the dugout, he'd caught her juggling the baseballs, a hint of a smile on her lips.

After the game, he'd celebrated with his teammates. They'd headed to Bruno's, a bar loud with live music and packed with groupies. Stryke had set his cell phone on vibrate, in hopes the blonde would call.

She never did.

The only call that came in was from a twelve-year-old boy named Tony Holmes—a boy who exuberantly thanked Stryke for the two souvenir baseballs that a blond hottie had tossed him as she'd left the park.

The lady had put Stryke down. Hard.

Disappointment shadowed him as he'd departed the head-pounding noise at Bruno's and strode to the parking lot. There, seated inside his McLaren, he'd talked sports with Tony for a solid hour. He'd promised the kid a signed jersey, to be picked up at the ticket window before their next home game.

Two weeks of road trips sent the team to San Diego, then on to Montreal. Returning home, the Rogues faced the Mets.

A passing look at the crowd as Stryke took the mound revealed the blonde and her friends once again seated behind the dugout. They were a row of stunning women, their interest held as much by the players themselves as by the sport. Several wore jerseys in support of their favorite Rogue.

The blonde had on another of her slogan T-shirts. He squinted to read the message: *Baseball Is All Wrong. A Man with Four Balls Cannot Walk.*

He smiled.

And she smiled back.

At the end of the game, he once again sent the batboy to find the blonde and give her his cell phone number.

Six days passed, and she didn't call. Neither did she show up at the park for three weeks. When she did, she was alone.

She sat higher in the stands. Yet she stood out in a red T-shirt, her light blond hair pulled into a ponytail beneath a Rogues baseball cap.

The Rogues lost to the Red Sox, four to five.

Stryke had pitched. And he felt like shit. He needed to be alone.

Avoiding the autograph hounds, he'd taken a side exit and crossed the players' parking lot to his McLaren. The silver Mercedes sports car would make for a fast escape.

His footsteps had slowed when he'd caught the blonde standing in the evening shadows. He'd thought her hot from a distance. Up close, she zapped him like a stun gun.

She was gorgeous.

When she was seated high in the stands, he'd been

51

unable to read the inscription on her latest T-shirt. Closing in on her, he'd been able to make it out: *You're the Baseball Player My Mother Warned Me About.*

"I'm not all bad," he'd told her.

"I'm not all good," she'd returned.

He'd liked her on the spot.

"Brek Stryker," he'd introduced himself.

"Taylor," she'd replied.

"No last name?"

"Not until I know you better."

He'd jammed his hands in the pockets of his jeans, cocking his head. "Why tonight?"

"The Rogues lost to the Red Sox."

"You're here to cheer me up?"

"You could say that."

Her cheering came in the form of dinner at a mom-and-pop diner that served homemade meat loaf and chicken casserole. Sensuality shimmered off her tight little body, hitting him with an eroticism that made his dick twitch.

He'd been hard from his second bite of meat loaf. He was so stiff by the time he'd finished a thick slice of apple pie à la mode and two cups of coffee, he'd sworn he couldn't slide from the booth—the pain was that great.

The night had been one to remember. It brought a vibrant, free-spirited woman into his life. A woman who'd proved a handful, with her spur-of-the-moment decisions and love of adventure.

It had taken two weeks for her to give him her last name—a name he'd recognized. He'd met her parents through sports clubs and athletic affiliations. Liv and Stephan Hannah were adrenaline junkies. Thrill seeking was their ultimate passion.

Taylor followed in their footsteps.

She skydived, snowboarded, and raced the rugged terrain of the Baja 1000. She ran full throttle, requiring little sleep.

She excited him, both in and out of bed.

After just one day apart, they would come together, wild and hungry and orgasmically explosive. Her flexibility amazed him. He found her scars sexy.

Her independence scared the hell out of him.

Taylor liked living on her own. Adjusting to being a couple had been difficult for her. The closer they'd grown, the deeper was his concern for her welfare. His protectiveness had provoked long arguments and the occasional full-blown fight.

Her parents' untimely deaths had grounded her for all of a month. She'd walked around like a zombie, yet refused to lean on him.

He'd never seen her cry. She'd never released the sadness that claimed her heart. In the end, she'd taken over the family business, guiding thrill seekers to the most dangerous and remotest places on the planet.

Stryke had held his breath from the second she boarded a plane until she returned. She was often gone for weeks at a time. He'd hoped asking her to marry him would keep her in Richmond.

It had not. She'd planned their wedding between white-water rafting with crocodiles on the Zambezi River and cliff diving in Acapulco. He'd known there was a risk she might be a runaway bride. He hadn't, however, believed she'd choose paragliding in New South Wales over attending their wedding.

He'd never fully shaken his anger and hurt.

Now, years later, as he sat slouched in the car seat, Stryke hated the fact that Taylor's memory could still invade his mind. *

She'd never looked back.

He'd never wanted to move forward without her.

Until Hilary Talbott. Hilary would never pack an athletic bag in the dark of night and be gone by first light. Nor would she run with the bulls at Pamplona or challenge African game.

Hilary was safe and sane, and would make a good mother.

Stryke wanted a family. And peace in his life.

While Taylor played in his mind, she'd never again have his heart. He wouldn't allow it. *Couldn't* allow it.

Starting his SUV, he pulled into the steady stream of late-evening traffic. He could live without the turkey sandwich. Just as he could live without Taylor Hannah.

He left her memory at the curb.

# CHAPTER FOUR

"Memories, huh?" Eve Hannah stared down Sloan McCaffrey with a practiced eye. "Are you looking for a week's worth of thrills or merely a few days to hit on my sister?"

The eight p.m. closing time had already come and gone when the prospective client had walked through the door, looking for Taylor. He'd introduced himself, then appeared put out to learn Taylor wasn't available. Despite his disappointment, he'd gone ahead and engaged Eve in a long and in-depth discussion of extreme sports.

It was now eight thirty. McCaffrey was slow to leave. "Well?" she pressed.

"I want both thrills and Taylor." The man with the shaggy black hair, cut features, and dimple in his chin grinned. An aura of tangible sin surrounded him; the crackle in the air was bold and electric and raised the hair on Eve's arms. "I want an adventure that will make me look good in Taylor's eyes."

Another male infatuated with her sister. Eve refrained from rolling her eyes. Taylor had been and always would be in love with Brek Stryker. She'd made a major mistake in leaving him at the altar. A mistake she'd lived to regret.

In countless sports, Eve had watched Taylor conquer

the odds and win. She hoped her sister had one more chance with Stryke. One small, life-altering opportunity that would bring them together again.

She didn't, however, share her thoughts with Sloan McCaffrey. He looked like the type who'd turn a deaf ear to anything he didn't want to hear.

Standing near the front windows, she went ahead and closed, then latched the indoor cottage-style blue shutters before turning to Sloan and saying, "Taylor's adventures are hard-core. You don't travel to be seen or to show off. What you do on the trip is for you and nobody else."

She straightened the burgundy leather chairs, then went on to neatly stack the magazines on street luging, mountain biking, and kite surfing. She flicked off the main overhead lights, discouraging anyone else from entering. Six sconces cast Sloan's shadow and her own on the brick wall.

Their enormous silhouettes flickered and wavered.

And touched.

Eve sidestepped, so there'd be less touching.

Her white gauze skirt swirled about her legs as she crossed to the counter. Leaning on the glass top, she asked, "What are you good at, McCaffrey? So I can spin you in a positive light."

"No need to spin." He was anything but humble. "I'm healthy and athletic. And don't break easily. My adventure needs to be scheduled in the winter. Off-season from the Rogues."

A Rogue. She should have guessed he played ball. The man had the strut and inflated ego of a jock. His good looks and rippling muscles had gotten him through life.

Eve was not impressed.

Drilling her fingers on the counter, she suggested, "How about rafting? Taylor takes an expedition down the Brahmaputra in November."

His forehead took on two crease lines.

"India." She gave him a geography lesson. "Thick jungle, wild elephants, and tribal people."

"Headhunters?" asked Sloan.

"Not for forty years."

A third crease deepened as he took it all in.

"Then there's the river," she continued. "You'll learn paddling commands, safety, and self-rescue, in case you're thrown overboard. You can expect legendary drops, thirty-foot standing waves, rapids, and a short stretch of class-six water."

He shook his head. "Not my adventure."

She contained her smile. "There's cross-country skiing on top of the world. You could test your endurance in Longyearbyen."

The creases in his forehead dug deeper this time.

"Norway," she informed him. "You need to be fit enough to draw a sled packed with eighty pounds of equipment. You'll ski eight to ten hours a day. Over the course of a week, you'll cover roughly ninety miles. You'll need to put up with temps forty degrees below zero."

"Taylor finds this fun?"

"She pushes herself mentally and physically."

"How would I prepare?"

"Hold a ten-pound frozen sea bass, then smash the backside of your fingers until you can no longer hold the frozen carcass. This prepares you for numbness and shows what little finger dexterity you will have. You can also strip down to your underwear in front of an open refrigerator. Place ten to twelve ice cubes around your testicles, and poor a gallon of cold water over your head, while repeating, 'I'm a thrill seeker. Greatest adventure of my life.'"

One corner of his mouth curved slowly. "I've had ice

cubes on my testicles. Cubes were in a hot female mouth and melted quickly."

"At the North Pole, you'll be lucky if your balls don't freeze and fall off."

"I'd like to keep my boys."

"Perhaps paragliding, then? Taylor glides competitively. Paragliders are fitted with radar equipment to track their global positioning."

"Radar equipment?" Sloan didn't sound enthusiastic.

"Your glider needs to be tracked in case of an unexpected thunderstorm. Not too long ago, a male glider got caught up in severe wind currents and was lifted thirty-two thousand feet. He was flying with the jumbo jets. He lost consciousness and control of the glider."

"Holy shit . . ."

"When the storm subsided, he came to, and eventually landed safely."

"I don't do lightning and thunder," stated Sloan.

"How about snowboarding, waterfall ice climbing, downhill?" she suggested.

"Put me on a mountain. I can downhill." He looked pointedly at her pale green T-shirt and read the inscription. "I want to 'Huck It.'"

She wanted his eyes off her breasts. Crossing her arms over her chest, she asked, "Do you know what hucking even is?"

He innocently lifted one arrogant brow. "Thought it was a misspelling."

Why was she wasting her time with this muscle-bound clown? "Hucking is when a skier throws himself off the mountain edge and catches big air. The skier—"

"—hopes to land a jump, especially on a soft-snow day," he finished for her. He scanned the shadowed posters and pictures on the redbrick walls, all remote yet famed locales to make a man's blood run cold.

He eventually read the challenge of La Grave. " 'Belong to the longer, faster, deeper crowd.' " He made the words sound more sexual than adventuresome.

Eve's heart tripped. And her body flushed. She hated the fact that she'd reacted to this macho jerk. "La Meije isn't for the vast majority of skiers," she said, recovering quickly. "It's an untamed, ungroomed, code-red terrain."

His gray gaze went wide. "Mountain sounds big, bad, and really, really scary."

"You'd be a total yard sale."

"I have no plans of wiping out and leaving my equipment spread out in a trail of mass destruction."

"Then you'd better pack humility and responsibility," she warned him. "It's no place for egos. La Meije has a way of making a man feel very small and very mortal. Get cocky on the mountain and Mother Nature will slap you silly."

"I can handle Mother Nature," he bragged. "I've got the gear for downhill."

"Owning gear and knowing how to use it are two completely different things."

"I've skills," he affirmed. "Chances are good I'll beat Taylor down the mountain."

"Hitting the base as a human snowball doesn't count."

"Real funny, Eve."

She'd thought so. Smiling to herself, she reached for the thick brown leather notebook that held Taylor's travel itinerary. Flipping through the months, Eve noted that her sister had scheduled a trip to La Grave for mid-December. Three of the four client slots were already filled.

"There's only one slot available," she told him. "The

adventure runs five days, right before Christmas. If you're interested . . ."

He scratched his stubbled jaw. "I'm thinking."

"If you have to *think*, you don't want the thrill." She took a step back from the counter. "Why not just ask Taylor out? Dinner and a movie could save on broken bones. La Meije is treacherous."

"Your sister likes action."

"Taylor's not on the go every second of every day. She exhales, just like everyone else."

"After we race down the mountain, we'll exhale together at the hotel, in my suite."

Wishful thinking on his part. Taylor never got involved with her clients. Her adventures were all business. Eve tapped her gold-link watch, reminding him, "Thrill Seekers closed at eight. It's now almost nine."

"It's been great talking with you too." His gray eyes laughed at her.

Eve didn't return his laughter. For some unknown reason, she'd wanted to scare him off any and all adventures. She didn't know why, but she'd felt a compulsion to do so. Like Taylor, she always went with her gut. "If you're not in any big hurry to end your life, take all the time you need to make up your mind."

"No hard sell?" Sloan strolled across the room to an armchair and made himself comfortable. He picked up a skiing magazine displayed on a side table and thumbed through it. "Thought you'd want my business. I expected you to be more persuasive."

Eve stared after him. The man didn't understand *business closed*. He lived life on his own time, and didn't care whether he inconvenienced others.

Seated now, McCaffrey looked at home among the shadows, his body as solid as the brick wall at his back, a poster boy for fitness. Sadly, he was slow to comprehend that a physique honed for baseball differed greatly from a body ready for downhill. On the mountain, even the most athletic of men discovered muscles he'd never known existed.

"I never push a client to kill himself," she finally answered. "Once you sign up, there are no refunds."

He slouched deeper in the chair. "You ever skied La Grave?"

Eve shook her head. "I'm not a thrill seeker."

"Yet Taylor is. Are you the postman's baby?"

She'd heard that question a thousand times. It hadn't bothered her until Sloan McCaffrey asked it. Suddenly prickly, she reached beneath the counter for a bottle of Windex and a roll of paper towels. She sprayed and wiped down the glass countertop, then picked her words carefully.

"Taylor inherited the sporting gene. I have the business sense. I travel with her to scout out locations so I can convey the risk factor to clients. I don't own equipment, nor do I ever plan to hand my life over to a mountain, wild rapids, or the deep blue sea."

"Not an ounce of daredevil in your soul?"

"I play it safe."

"I want to play with Taylor." Sloan tossed down his magazine, then rose from the leather chair. He crossed back to her, his shadow on the wall big and imposing and once again touching hers. He had an easy roll to his hips. His expression was smug. "How much?" He reached into his back pocket for his wallet. His gray T-shirt separated from his jeans, and Eve caught the number three tattooed over his groin.

Sloan caught her checking out his tat. "A warning to women," he explained. "Three dates and I'm gone."

"What if the woman you're dating has a 'two' tattoo rule?"

"Makes it easier on me."

Eve rolled her eyes. She'd met a lot of men through Thrill Seekers. None were as arrogant and into themselves as Sloan McCaffrey. The man was an ass.

"La Grave will run you ten grand." She drew an information packet from a drawer behind the counter and handed it to him. "Inside you'll find a list of equipment as well as names of several insurance companies who offer high-risk policies. Be sure your travel insurance is fully paid up prior to departure. You might want to increase your life insurance as well. The hotel will require that you leave a next-of-kin address and your medical insurance details at the reception desk before you head up the mountain. Makes it easier on Taylor."

Sloan extracted a check from his black leather wallet and wrote it out for the required amount. He slid it across the counter to Eve. Their fingers brushed, the tips sparking, as if they'd both scuffed their feet across the carpet, producing static electricity.

He looked at her strangely.

She dropped her gaze.

Drawing her hand back, she slipped the check into a bank bag, then shook her head disbelievingly. "The price men pay to be with my sister."

"Obviously I'm not the first."

"Nor will you be the last."

"Taylor's hot. The trip's well worth the money."

"My sister's an excellent guide. If you listen to her and don't spit in Mother Nature's eye, you'll have the adventure of a lifetime."

"Why don't you come along?"

To her surprise, Sloan leaned across the counter,

fingering a tendril of hair that had escaped her French braid. Calloused skin brushed against her neck, and she flinched, her breath catching on the way out as he tucked the loose strand behind her ear.

Intimate and dangerous.

His gaze lingered on her lips, and she licked them self-consciously. The man made her nervous.

With a light tug on her braid, he stated, "I've always wanted to do sisters."

"Taylor and I don't share men." A split second of vulnerability and he'd played her. She slapped his hand away.

Sloan McCaffrey knew that if he smiled, Eve Hannah would rip him a new one. The lady was a ballbuster. He wasn't sure what he'd done to tick her off, but from the onset, she'd been cool and sarcastic. He hadn't been able to warm her up.

Teasing her had seemed fun, for him anyway. Yet she hadn't cracked a smile. Not even a twitch of her lips.

He figured Eve needed sex. Most women this uptight could use a quick slam-bam, just to relieve the tension. She was pretty enough, but her attitude sucked. As she stood before the computer, her posture was protective, as if she were defending herself against the world.

A man dedicated to foreplay and follow-through, he'd like nothing more than to unwind that tight-ass braid and watch the dark blond strands tickle low on her spine. He'd like to bite her lip, suck her sharp tongue into his mouth, tangle with her until she went soft and pliant.

She'd fight him.

And he'd win.

One dusk-to-dawn with her, and—

"I thought you'd be closed by now." Taylor Hannah's appearance took Sloan by surprise. "It's dark in here."

"We're supposed to be closed." Eve looked pointedly at Sloan. "Last-minute customer."

Sloan ignored Eve's jab. Taylor took his breath away in her red tank dress and turquoise-jeweled sandals. He loved tanned, toned women with the strength to crack a walnut with their thighs. Taylor was a nutcracker—of that he was certain.

Eve looked up and smiled at her sister.

Metal flashed, and Sloan blinked. Eve had braces. He wouldn't have known she even had teeth had Taylor not shown up. Eve didn't smile nearly enough. She had a soft, single dimple and a sweet curve to her mouth, surprisingly nice.

"I've signed Sloan McCaffrey for La Grave," he heard Eve say. "He's willing to risk life and limb to challenge the mountain."

"My kind of guy." Taylor's approval came with a wink and a handshake. "There's no better place to play with the elements than the Alps. You're so high on the mountain you almost brush against the clouds and can nearly kiss the sky."

"Thin air and altitude can make you both tired and drunk, if you're not careful." This from Eve.

Damn, Eve was a downer. Taylor, a wet dream. Shaking Taylor's hand, he waited for the static zing he'd felt with Eve, yet got nothing beyond her soft, dry palm. *Shit fire.*

Cutting his gaze to Eve, he caught her once again watching him with her snippy disapproval. The woman needed a man to back her against a brick wall, lift her flowing white skirt, and rock her hips into tomorrow.

Turning back toward the friendly sister, he asked, "Any chance we could hook up before La Grave?"

Taylor slowly shook her head. "Sorry, no time. I'm bound for Africa on Monday. Desert hiking in the Sahara.

I have weekly trips scheduled for the rest of the year. I won't be returning to Richmond until Thanksgiving."

That news sucked. "How's your knee?"

Taylor hesitated. "I'm holding my own."

*Barely* holding her own. Sloan caught the ACE bandage that wrapped her knee as she stepped around the counter. She walked with her weight on the outer edge of her foot. Short, precise steps kept her balanced. Given the clench of her jaw as well as the white lines that bracketed her mouth, she was in pain. No way would Taylor be trekking the Sahara in four days.

"I came to check on Addie's party," Taylor announced, addressing Eve. She crossed to a filing cabinet set against the brick wall, opened the top drawer, and plucked out a manila folder. Flipping it open, she ran her finger down the typewritten page and nodded her approval. "The caterer, decorations, RSVPs, everything's come together. Addie's birthday is good to go."

A birthday party? Sloan didn't care who Addie was; he wanted an invitation.

"I've added Jacy and Risk Kincaid to the guest list," Taylor told Eve as she closed the file and returned it to the cabinet. "Addie adores them both."

"Mayor Talbott invited himself," Eve informed her sister. "Addie's involvement in senior citizen reform caught his attention. I think Talbott's more interested in a photo op than allocating funds for community transportation."

Taylor sighed. "Seniors could use those buses. Many no longer have their driver's licenses, and they can't get around town. Maybe if we all jump Talbott at the party, he'll make a commitment."

Seniors in need of transportation—Sloan stored the information.

"We'll definitely work toward that goal," Eve agreed as

she collected the printed receipt on Sloan's itinerary and slid it across the counter to him. He noticed she avoided any contact this time around. "Jingle bells." She gave him a tight-lipped smile. "May you live to put out milk and cookies for Santa on Christmas Eve."

The woman didn't believe he'd return in one piece. He had every intention of enjoying the holiday. Maybe even enjoying it with Taylor. Surely she'd be home for Christmas.

"Stop back anytime," Taylor invited as he strolled toward the door. "Eve's here every day to show videos on the various locales and to answer questions. Even the most hard-core thrill seekers get the jitters before a trip. Eve's good at soothing nerves."

*Soothing?* Eve had the personality of a porcupine. "No jitters," he assured Taylor. "I've nerves of steel."

"Easy to say now." Eve's words hit him square between the shoulder blades. "Wait until you face an uninterrupted vertical drop of five thousand meters. You'll be quaking in your snow boots."

"I don't quake," he tossed back. "The only time I shudder is in orgasm."

He caught Eve's reflection as he shoved open the glass door and walked into the night. Her jaw had dropped and her eyes had gone wide. Her braid had worked its way over her shoulder, the tight-ass tip tweaking her right breast.

Satisfied he'd shaken her up, he left her to imagine his shudder.

# CHAPTER FIVE

Anger shook Eve Hannah when she faced Sloan McCaffrey four days later at the front door of Addie's town house. "You're crashing my eighty-year-old grandmother's birthday party?" Her tone was disbelieving. "Are you out of your mind?"

"I like older people," he said defensively. "I had no plans for the evening, so I thought I'd drop by."

Eve stared at the broad-shouldered man in the gray T-shirt, black leather vest, and distressed jeans. His hair was still damp from a recent shower. He hadn't bothered to shave for what appeared to be days.

A motorcycle helmet hung from his left hand. She looked down her nose at the big, bad bike parked on the lawn. "Is that your ride on the new sod?"

"It's a 1951 Vincent Black Shadow," he said proudly. "Hand-assembled. There are only eighteen hundred in existence."

"Shouldn't it be showcased? Preserved in a garage?"

"I'd rather show it off."

"You could have left it on the street."

"Parked between the golf carts and three-wheel bicycles?" He was all shock and indignation. "No way in hell. It stays on the grass. I don't want it scratched."

Unmovable, disagreeable man. Sloan remained before her, one booted foot on the brick stoop, the other between the door and jamb, trying to weasel his way inside. On either side of the door, flowering peach-and-fuchsia-colored impatiens in giant white ceramic planters scented the air in welcome. The late-afternoon sun hit Sloan's back, casting him in dark shadows.

"Who gave you my grandmother's address?" asked Eve.

"I overheard Risk Kincaid discussing the party in the clubhouse," he admitted. "Briarwood Village is a maze of streets. The house numbers are painted on the curb and hard to see. I drove by Addie's town house twice."

"You should have kept on driving."

The man had brass balls, showing up uninvited. His desperation to see Taylor irritated Eve. She was about to shut the door on him when he thrust a box into her hands. Gold metallic paper and a red silk bow suggested he'd had it professionally gift wrapped.

"I came prepared. I brought Addie a present," he said. "I'm a considerate, caring guy."

Eve shook the box. "Does it have a plug?"

"It's not an appliance."

"What is it?" She didn't want any surprises.

Sloan shrugged. "I grabbed it from my girlfriend closet—"

"Girlfriend closet?"

"I stockpile gifts. That way when I break up with a woman, I can give her a present when she leaves. Makes her happy, and I come off as the good guy."

Eve imagined the worst. "This gift could be a black teddy or a red thong?"

"Or a vibrator."

"Go home." She shoved the box into his chest.

He made a face, rubbing his left pec. "What's your hang-up, Eve?"

"My granddaughter has no hang-ups," asserted Addie Hannah as she came up behind Eve. "She's smart and pretty and a very good judge of character. Who, young man, are you?"

Eve watched Sloan study Addie. The two-story residence appeared overly large for the small woman who looked back at him questioningly. Even at her advanced age, Addie remained active. Tanned to a berry brown, she looked amazing with her braided white-blond hair, pale blue eyes, and "toned bones," as she called them. Attired in tennis whites, she clutched a Yonex racket in her right hand; in top-of-the-line Nikes she looked ready to receive a serve.

"I'm Sloan McCaffrey, ma'am," he stated. "Happy birthday."

"You're a guest I've yet to meet." Addie looked him over. "A friend of Taylor's or Eve's?"

He didn't miss a beat. "Eve's."

Eve caught the wicked gleam in his eye as his slow grin spread.

"I guess your granddaughter hasn't mentioned me, as we've just started dating."

*Dating?* Eve's mouth puckered as if she'd sucked a sour candy. Her throat closed; no words rose to refute his claim.

Addie tilted her head. "She hasn't mentioned you, son."

"Give her time," he said, straight-faced. "Once she starts talking about me, she won't be able to stop."

Addie slapped her tennis racket against her thigh. "You look athletic. Ever play football?"

"I played both football and baseball in college," he replied. "I've just come up from six years with Triple-A ball. This is my first year with the Rogues."

Addie looked thoughtful. "My granddaughters and their Rogues."

"Ma'am?" Sloan didn't understand.

Eve wasn't about to explain Taylor's past relationship with Brek Stryker. Let Sloan find out for himself.

Addie wasn't finished studying him. "McCaffrey." She paused, squinting hard. "You're the new reliever who allowed two home runs in the fifth inning against the Minnesota Twins during your major-league debut. Made the record books, I believe."

Sloan dipped his head and admitted, "That was me, ma'am. My life flashed back to the minors while I was standing on the mound watching two Twinkies pound my best heat. Had Brek Stryker not spoken on my behalf to the general manager, I'd be back in Triple-A. Stryke carries a lot of weight."

Addie patted him on the shoulder. "You've got the worst out of the way."

"Season's still young," muttered Eve.

Sloan *tsk-tsk*ed. "Not nice, sweetheart."

He then handed Addie the gift Eve had rammed into his chest. "Eve's spoken so highly of you," he said, his voice smooth and sincere. "Even though we've never met, I feel I know you, Addie. I wanted to drop off a gift."

"He has no plans to stay," Eve said so fast her words ran together.

"How very thoughtful." Addie accepted the gift. "Any man who bears a gift is welcome to join the fun. Steaks are being barbecued out back, and the bar's set up on the patio."

Addie stepped back to let Sloan enter. It took Eve a moment longer to allow him entrance. When Addie moved ahead of them down the hallway, Eve elbowed Sloan in the ribs, her voice tight. "*Dating?* You lied to my grandmother."

"Tonight's our first date. The lie got me into the party." Sloan slid his arm about her waist and drew her to him. "I think we need to keep up appearances. People will expect us to be into each other."

"You're not into me; you're into Taylor." She tried to pry his hand off her hip. He had big hands and a tight grip. "I won't be the placeholder between your last lover and my sister. I refuse to play along."

"Party pooper." He pulled her even closer. "Loosen up, Eve."

"You think I'm uptight?"

"You've got a broomstick up your ass."

She dug in her heels.

He sighed and stopped as well. "Now what?"

She turned toward him in the narrow hallway, and their hip bones collided.

She wiggled.

And he widened his stance.

Her apple green cotton skirt twisted and teased between his blue-jeaned thighs. He held her so tight, the pearl buttons on her yellow silk blouse dimpled the soft leather of his black vest.

Her nipples puckered.

Something other than his keys poked her belly.

Heat migrated south. "You . . . you're not—"

"Thinking with my dick? Damn sure am." He gripped her bottom. "Stop brushing unless you want me."

Want him? A man who no doubt called out his own name during sex? She stilled, clenching her teeth until her jaw ached. "I don't want you at this party."

"I'm not going to ruin anyone's fun."

Her fun was already ruined. "Just leave. I'll tell Addie you remembered a previous engagement."

"My only commitment's to you, sweetheart. My entire evening's free."

She flattened her palms against his chest, pushing him back. "Are you for real?"

"I can be real, given the right incentive."

She thumped his shoulder. "If you twitch one more time—"

"Sorry, twitching's beyond my control."

His hands stroked up and over her butt before he set her away from him. A room opened left off the hallway, and he ducked across the threshold. Afraid he'd steal the family silver, Eve followed. She caught him adjusting himself.

"Better now." He took two deep breaths and looked up. His interest was instantly held by the hundreds of framed photographs that drew the viewer into the lives of Liv and Stephan Hannah. From black-and-white to color, the pictures captured their extreme sports. Photos of Taylor's adrenaline highs were also scattered throughout.

Sloan admired a picture of Taylor waterfall ice climbing. "A lady and her icicles. Not many men would challenge life as she does."

Only Brek Stryker had dared. "Taylor's in a league of her own."

"Your sister's fearless."

He continued to circle the room, a room done in shades of sage and lemon sorbet, everything soft, warm, and inviting. As he closed in on one particular corner behind a green-and-gold paisley couch, Eve moved to intercept him. She snagged his arm and attempted to tug him beyond the next cluster of photographs.

The man was not to be tugged.

"This you?" He studied a picture of a young girl on horseback. "Damn, you're pale as a ghost."

"It's a black-and-white photograph."

"I can sense your fear."

Eve bit down on her bottom lip. She hated opening her life to this man. "I was eight. My parents thought I'd enjoy horseback riding."

"They were obviously wrong." His eyes narrowed sharply. "You're holding on to the saddle horn for dear life."

He hadn't yet noticed her tears—

"You're crying."

The man was too observant.

"You're bawling here too." He'd moved on to another photograph, one that pictured Eve clinging to her father's leg after riding the Matterhorn at Disneyland.

"I'm not a fan of roller coasters," she said stiffly.

He moved to the next picture. "Appears you weren't a fan of Santa either."

Eve knew the picture. At age four, she'd been petrified of the red-suited man with the white hair and beard. His merry, "Ho, ho, ho" had stood her hair on end. Tears had flowed. The elves had given her nightmares.

He ran his finger along the frame of the next photograph. "Nor did you enjoy climbing trees."

The big oak in the backyard. She'd climbed two rungs on a ladder that led to a tree fort when she'd stopped, afraid of heights. Taylor, at her back, had pressed her shoulder into Eve's bottom and pushed her another notch. Taylor was all laughter and fun, whereas Eve wanted nothing more than to feel the earth beneath her feet. Her expression shouted, *Get me down.*

She cringed as he took in the next photo. "You running from a duck?"

"It was at a petting zoo. I ran out of sunflower seeds, and the duck was still hungry. He came after me. Nipped my heel."

He lifted a brow, the corners of his mouth itching to smile.

"I was five, and the duck outran me. The bite hurt." Her face hot, her hands clenched, Eve drew herself up. "Can we move beyond my crying corner?"

"Bad memories?"

"All memories with my family were good. Some were just more stressful than others. Even though I wasn't athletic, competitive, or an adrenaline junkie, I was never left out of family functions. There were times my parents and Taylor held back because of me. Eventually I chose to stay with Addie when they traveled."

"You and Addie are close?"

"Close as mother and daughter." He'd learned enough about her, she decided. Eve nodded toward the door. "Let's go."

"Go, as in joining the others? Or go, as in I'm supposed to leave?"

"Can I get you to eat and run?"

"No man hurries through a steak."

He moved to stand before her, a broad-chested man who weighed about two-ten before the appetizers. Holding out his hand, he requested, "Date me for two hours?"

"Not for five seconds."

"Your grandmother thinks we're a couple."

"Whose fault is that?"

He let his hand drop. "I think fast on my feet. It seemed right at the time. You don't want to disappoint Addie, do you?"

"I don't want my name linked with yours."

"Why the hell not?"

"You have a three tattooed on your groin."

"For you, I'd go four dates."

"Give up, McCaffrey. I don't like you."

"I like myself enough for both of us." He shifted his stance, ready to move on. "Where can I find Taylor?"

He'd rather be with her sister. Eve's heart squeezed for six surprising seconds. "Taylor's on the patio," she told him. Retreating to the hallway, she pointed to the sunshine-hued tiles. "Follow the yellow brick road. Twenty feet and you'll bump into her."

"Where will you be?"

"Anywhere you aren't."

*"Quack, quack."* He nipped her on the neck on his way to the doorway. Gooseflesh rose on her entire body.

Twenty steps and Sloan McCaffrey easily found the patio, a screened expanse of gray slate and lavender-cushioned Adirondack chairs. Red streamers fluttered on the breeze, and blue, white, and yellow balloons dangled from the ceiling, festive and colorful.

A horseshoe pit bracketed one side of the porch; a flower garden bloomed on the other. Tennis courts and a clubhouse were visible off in the distance.

Sloan located his teammate Risk Kincaid and his wife, Jacy, beneath an enormous outdoor tent. Positioned around a gas grill, a dozen or more tables were set up for dining. Risk stood over the grill, turning steaks. Jacy lounged beside him on a vinyl chaise. Big, round sun-glasses shaded her face; the red polka dots on her white sundress matched her hair. Grecian sandals laced up her calves. She had nice calves.

The scent and sizzle of a juicy steak made Sloan hun-gry. He was glad he'd chosen Addie's birthday for dinner. He hoped they'd eat soon.

He found the nicer sister behind the bar on the patio.

Taylor was surrounded by a sophisticated and fit group of senior citizens, all casually dressed and nurturing cocktails.

In her aqua halter top, skinny black jeans, and bare feet, Taylor could make a man go hard. Her toenails were painted bright red. Several toes were banded in gold rings.

He felt neither twitch nor rise.

He was dead from the waist down.

And not happy about it.

He ducked beneath the HAPPY BIRTHDAY sign, bopped a balloon aside, then drew himself up on a bar stool. Trays of appetizers lined the bar. Sloan sat and watched Taylor mix drinks.

She knew her cocktails. She shook an apple martini, blended a piña colada, and added a cherry to a Manhattan. She wrapped up an order for a rum and Coke, then turned to him. "Hello, party crasher."

"Word spreads fast."

"Addie mentioned that Eve's date had arrived." One corner of Taylor's mouth turned up. "I know for a fact Eve's not involved right now."

"Can't picture Eve involved with anyone ever." Sloan scooped a handful of mixed nuts from a glass bowl on the bar, only to pick out the cashews. "She's too uptight."

Taylor looked at him strangely. "Eve, uptight?"

"Damn sure is."

Taylor pointed toward a dozen older men clustered about a horseshoe pit just off the patio. Eve stood among them. "She looks relaxed now."

Sloan's gaze drifted over Eve Hannah, who was getting a lesson in pitching horseshoes. Directly behind her, a slump-shouldered man set Eve's hips, then helped draw back her arm. He deliberately held on to her forearm even after she'd pitched the horseshoe.

Eighty hitting on thirty? Gramps should have released Eve immediately after the toss. Yet he was still hanging on.

The horseshoe landed in the sandy pit, a good three feet from the metal stake. Eve's second attempt landed a ringer. She smiled so broadly both her dimple and braces flashed. Her coach patted her shoulder.

"Who's the old guy?" he asked.

"Edwin Sweeney, horseshoe champ of Briarwood Village."

"Looks like Eve's found her sport." Sloan sampled a miniquiche. Tasting spinach, he pulled a face and went back to his cashews.

"Eve may not be athletic, but she's artistic," Taylor said as she popped the top on an Amstel, then poured it in an iced beer mug for one of Addie's guests. "She paints. While I was drawing stick figures, she mastered seascapes. She has a small studio downtown above Thrill Seekers. She has an upcoming show at Fine Arts next month."

"Good for her." He snagged a maraschino cherry from the condiment tray and sucked it off its stem. Rolling it around on his tongue, he said, "I get claustrophobic inside. I'm a sportsman. I come alive outdoors—"

"At the ballpark and on the mound." Taylor read him well. "You perform best with eighty thousand fans shouting your name."

"A definite rush."

Eve had stopped pitching horseshoes and now approached the bar. "No one will be cheering you down the mountain when you ski La Grave. The swoosh of your skis, the voice inside your head screaming, 'Stupid, stupid, stupid,' will be all that breaks the silence."

Sloan had long tired of Eve's sarcasm. He turned, about to tell her so, but lost his train of thought. Less than a foot separated them. He got caught up in her sunburned nose and unbuttoned blouse, opened because of the heat. A lacy cream camisole peeked out, as did the swell of her breasts.

His penis perked up. Damn, his dick had poor taste in women. He kept right on staring until Eve jerked her blouse together and once again buttoned up.

She spoke directly to Taylor. "Addie's getting ready to open her gifts. She wants everyone to gather by the porch swing."

Her sister immediately rounded the bar and moved toward the crowd surrounding her grandmother.

Sloan slid off the bar stool.

Eve blocked his path. "Tell me your present's appropriate for an eighty-year-old woman. I don't want Addie embarrassed."

"There will be blushing if she hits the switch and the G-Swirl buzzes."

She swatted his arm. "You jerk."

Sloan pulled back. Eve was slaphappy.

He watched Eve watch her grandmother as Addie opened a huge pile of gifts. Eve chewed her lip through the gift certificates, boxes of sugar-free candy, and aged brandy.

Risk and Jacy Kincaid presented Addie with a pink cellophane basket packed with gourmet coffees and cookies. Taylor added a new tennis racket and sleeves of tennis balls to the pile of gifts. Addie stood up and swung the racket from side to side, then declared it perfectly balanced.

A soft admiring "aw" rose from all those gathered as Addie carefully removed the brown wrapping paper from Eve's gift.

"The Old Cape Henry Lighthouse." Emotion brightened Addie's eyes. "One of my favorite landmarks. I thought you'd planned to sell this piece at your next show."

"Once you admired the painting, it was yours," Eve told her grandmother.

"I've always loved this old lighthouse." Addie propped the painting up against the back of the porch swing for all to see. "You captured its history, Eve: an old, yet proud beacon at the entrance to Chesapeake Bay."

For all Eve's snippiness and sarcasm, Sloan had to admit she could paint. Drawn against a weather-beaten sky, the tall octagonal structure cast the viewer into the lighthouse keeper's life, a solitary and lonesome existence amid hewn stone, narrow lookout windows, and oil-burning lamps.

Lost in the painting, Sloan felt the shift in the wind, saw the dark clouds racing, heard the waves pounding the shore. The lighthouse would withstand the heavy rainfall, as would the ships entering Norfolk harbor.

"I'll hang it this evening," Addie said to Eve.

"I'll stick around and help you," Sloan offered. "I have a suggestion as to which wall would catch the best light."

That wall was Eve's crying corner. It was time to replace her childhood photographs with this painting. For some unknown reason, her tears bothered him. She'd grown up in Taylor's adventurous shadow, afraid of Santa Claus and ducks.

"Next you'll be rearranging my grandmother's furniture," Eve objected.

He made a recommendation: "Angle the coffee table between the sofa and armchair and you'd have more walking space."

"The table stays right where it is."

Anticipation built as Addie opened Sloan's gift, a gift she'd saved for last.

"Don't let it be a vibrator," Sloan heard Eve pray as Addie stripped away the red bow and gold paper and slowly lifted the lid on the box.

Eve held her breath

Sloan hoped she'd turn blue.

A perplexed Addie reached into the box and removed a large engraved gold disk. " 'McCaffrey's Transport'," she read, then looked questioningly at Sloan. "I don't understand."

He edged forward until he was close enough to speak directly to the older woman. "I know many seniors can no longer drive and that you're an advocate for safe public transportation. Even though you may be able to convince the mayor to set up a service, I'm your driver until he gets the buses on the road. Twice a week, I'll take you and a group of friends to the mall, the restaurant of your choice, the theater, you name it. My cell phone number is also engraved on the token. Give me twenty-four hours' notice, and unless the Rogues are playing out of town, I'll get you where you want to go."

"Driving Miss Addie."

Sloan didn't have to turn around to know who'd uttered those words—they came from the sarcastic sister.

Addie patted his arm. "I accept your gift, and thank you, son. You're very generous with your time."

Approving nods from the guests followed Sloan as he walked back to Eve and Taylor. "Impressive," Taylor commented.

"Suck-up," Eve muttered.

"Addie loved your gift. She's ready to adopt you." Taylor squeezed his arm.

Sloan caught Eve's shudder.

He didn't give a rat's ass what Eve thought. He'd done right by Addie; that was all that mattered. He'd crashed her party, yet given an appropriate gift. No one could fault him now.

No one but Eve. "You played me." Her words struck low, her punch high.

A punch straight to his upper arm. Sloan's muscles spasmed. He grabbed her by the wrist and tugged her back near the bar out of earshot. All the guests had their backs turned to them. "Stop with the jabs; that's my pitching arm," he growled. "Damn straight I played you. You're sarcastic as hell and have me pegged as an ass. I'm not that bad."

"You're the very worst." Her eyes were livid, her tone tight.

Sloan stared at her. She was all fired up, her color high, Eve Hannah looked hot—hot enough for him to give her a second look. Her eyes flashed, and the pulse at her throat beat wildly.

As wildly as that of a woman about to climax.

Her heat drew his own.

His groin burned.

His dick strained against his zipper.

He'd be full-blown in a matter of seconds.

Wickedness pushed him to say, "Want to know what I'd have gotten you, had it been your birthday?"

Curiosity pursed her lips before she shrugged. "I couldn't care less."

He read women, and knew she wanted to know. So he told her: "A gift from Good Vibrations. And it's not a Beach Boys CD."

"A gift that runs on batteries?"

"You're quick, Eve. My women like Intimacy Kits."

"I'm not one of your women."

Definitely not one of his women. Sloan McCaffrey would never have a tight-ass in his life. Yet he had the sudden urge to provoke, to get her so worked up she squirmed.

He leaned in closer so his breath warmed her ear. "For you, I'd have gone with the deluxe kit."

Her eyes widened, and her blush deepened. Yet she didn't pull away.

"The deluxe includes *Naughty Nights*, an erotic novel that tucks you in and turns you on."

He heard her swallow.

"Then there's the chocolate thong. The heat of your body melts it down. Mm-mmm, good."

The tip of Eve's tongue wet her upper lip.

"And the Tickle-Popzzz. Green and purple guilt-free pleasure treats. The soft, vibrating rubber suckers are perfect for massaging those sweet spots that need a little extra attention."

Her breathlessness amused him.

"The kit also comes with a tangerine massage cream that makes you tingly all over." He took her hand and very slowly rubbed his thumb over her wrist. "You could use a tingle, couldn't you, Eve?"

Hot little shivers made her fingers twitch, and she clenched her hand to still the sensation.

He moved his hand to her hip, finger-walking across her belly—a surprisingly flat little belly. "You'd like the spearmint lubricant. The gel works to keep things warm and slippery."

Sloan swore he felt her stomach flutter.

Her lips had parted, and her eyelids had gone heavy.

His next words brushed her cheek. "The G-Swirl's my favorite. It has three speeds and is waterproof." He nipped one corner of her mouth. "Beats the hell out of bathing with a rubber ducky." Then he quacked.

His *quack* broke her trance. Eve stepped back so quickly,

she bumped into the bar. She rubbed her back and glared at him, more embarrassed now than angry. "Save your deluxe kit for someone else's birthday. You'd never be on my guest list."

"A shame, sweetheart. You could use a buzz."

"You should get your head out . . . out—"

"—from between a woman's thighs," he said around her stammer.

"There's more to life than chocolate thongs and flavored lubricant."

"Maybe so, but both make life sweet."

She shook her head, her cheeks now as red from embarrassment as they were from anger.

He hadn't meant to make her uncomfortable, only to tease her. Somehow he'd crossed the line. Her narrowed stare made him feel shallow and small. He didn't like the feeling.

In his mind, sex toys were to foreplay as warm-up pitches were to baseball. Both left the body well oiled and fluid and ready for action.

Yet the buzz of a vibrator would probably send Eve screaming from the bedroom. She'd never crack the spine on an erotic novel. Never get tangerine tingly.

He jammed his hands into his jeans pockets. He didn't want Eve totally ticked for the remainder of the party. He gave an inch. "Addie's your grandmother. You've thrown her a great party. If you want me to leave, I'm gone."

Eve blinked, blew out a breath that fluffed her bangs, and sighed heavily. Her mental debate lasted longer than he liked.

"Steak and cake," she finally said, "but be gone by the Bunny Hop."

"You hop?" It was hard to imagine her having fun.

"I'm the lead bunny."

83

Sloan couldn't help himself; he threw back his head and laughed out loud.

Eve fought her smile and lost. Her braces and one deep dimple flashed for two whole seconds, then were gone.

"Truce?" he asked.

"We'll never come to terms, McCaffrey," she said with conviction. "It is, however, Addie's day. She's all that matters." A short pause. "Go flirt with Taylor."

"That I can do."

Addie had opened her last gift and announced that it was dinnertime. Sloan got in line behind the seniors as they filed by Risk Kincaid at the grill and selected a steak. His wife, Jacy, stood by his side—a gorgeous woman, even in her quirky clothes.

"Which sister are you hitting on?" asked Risk as he dropped a T-bone onto Sloan's plate.

"The sweet one."

"Eve?"

Sloan frowned. "How can you call her sweet?"

"Eve's known as sweet, Taylor as sexy," Risk informed him.

"Eve invited me, but I'm interested in Taylor."

Risk looked at Jacy. "We heard you invited yourself."

Damn, did the whole world know he'd party-crashed? "I was at Thrill Seekers a few nights ago booking a trip when I overheard the ladies discussing the party and Addie's transportation problem. I knew I could fix it."

"You fixed it just fine," Risk said. "Taylor and Eve have full lives. Addie will soon have you on speed dial." He served up two thick tenderloins to an elderly man and woman, then asked, "You have a decent vehicle?"

"I'm looking at vans tomorrow."

"I'll go halves with you."

Sloan looked at the big man who played center field. Risk Kincaid was relaxed in social situations, yet came on hard on game day. He was known for his community involvement and accessibility to those in need. "I can afford the van," Sloan stated.

Risk cut a glance to Jacy. "It would please my wife greatly if I participated in transporting the elderly."

"If I'm happy, Risk will be grinning like a fool." Jacy slid one arm about her husband's waist and squeezed him tightly. Risk responded by dropping a light kiss on top of her red head. They were an openly affectionate couple, comfortable in each other's company.

Sloan admired what they had. On dates, he had women bumping and grinding and climbing his body. But he'd never stuck with one woman for more than three dates. Commitment and permanence were lost on him.

"Nice going, Sloan," Jacy complimented him. "Addie's in good shape and financially secure, but most of her friends are legally blind and on fixed incomes. Many haven't driven in years. Taylor told me that Addie has a trick right knee and that it locks on occasion. She refuses to drive for that reason. Your van will give the seniors lots of freedom."

"I'm certain several of the other Rogues would give one night a week to help out too," Risk said.

"I want Addie's gift free and clear of community-service hours," Sloan said firmly. "Anyone who transports, drives on his own time, not team time."

Risk nodded. "Agreed. I have a friend at the Dodge dealership. After practice tomorrow, we'll check out the Sprinter. It's durable, and with custom bench seats you could fit twelve."

"Let's get it done," Sloan agreed.

"You're a good man." Jacy smiled at him.

*Tell that to Eve*, he wanted to say, but let it pass.

"Go eat your steak before it gets cold." Jacy nudged him on. "There's a buffet laid out beneath the tent."

Sloan went to the buffet. He was one hungry man. He took heaping helpings of pasta salad, coleslaw, and corn on the cob. When he couldn't decide between a sweet or a baked potato, he took both, and piled on the sour cream.

He checked the tables for Eve and noted that she'd slid in between Addie and her horseshoe partner, a tight fit. No room for him there. He carried his plate back to the bar, where Taylor continued mixing drinks.

"Share my steak?" he offered.

"M-mm, maybe a bite. I'm not too hungry."

"Your leg's hurting you," he guessed.

She wasn't the type of woman to complain. "I ignore pain."

"You shouldn't be standing."

"I'll be off my feet shortly. Once the coffee is—"

*Is what?* Sloan took a bite of steak, waiting for her to finish her sentence. She never did. Taylor's gaze was fixed on the patio doors, and she'd gone pale.

He chewed and swallowed, then scanned the five new arrivals. He recognized Mayor Talbott from his picture in the paper, as well as Stuart Tate, his campaign manager. Then there was Brek Stryker and a pretty brunette, whom Sloan assumed was his fiancée, Hilary Talbott. As well as a photographer.

He saw Addie set aside her plate and rise to greet the mayor, manager, and brunette with a handshake and a smile. She next embraced Brek Stryker with a welcoming hug, as if he were family. Addie pointed to the bar, offering drinks.

All eyes came to rest on Taylor.

The mayor and manager nodded.

The brunette frowned.

Stryker's stare went from narrowed to hungry in six seconds flat. Hungry for steak, birthday cake . . . or Taylor Hannah?

For a solid minute Taylor and Brek openly stared, their gazes locked as tightly as any two bodies during sex. Singed by their sexual vibe, Sloan patted down his clothes, checking for fire.

*What the hell?* No one had told him that Stryke and Taylor knew each other. Yet it was obvious they packed a hot and heavy history.

A silence settled over the party.

The mood went from cheerful and loud to a funereal hush as gazes darted between the thrill seeker and the starting pitcher. It was obvious that everyone but Sloan knew about their past. Closemouthed Eve must have been laughing her ass off behind his back as he came on to Taylor, a woman who'd turned white as a sheet.

Gone was the daredevil with spirit and energy to burn. In her place stood a vulnerable woman barely holding her own.

Taylor's hands visibly shook as she measured coffee from a canister into the fifty-cup urn. Grounds spilled onto the shelf behind the bar. It took her two tries to plug in the coffeemaker. She then brought out the after-dinner liqueurs, offering the guests their choice of absinthe, Kahlua or crème de cacao.

Observant to the point of annoying people by what he saw, Sloan took it all in.

Only a man could make Taylor so edgy. That man had to be Brek Stryker. There was some major drama going down.

Amid it all, Sloan's steak called to him, thick and juicy and pink in the middle. He sliced off a big bite, chewing thoughtfully. He liked a party with a lot of action.

"Beck's," he requested of Taylor. When she didn't immediately respond, he threw a cashew at her. The nut bounced off her bare shoulder and got her attention. "Beer," he reiterated.

She poured him a Bud.

The lady was definitely distracted.

He set down his fork, reached across the bar, and laced his fingers with hers. "Want to touch my tattoo?" he teased to ease her tension.

A small smile curved her lips, and she managed to exhale. "Eve told me about your three."

Eve. Sloan groaned.

"Behave yourself, McCaffrey. You're her date for the party. No two-timing her."

"She told me to flirt with you."

"But did she mean it?"

Of course she meant it. Eve had no interest in him. None whatsoever. He looked across the tables to where she was chatting with Addie, her horseshoe partner, and five other guests. Eve had them leaning toward her as she related a story that held everyone's interest.

Taylor caught him looking at her sister. "Go join them. I'm fine behind the bar."

"The bar can't protect you like I can."

"Protect me from what?"

"Whatever or whomever broke your heart." He glanced

toward the sliding patio doors and saw Hilary Talbott leave her group and wind her way toward the bar. Brek Stryker was right behind her. "Put your game face on, Fearless," Sloan warned. "We're about to play hardball."

# CHAPTER SIX

Taylor's chest squeezed so tightly she thought her heart would burst. She'd known Mayor Talbott would make an appearance at Addie's party; she hadn't, however, expected Brek and Hilary to show as well. Yet there Brek stood, tall and handsome, his supportive palm high on Hilary's spine. A man protecting his woman.

Hilary . . . the woman who owned his heart. She looked stylish in her red blazer and gray skirt, complementing Brek's more casual appearance in a white button-down and navy trousers.

Unable to escape, Taylor returned Brek's stare. His expression was fixed, unreadable—a man who gave nothing away.

Her ears buzzed and her body hummed as Stryke and Hilary crossed to the bar, and Sloan McCaffrey closed in on her.

Sloan . . . For all his jock ego and cockiness, he was doing her an enormous favor. He was hanging out at the bar, paying her the attention of six men. The man could charm.

Had Taylor been several years younger, she might have taken Sloan for a test drive. He'd proven today that he could be her friend. But because she'd already had Brek

Stryker, she wanted no other man. Stryke was her once-in-a-lifetime love. She'd never forget him, even after he'd married.

"How do you know Stryke?" Sloan lowered his voice discreetly.

"We were close once."

"Close as in sharing a cup of coffee or doing the dirty?"

"That's none of your business."

"I'm sizing up the competition," he told her. "Are you only into starters or will you date a reliever?"

"I'd date the closer if I liked him."

He cut into his steak and offered Taylor a bite. "Pretend the steak melts in your mouth. Moan a little."

She ate off his fork, a friendly yet intimate gesture. However tasty the food, she couldn't bring herself to moan.

"Want to round my horn?" Sloan used the baseball term as a sexual invite just as Hilary and Stryke reached the bar.

Taylor barely managed to swallow.

"McCaffrey," Stryke acknowledged before he looked at Taylor, a flatness in both his tone and expression.

Hilary, on the other hand, studied Taylor with shy interest. "I'm Hilary Talbott." The soft-spoken brunette introduced herself with the polite formality of a politician's daughter. She looked from Sloan to Taylor. "I believe you know my fiancé, Brek."

Taylor had once known him inside out and buck naked—a man of strength and pride, who was engagingly open to love.

That man was long gone. His cool detachment told her she was a dead memory.

"I'm Taylor Hannah, Addie's granddaughter." She

fought to keep her voice steady, did her best to be cordial.

"Sloan McCaffrey, party crasher," Sloan introduced himself.

Hilary recognized him. "You climb onto that little hill and throw pitches after Brek." It was obvious she didn't know a lot about baseball.

"I'm the reliever," Sloan explained. "I take over where Brek leaves off." *Both on and off the field.*

The words unsaid were heard the loudest—a most daring comment on Sloan's part. Taylor noticed the hard set of Brek's jaw. Only Hilary looked blank and out of the loop.

"What can I get for you?" Taylor wanted to mix their drinks and move them on. She'd never wanted to meet Hilary. Never wanted to know whom Brek had chosen after her. The pain of seeing the two of them together was physically debilitating. She could barely breathe. Every muscle in her body ached from holding herself so stiffly.

"Scotch for Daddy and Stuart," Hilary requested with a sweet smile. "I'll have a vodka gimlet, and Brek will have . . ." Her expression went blank.

Taylor waited for the woman to say, "Club soda with citrus." Hilary never did. Her puckered brow indicated that she couldn't remember what her fiancé drank. Stryke looked concerned as well.

During Brek's time with her, Taylor knew he hadn't indulged during baseball season. He'd kept his body at a high-performance level. She wondered whether he drank now or still abstained. She stood quietly, awaiting his order.

"Club soda and citrus," he finally said.

Taylor exhaled her relief over his choice. She was glad some things hadn't changed.

Across the bar, Hilary hooked her arm through Brek's. She looked up at him with her big brown eyes. "Did we decide on a restaurant for dinner? Daddy thought the Prime Club might be nice, but Stuart and I prefer Chesapeake Landing. I'm in the mood for seafood. How about you?"

Stryke shrugged. "It doesn't matter, as long as it's an early night."

Taylor caught Hilary's pout. "I respect your curfew; I just wish you could stay up past eleven on occasion."

"Maybe I could," he agreed, "in the right circumstances."

Memories hit Taylor hard. She'd always looked forward to his curfew. She and Stryke would strip and race for bed. Neither had slept until the early morning hours, yet he'd still gotten up with the alarm.

Closing her mind to what once had been and would never be again, Taylor set the three alchoholic drinks on the bar, then poured club soda for Brek. She squeezed fresh lemon and lime wedges into the soda, then floated several orange slices on top.

"Another Bud, sweetheart." Sloan held up his beer glass as Hilary and Stryke picked up their drinks.

Her fingertips damp, Taylor lost her grip on the glass Sloan passed to her. It slipped through her hand. At any other time, she could have caught the glass before it hit the floor; her reflexes were that sharp. Not today, however. Her muscles froze, and she watched as the glass hit the slate tile near her right foot and shattered loudly.

"She's barefoot," she heard Sloan say.

She damn sure was. Flecks of blood now patterned her toes. She stepped back, only to feel splinters of glass bite into the ball of her foot.

Angry with herself for being so clumsy, she searched

behind the bar for a broom and dustpan. Locating them on a bottom shelf beneath a lemonade pitcher, she quickly bent to clean up the mess.

Pairs of low biker boots, gray suede pumps, and leather loafers rounded the end of the bar as she worked.

"You're bleeding; I'll finish up." Sloan hunkered down beside her and took the broom and dustpan right out of her hands.

"It's nothing." She tried to wave Sloan off.

"Glass in your foot is something. You don't need an infection." The statement came from Brek, without any inflection of concern.

Emotionally drained, Taylor straightened. "I'm fine. Just fine." Her knee, swollen and sore, suddenly popped. Her leg buckled and she pitched forward.

It was Stryke who reached for her.

Stryke who caught her.

Stryke whose hands curved about her hips and kept her upright.

Stryke who lifted and swung her over the remaining shards of glass before she could cut herself further.

Stryke who then stepped back and let her limp toward the powder room. Alone.

Taylor set her shoulders and straightened her spine, a physical warning to those gathered not to follow her.

"Should I help her?"

Hilary's question had Taylor limping a little faster. No matter her good intentions, the very last thing Taylor needed was Brek's fiancée playing nurse.

She made it to the powder room below the staircase and closed the door. The scents of lemon potpourri and lavender bath soaps soothed her, fragrances that would always remind Taylor of Addie.

Suddenly tired, she leaned against the jamb and closed

her eyes. Brek's arrival at Addie's party with Hilary was a real killer. Did he hate her so much he wanted to publicly humiliate her, as she'd once humiliated him on their wedding day?

Placing her hand over her heart, Taylor wished she could push back the pain. She'd never have believed her chest could hurt so much. She felt vulnerable. Totally lost. Completely crushed.

And very much alone.

A knock on the door brought her heart to her throat. "Taylor, it's Hilary Talbott. I'm coming in."

A push on the door nudged Taylor forward. Hilary peered in. "Let's clean your foot."

*Don't be nice to me.* Taylor opened her eyes, her gaze unfocused. "I can manage on my own." Her voice sounded out-of-body.

Hilary glanced down at Taylor's toes. "There's a lot of blood."

"Superficial cuts," Taylor assured her. "They look worse than they are."

"Let me be the judge." Hilary stepped fully into the powder room and motioned toward a stool covered in yellow satin. "Sit down, please."

Hilary had come to care for Taylor. Only outright rudeness would send her away.

Taylor sank down on the stool.

Hilary then proceeded to study the contents of the medicine cabinet. She set out a bottle of peroxide, a magnifying glass, a pair of tweezers, several cotton balls, and a tube of Neosporin, along with three large Band-Aids.

"What can I hand you first?" Hilary asked.

Taylor slowly slid off her toe rings, crossed her right foot over her left knee, and examined the cuts. They were worse than she'd originally thought. Deeply embedded glass poked from the ball of her foot. Fine splinters stabbed her toes. It would take some time to doctor her foot.

"Tweezers," she finally managed.

Hilary quietly handed them to her.

The silence held as Hilary watched Taylor work on her foot. Every time Taylor blew out a breath and looked up, she met Hilary's stare.

A rather intense stare, for a woman known to be shy. Taylor sensed that Hilary was sizing her up.

The tick of the powder room clock registered less than a minute before the brunette bit down her bottom lip and said, "I like Brek a lot. He's a good man."

*Like him?* Hilary's choice of words surprised Taylor. *Like* was appropriate for friends, dogs, flavors of ice cream, and a good book. Not for the man Hilary was about to marry.

Taylor had no desire to discuss Brek.

Hilary, on the other hand, did. "I, um, know this is awkward, but I need your advice," she softly continued. "Even though Brek never talks about you, I know you were once engaged. Tell me how to make him happy. I don't want to make the mistakes you did."

Taylor's mistakes. *Don't leave him at the altar and you'll be fine.* That didn't sound quite right. But it was all Taylor had to offer.

Her time with Brek had been sacred. She'd screwed up royally. Admitting this to Hilary would open wounds and leave more scars.

"Peroxide, please," was all she could manage.

Hilary was slow to hand her the disinfectant, so Taylor reached for the bottle herself. Forgoing cotton balls, she poured the peroxide straight onto her foot. The disinfectant bubbled, turned white, and her toes started bleeding again. She grabbed a hand towel and blotted her foot.

There was a shuffle of feet, and Sloan McCaffrey appeared in the doorway. "Glass is all cleaned up," he told Taylor.

"We came to check on you," Eve put in, as both she and Addie peered around Sloan.

Taylor welcomed their arrival. "My foot is fine," she assured her grandmother. "Go back to your guests."

Addie nodded. "I'll be close by."

Eve, however, stayed.

Sloan crossed to Taylor, hunkering down beside the stool. He ran one finger over the ball of her foot, then across her toes.

"I'm still feeling glass," Taylor told him.

"Let's take a closer look. Magnifying glass," Sloan requested.

Hilary dropped it on his palm.

Sloan made three attempts at removing the glass before Taylor stopped him. "You're pushing the glass in, not picking it out." She took back the tweezers.

Sloan apologized. "I never meant to hurt you, sweetheart."

Hilary was watching them closely. "You two a couple?"

Sloan looked from Taylor to Eve. His grin curved slowly. "Eve's the only sister who's seen my tattoo."

Hilary looked confused. "I thought you were with Taylor."

"Enough of me for both of them," answered Sloan.

Taylor rolled her eyes, and Eve pulled a face.

Hilary, on the other hand, contemplated his remark. "I'd heard the players brand themselves."

"Adds to our mystique," Sloan explained. "I have the number three; Brek has 'Strike Zone.'"

Hilary fingered a brass button on her red blazer. "So I've heard."

*Heard, not seen?* Taylor went still—so still she wondered if her heart had stopped beating. Was it possible Hilary and Brek had yet to sleep together?

Hilary a virgin?

Brek celibate?

Hard to comprehend. Brek was a physical man. He'd wanted Taylor as often and as badly as she'd wanted him. They'd been as active in sex as in sports. Dusk to dawn, they'd welcomed the sun with a smile on their faces.

"Ah, there you are, Hilary." Stuart Tate had located the mayor's daughter. "Your father requests your presence. He'd like you to meet his senior constituents."

"Excuse me," Hilary said as she stepped around Sloan.

Tate eased back to let her pass as well. He then pressed his palm to her lower back and followed her out.

Sloan nodded toward the door once Hilary and Stuart had moved beyond earshot. "They're pretty chummy."

"They're working together on the campaign," Taylor suggested.

"Goes beyond work." Sloan stood up. He hitched his hip on the powder room vanity and crossed his arms over his chest. "Try sexual familiarity."

Startled, Taylor lost her grip and she tweezed her little toe, slicing skin. She winced. "Jacy speaks highly of Hilary. The woman's sweet and reliable and dedicated to Brek."

"No dedication there."

Taylor's chest compressed and her breath locked in her throat. "You're wrong, Sloan."

"I'm calling it like I see it."

"Prove it," Eve challenged.

"I caught the look in Hilary's eyes when she first saw Stu. She's seen the man naked."

Eve's eyes went wide. "You got all this from a look?"

"Her look and his palm," Sloan stated. "A man's hand on a woman's ass is the universal sign they're lovers."

"You need glasses."

"I saw what I saw, Eve." He stood firm. "I'm sure Stu removed his hand by the time they joined the others."

"Brek's not blind." Taylor exhaled. "He'd know if Stuart was making a move on his fiancée."

Sloan shrugged. "A man sees what he wants to see. It all depends how much Stryke's into his woman."

"Maybe you're reading more into the situation than is warranted," Eve said, looking unconvinced.

"Maybe I am; maybe I'm not."

Silence hung heavy as Eve and Sloan faced off, glaring at each other. Taylor took in their confrontation and found it amusing. Their dislike sparked like loose wires—wires that, if ever connected, would shock them both into tomorrow.

Sloan's observations left Taylor thinking. She refused to believe Hilary was cheating on Stryke. Surely Sloan had misinterpreted Hilary's look and Stuart's palm on her back.

It had to be a mistake.

"Take care of your foot." Eve patted Taylor on the shoulder. "I'll be back to check on you."

Taylor nodded and returned to work on her foot.

"Taylor." Sloan said her name so softly, she wasn't certain she'd heard him. Glancing up, she found he'd gone all serious on her. "I wouldn't have come on so strong had I known you cared for Stryke."

"You flattered me with your attention," she said, easing his tension with a smile. "Brek lost interest long ago."

"You're a thrill seeker and a total turn-on."

"Compliments are always welcome."

His dark brows drew together, and genuine curiosity

darkened his gray eyes. "What happened between you two? A miscommunication? A fight?"

She blew out a breath. "It wasn't like that."

"What was it like? The man was a fool to leave you."

"Not quite the fool you think," Brek corrected from the doorway, where he now loomed, tall and broad shouldered. His eyes were narrowed, his mouth hard. The powder room felt suddenly small and very crowded. "I never left Taylor; she left me—at the altar on our wedding day. She chose paragliding over our vows."

"Holy shit." Sloan McCaffrey coughed into his hand. "Must have been one hell of a glide."

Stryke took in the scene: Taylor sitting on the stool, her foot slightly swollen and already turning black and blue from the embedded glass; Sloan leaning negligently against the vanity, bold in his pursuit of Taylor.

His chest tightened at the reliever's interest. He shouldn't have felt a thing, yet he did. Pain wedged between his ribs like a spike, and his muscles felt roped and knotted.

"I shouldn't have pried," Sloan finally said as he pushed off the vanity and moved toward the door. "Later, Taylor."

Stryke stepped aside to let him pass.

Which now left him alone with Taylor and her tweezers.

"Addie asked that I check on you," he told her.

She blew him off. "A few more splinters and I'm ready to Bunny Hop."

Bunny Hop, his ass. The stubborn woman couldn't even stand.

She sat, her spine curved, her concentration back on her foot and off him. Wisps of blond hair curved against her cheekbones, her face in profile, slightly drawn, her lips tight. Her breathing was shallow. He could barely detect the rise and fall of her chest.

She hadn't looked at him since he'd entered the powder room. She was waiting for him to take the initiative and leave.

He wasn't going anywhere.

He took a step toward her. "Need help with your foot?"

"*No*," she said so abruptly, and with so much force his own heart kicked.

A growl rose low in his throat. To hell with what she wanted. He held the advantage. Taylor had a hurt foot and a bad knee. She couldn't run either fast or far from him. He was staying—whether she liked it or not.

He dropped down beside her.

She jerked back.

"Don't touch me." Her words were edged with the same unhealed pain he felt when he was near her.

Despite her resistance, he secured the tweezers and her ankle. He pressed her heel to his thigh, then wrapped one hand about her calf to hold her still.

She quieted.

Her nearness scented the air with Amber Nude. The fragrance reminded him of restless nights and heated sex.

So much sex—both rough-and-tumble and slow and languid—as well as long moments of doing nothing more than holding each other.

"You need my help," he insisted. "I've doctored you more times than I can count. Give me five minutes, and if I haven't removed the glass, I'll leave."

She looked at him then, a woman torn between dealing with his doctoring and dealing with him as a man. "You need to be with Hilary, not here in the powder room with me."

"Hilary doesn't have glass in her foot."

He poured a capful of peroxide between her toes, then took up the task of removing the tiniest shards of glass.

He'd always liked her feet, narrow with sexy toes. He knew they were ticklish. Yet now wasn't the time to make her giggle. Those days had long passed.

"Four minutes," Taylor counted down the time on the vanity wall clock, the tick loud in the ensuing silence.

Stryke moved to the ball of her foot. He'd removed the last piece of glass by the time Taylor said, "Thirty-five seconds."

He ran his fingers along her toes and across the bottom of her foot, making sure he'd gotten it all. Without conscious thought, he stroked her ankle. His thumb drew a soft circle over the bone before she pulled her foot back.

"Thanks, but I can take it from here," she told him.

She stretched then, reaching over his shoulder for the Neosporin and Band-Aids on the vanity. His shoulder flexed as her breast unexpectedly brushed his upper arm, and her sleek side came in contact with his chest.

The sensation was as intense as it was irreversible, a commingling of heat, a compression of flesh.

He could tell she was debating whether to pull back or to collect the items. In the end, she sucked it up and grabbed what she needed, then dropped back on the stool.

Pushing to his feet, Stryke looked down on her fair head, the slender column of her neck, the firm set of her shoulders. He had something to say, and needed to get it off his chest. "I apologize for showing up at Addie's party."

Taylor cautiously met his gaze. "It wasn't purposeful?"

He tucked his hands into the front pockets of his dress slacks and shook his head. "Despite our history, I'd never go out of my way to embarrass or humiliate you. There was no reason for you to meet my fiancée. I thought we were headed to dinner. I had no idea until I was in the limo that the mayor planned to stop here for a photo op. If I could have avoided Addie's birthday, I would have."

She nodded. "I appreciate your honesty."

"I've always been honest with you."

"I'm the one who never came clean." Her expression turned thoughtful as she spread the Neosporin and strategically placed the Band-Aids between her toes. "I owe you—"

"Nothing, Taylor." He refused to touch on their past. "Now's not the time."

Her lips compressed. "Will there ever be a time?"

"Afraid not."

She looked a little sad as she absently rubbed her knee—a gesture not lost on Stryke. He knew her knee hurt her more than she'd ever let on. "Tell me you're not desert hiking on Monday." The words escaped him, spoken with more concern than he would have liked.

"I thought you wanted me gone."

"I do, but not if you're hurt."

She eased to her feet and stood before him, her weight on her good leg. Her smooth forehead reached his chin, a forehead he'd so often bent and kissed, just for the pleasure of it. Not today. Not ever again.

She angled her head to meet his gaze. "I have an appointment with an orthopedist on Monday. My trek across the Sahara is postponed for a week."

"Another week in Richmond, huh?"

"The Rogues are on the road," she reminded him. "You play a three-game series against Kansas City, then four games in Detroit, followed by a weekend doubleheader in Louisville. Our paths won't cross."

*Might never cross again.* A hollowness gripped him, one

he might never fill. It frustrated him that this woman who'd once ditched him still complicated his life and touched his soul.

He forced her from his heart, closing his mind to thoughts of what might have been. He could never go back. What they'd had was dead.

"Brek, we're about to leave." Hilary Talbott had come for him. She stood small in the doorway, hesitant, but clearly hopeful he was ready to join her.

Stuart Tate was at her back. Always at her back. Sometimes he stood so close, Stryke didn't know where Hilary left off and Stuart began. He'd questioned Hilary about Tate's need to shadow her. Hilary had explained that her father had asked Stuart to keep tabs on her during the campaign. The mayor hadn't wanted her lost in the crowd or uneasy at any function.

That still didn't explain Stuart's liberties. Stryke had noticed the campaign manager's hands on Hilary: a touch to her arm, a palm on her back. He needed to have a man-to-man with Stu when the time was right.

Maybe tonight. Maybe tomorrow. Maybe next week. Whenever the opportunity presented itself.

"I'm with you," he told Hilary. He then cast one final look at Taylor—and wished he hadn't. Sadness flickered deep in her sea green eyes, as if she had regrets she'd never voiced. There was no need to hear them now. They were on two different life paths, and his led to dinner with Hilary Talbott. "What restaurant did you decide on?" he asked his fiancée.

"Stuart and I persuaded Daddy to dine at Chesapeake Landing." Her, "Work for you?" came almost as an afterthought.

Stryke liked seafood, although tonight he'd have preferred the Prime Club. The chef grilled a mean filet.

He'd caught Risk Kincaid's eye out by the barbecue. Stryke would have liked nothing more than to pull up a lawn chair and enjoy a meal with Risk and Jacy.

Instead he moved toward Hilary. And Stuart.

Glancing back at Taylor, he cast over his shoulder, "Take care of your knee."

"I'm a fast healer. I'll be gone soon."

*The sooner the better.*

Her life course was set.

And so was his.

Then why did he already miss her?

"Brek Stryker's in love with Taylor Hannah."

Hilary Talbott ignored Stuart Tate. She sucked his words into her mouth, then stabbed him with her tongue. Hot, needy, and demanding, she bit his lip, securing his silence.

She hated a man who talked during sex. Stu had gone on nonstop since sneaking through the back door of her condo. He'd drawn a ragged breath when she'd stripped off his clothes and shoved him down on the horseshoe-shaped sectional. He'd then gone off on another tangent, even when she'd taken him in her mouth and given him a blow job that should have shut him up for the entire night.

Now in bed, he rambled on and on. "You'd better hope Taylor leaves town soon. She's about to screw up your father's campaign."

Stuart was going to talk her to death.

She reached for a condom on the nightstand and tore it open. He grunted as she roughly rolled it on. The latex tip hung longer than his rod. Why he bought Magnums for his millimeter peter was beyond Hilary. The man had penis envy.

She stuffed him inside her, then bucked wildly to get him fully hard.

*"Grind."* Hilary wanted satisfaction, and Stuart was slow in getting her off.

He'd perfected a hip twist that always did the trick. Yet tonight he was all pump, and each time he pulled back he lost penetration, which frustrated her enough to growl, *"Stick it,* Stu."

She dug her nails into his hips.

Stuart yelped.

Then she directed his drive, spanking his ass when he slowed.

Tate grunted in her ear. The sweat from his upper lip slicked her cheek. His breath beat against her neck, hot and wet as he licked the base of her throat.

He ground so hard, she swore he'd bruise her hip bones. The pleasure-pain made her light-headed. She was almost there. . . .

Stuart withdrew. "Take off Stryker's ring and put mine on," he demanded.

Hilary lost her mind. "Change rings, *now?*" Her shriek hurt her own ears.

He teased her opening with the tip of his penis.

Sensitive, wet, and on the verge of orgasm, she swore a blue streak as she tore off Brek's ring and threw it across the room. She rolled onto her side, tore open the top drawer of her white-lacquered nightstand, and retrieved the ring Stu had bought for her with one of Brek Stryker's donations to father's campaign fund.

Showcased on her finger, the pink diamond shone large, brilliant, and outrageously expensive. Hilary felt she deserved every carat. She'd catered to her father's political ambitions long enough. She didn't care if he was elected mayor for a second term. She did, however, plan to skim enough money from his campaign fund to move from Richmond.

*"Happy?"* She lunged at him, bit him on the shoulder. Marked him with her uppers.

He penetrated her once again, went with the hip twist, and she climaxed within seconds. Her orgasm would have been stronger had he not insisted she change her ring, but she'd demand seconds as soon as Stuart caught his breath.

She pushed him off her and settled against her pillows—imported feather pillows with creamy satin cases.

Stuart removed his condom, tossed it in the trash, then rolled onto his side to face her. "Within a month, Brek will be breaking off your engagement. The man wants Taylor."

"He has too much pride to go back to her."

"It's passion, not pride, that's making him hard."

"You think I can't hold him?"

"Not even with sex."

Stuart's words hurt, yet Hilary knew them to be true. The photo op between her father and the senior constituency had backfired. She'd planned an in-your-face with Taylor Hannah, yet Hilary had been the one to get an eyeful.

She'd witnessed Brek's stunned and unguarded expression when he'd first caught sight of Taylor behind the bar at her grandmother's birthday party. It had been open, honest, and animal hungry. The spark between the two was as incendiary as it was painful to her.

Brek had masked his emotions, but it had been evident that his feelings for Taylor weren't as dead as he claimed.

Hilary knew she couldn't change how Stryke felt about the thrill seeker. She had no reason to try. Brek was a means to an end, nothing more. She believed him an honorable man. He wouldn't dump her overnight.

"One final donation and we're set for life."

"You're pressing your luck," Stuart worried.

"It's luck to press. I have nothing to lose." Hilary punched her pillow. "My life sucks. I hate working for my uncle. There's no advancement in his firm. Uncle Matt has two sons. They're a shoo-in for the next vice presidents. I will remain an administrative assistant until I turn gray."

Her scowl deepened. "I also hate being the token sweetheart in this campaign. Daddy sees me as a lightweight. He pats me on the head like the family dog. I'm tired of smiling, shaking hands, and being nice to voters."

Stuart ran a finger down her bare arm. "Hang in there. We'll be in Costa Rica by the end of June. We close on the oceanfront villa next week."

His words calmed her. Stuart might not be much to look at, but they both dreamed the same dream. He was as conniving and greedy as Hilary. They made a solid couple.

From the onset of the campaign, they'd played with the notion of what it would be like to be rich—filthy, stinking rich. They'd fantasized about Costa Rica, the lush beaches, warm weather, and low cost of living.

Their fantasy had become a reality when Brek Stryker walked into campaign headquarters and made his first donation. They'd realized then that skimming funds could set them up for life.

They'd done more than skimmed. They'd dipped deeply.

Hilary had found that managing both Stuart and the money came easily. Their offshore account was setting fat.

"Playing nice with Brek Stryker is getting old," she confessed. "He's become inattentive—"

"And harder to handle."

That, too, Hilary had to agree.

Brek . . . The very thought of the man made her shiver. She found him intimidating. His size and larger-than-life persona overwhelmed her. He filled a room, commanded attention. No one should be that good-looking, wealthy, and physically skilled.

"Brek's as high-profile off the field as he is at the park," Hilary complained. "Throughout the campaign, he's gotten more media attention than my father. Crowds rush him, wanting his autograph and an interview. Few listen to Daddy's speeches. Speeches *you* write."

"My speeches blow hot air," Stu stated. "Brek Stryker's a celebrity. He's drawn more attention to your father's campaign than a million dollars' worth of advertising ever could. He'll back Wayne as long as your old man supports the Boys and Girls Clubs of Richmond."

Hilary smiled up at the ceiling. "Brek will shit a brick when the city budget cuts eliminate those clubs."

"Cross Brek Stryker, and he'll be a force to reckon with." Stuart raised himself on one elbow, looking down at her. "We need to pull back. Your sweetness and dedication can't hold him now. There's a shift in the wind. Her name is Taylor Hannah."

Stuart was right. In their earliest days together, Stryke had been drawn to her shyness and stability. Those attributes had held him once, but wouldn't over time.

He'd had no closure with Taylor. It was obvious she still lived in Brek's heart and mind. Hilary couldn't shut the woman out. The starting pitcher needed more than a gentle smile and a soft touch. He needed Taylor Hannah.

The thrill seeker exuded a beauty born of self-confidence and good genes. Men would always do a double take when they saw her. They'd stand taller, suck in their guts, and wish they had nine-inch dicks.

No woman would stand up to a comparison. Taylor's

natural beauty made cosmetics obsolete. No female deserved cheekbones so sharp, nor a mouth so lush that men would fantasize over her kiss.

Hilary punched her fists into the mattress and admitted, "Brek's grown restless. The man has needs."

She'd felt those needs in his embrace. He'd never pushed her for sex; an occasional kiss satisfied him. Until now. She could tell by his increased heat, the constant flexing of his muscles, the ridge beneath his dress slacks, that he was a man needing his woman.

Ring or no ring, Hilary was not Stryke's woman.

She was committed to Stuart Tate.

Her plan was to leave before election night. She and Stuart would be long gone by the time her father read his concession speech. He had no chance of winning. Wayne Talbott was old and out of touch with today.

His opponent, Scott Beatty, was young, innovative, and presented himself well. His television ads spoke to the people; his radio time was carefully calculated to capture the most listeners.

Hilary had purposely limited her father's communications to fifteen seconds. Less money spent on media meant more money in her pocket. She'd sold her father out.

There'd be a landslide vote in Beatty's favor.

Hilary would applaud his win from Central America.

# CHAPTER SEVEN

Rogues verse Colonels. Louisville, Kentucky. The stadium shook with shouts and foot stomping. The sellout crowd was as frenzied and loud as at any World Series championship.

Bottom of the ninth, and Brek Stryker stood on the mound, his nerve endings charged. Two additional outs and he'd have thrown a no-hitter. It would be the sixth no-hit game of his career, and would tie his father's record.

Brek wanted this win. Badly.

The Rogues were on a hot streak. And Brek was at his personal best. The team had swept both the Royals and the Tigers, and were about to sweep the Colonels. A win today and Richmond would rank first in the National League East.

Throughout the week, the team had played all out. There'd been few strikeouts and no errors. Everyone had been on their game.

The Bat Pack had hit as many home runs as on-base singles.

Defensively, the team played like action heroes. Risk Kincaid covered center field on bionic legs. Right fielder Psycho McMillan came off the ground for fly balls as if he wore a jet pack. Third baseman Romeo Bellisaro bare-handed the ball to first so many times he had no need for his glove. Shortstop Zen Driscoll had picked up hoppers and short pop-ups with well-oiled precision.

Brek hadn't shaken off Chase Tallan once. The series of signs had brought an unbeatable rhythm and cadence between pitcher and catcher. Strikes came fast as Brek pitched to the catcher, not the batter.

It was late Sunday afternoon. The sun now edged his shoulder, and shadows scored the outfield. No one warmed up in the bullpen. He was set to go the full nine innings.

Rogues led the Colonels six to nothing.

He rolled his shoulder, eyeing the next batter. Randy Hampton. Ham hadn't had a hit in his last sixteen times at bat. The man was due.

Brek cut a glance at the on-deck circle and spotted Kason Rhodes. Rhodes swung a hot bat. He had wild eyes and led with his chin.

Fans called him "Mental."

Brek swore Kason was Psycho McMillan's twin, separated at birth. Both had similar looks, indiscriminant wild streaks, and could bat the cover off a ball.

While Psycho often swung at the unhittable pitch, Kason was known for his discipline and patience. The man would wait a full count before taking his swing. He seldom hit out of his strike zone. Rhodes ranked first in home runs in the American League. Psycho sat on top for the National.

Brek took a deep breath, then attacked Randy Hampton. He threw across his body, sliding in a fastball for a swing and a miss. Strike one.

Second pitch, and Hampton hacked at Brek's slider. The ball went foul to the mighty roar of Chewbacca. The stadium had a sound system that brought *Star Wars* to Lindenberry Park.

Fans fought for the fly. Strike two.

Brek returned to his fastball.

A checked swing by Hampton. Ball one.

A final cutter, and Ham whiffed. Strike three.

He went down, to the dismay of the crowd.

Angered, Hampton threw both his bat and batting helmet, and was immediately ejected from the game.

Brek had one batter to go for his no-hitter.

*Get him before he gets you.* His father's coaching came to mind. Brek couldn't afford a mental mistake.

Marshaling all his concentration, he honed in on Kason Rhodes, a man whose eyes had narrowed to a squint. There was an intense flare to Rhodes's nostrils and a curl to his lip as he dug in; his stance was so tight his muscles bulged.

Brek's windup was precise, his delivery strong.

A breaking ball, down and in.

A hard smack by Rhodes, and wood went flying. Brek ducked to get out of the way of the broken bat. The ball shot upstairs, bounced off the upper deck. Foul, strike one.

Fastball, outside. Ball one.

Cutter on the corner. Strike two.

Changeup. Rhodes checked his swing, and the home-plate umpire ruled that he had not gone around. Ball two.

The Rogues' pitching coach, Danny Young, disagreed with the call. He tore off his baseball cap, stormed out of the dugout, and shouted several choice phrases at the umpire.

The umpire warned Young to sit down and shut up.

Young kicked dirt and begrudgingly returned to the dugout. His cap was still off in protest.

The stadium became a living thing. Louisville fans cheered Rhodes to hammer it out of the park. The Richmond crowd screamed just as loudly for a no-hitter.

The catcher signaled a slider.

Brek delivered.

High and wide. Ball three.

Full count.

A final signal from Chase Tallan, and Stryke wound up for the last pitch. He knew that if the ball was anywhere within Rhodes's area code, the man was going to swing.

Rhodes swung with bad intention, and caught a piece. Low, and as straight as a speeding bullet, the ball shot between first and second base.

Psycho McMillan rushed in from right field and made the save, but not before Rhodes earned a double.

Brek Stryker exhaled his disappointment on a low hiss. *Son of a bitch.* He'd gone from no-hitter to a one-hitter in the blink of an eye.

He *felt* Kason Rhodes behind him on second.

*Felt* the power of the man ready to steal third.

No way in hell would Rhodes reach third. Brek couldn't let the man's hit take away from what he'd accomplished today. It was time to wrap up the inning.

Game face on, he went after the next batter, Sam Wells. Wells could swing the lumber. The man had power and pop. Brek refused him both.

The catcher signaled, and Brek threw a succession of fastballs.

The count soon stood at one ball, two strikes.

Wells expected a changeup.

Brek tricked him with a fourth fastball.

Wells swung as if his life depended on it.

Strike three.

Wells stood in the batter's box, head bent, breathing hard, disbelieving his fate.

On the field, the Rogues crowded Brek with whoops and slaps on the ass. Amid the congratulations, he caught Kason Rhodes from the corner of his eye as the man moved off second and edged past the celebration, heading for the dugout.

Their gazes locked for a split second. Rhodes's brief nod recognized Brek's accomplishment of a one-hitter. His smirk reminded Brek that he'd been the batter to steal his no-hit game.

The Rogues would face the Colonels at home in two weeks. Brek would strike Rhodes out in their next confrontation. No one came to his park and bested him a second time. No one.

After an hour's worth of interviews and a twenty-minute shower, Brek was ready to head back to Richmond. Win or lose, tradition demanded that the team sit down and share a meal before they flew home later that evening.

"Yeah, I'm free tomorrow; let me know what time to pick you up, Addie."

*Addie?* Brek turned slightly. Two lockers down, Sloan McCaffrey cupped his cell phone between his ear and shoulder as he tugged on a pair of khakis.

"Riverside Mall works for me." Sloan sounded agreeable. "I'll treat everyone to dinner, and then you can shop."

Stryke saw Sloan duck his head and scrunch his face. "Sure, Eve's welcome." Short pause. "How's Taylor doing?"

Hearing Taylor's name caused Brek to look fully at Sloan. The fact that the reliever had asked about Taylor shouldn't have affected him, yet it had. Affected him so strongly it took every effort to slide his arms into his pale blue dress shirt and button it, then knot his silver-and-blue-striped tie.

"Tell Taylor I'll visit her in the hospital," Sloan went on.

*Hospital?* Brek stood as still as he did on the mound before his windup. Tension swelled his chest. A charley horse threatened his calf. What the hell had happened?

"See you soon, Addie." Sloan disconnected. "Hey, Kincaid," the reliever called down the lockers. "Addie said, 'Good game.' "

Risk nodded and continued dressing.

A need-to-know had Brek stepping toward Sloan and asking, "Taylor?"

Sloan shot his arms through his white T-shirt and stared Brek dead in the eye from the neck hole. "What about her?"

"I heard the words 'Taylor' and 'hospital' in the same sentence."

"Eavesdropping on my call?" He tugged down his shirt.

"Anyone within twenty feet heard your conversation."

"And your concern comes from where?"

*What a shit,* Stryke thought. Why was McCaffrey pushing his buttons? He'd simply asked about Taylor, and expected a straightforward answer, not some runaround as to what he was to her.

"Taylor's knee was banged up when I last saw her at Addie's party." Stryke kept his temper in check by speaking slowly. "I knew she was planning to see an orthopedist this week. I didn't, however, know she was scheduled for surgery."

Sloan further agitated Brek by sliding into his Nikes. He tied both athletic shoes before saying, "Her X-rays showed a torn ACL. While you were pitching a one-hitter, she was under the knife."

ACL, her anterior cruciate ligament—one of the worst sports injuries imaginable. Unlike other injuries, the ACL would never completely heal. The ligament kept the knee stable. It was essential for jumping, running . . . skiing.

A thrill seeker could be sidelined for life with that kind of injury.

Brek's jaw worked. "She okay?"

Sloan snagged his brown sport jacket from a hook in the locker. He shook it out and took his sweet time putting it on. After combing his hair, he finally answered, "Taylor's in recovery at Richmond General. Addie said the surgery was successful, but that Taylor's facing a slow recovery."

Slow and Taylor didn't walk hand in hand. She'd want full mobility in her knee a day after surgery. And it wasn't going to happen.

"Thanks."

"For what?" Sloan shrugged. "Telling you the condition of an old friend? That's what Taylor is to you, right? An ex?"

Stryke didn't take the bait. Instead he turned back to his own locker, rolled his shoulders, and blew out a breath. Taylor wouldn't make a great patient. She'd need someone to tell her not to push herself. Someone to reassure her she'd be fine.

Stryke wondered if Sloan was the man for the job. Could he keep Taylor calm? Would Sloan know when to let Taylor vent, and when to hold her if she needed his strength?

Pretty damn doubtful.

Brek closed his eyes, mentally restraining himself. He had no reason to rush to Taylor's hospital bed. No reason at all. They were estranged.

Taylor didn't need him.

He definitely didn't need her.

Yet a sense of urgency claimed him. He knew he'd never sleep if he didn't check on her. A quick glance in her hospital room, and he'd back out of her life for good.

Eyes wide open now, he reached for his navy slacks, socks, and shoes, and dressed quickly. Ready to travel, he hooked his sport coat on his finger and crossed the locker room in search of Guy Powers.

Forty minutes later, Stryke stepped from the team owner's private limo and took to the tarmac to board the corporate Cessna. Powers hadn't raised a brow at Brek's request to return to Richmond ahead of the team. Guy had made the necessary calls, and Stryke was on his way.

The private jet would return for Powers later that evening. Stryke knew that behind-the-scenes negotiations were taking place between Powers and his ex-wife, Louisville Colonels team owner Corbin Lilly.

Corbin was as beautiful as she was powerful. As the only female owner in major-league baseball, she brought class and distinction to the old boys' club. Stryke knew midseason trades were already under discussion.

It was rumored that Kason Rhodes had recently waived the no-trade clause in his contract. The left fielder could be wearing another team uniform in July.

With Ryker Black, the Rogues' own left fielder, on the disabled list with a pulled hamstring, Powers needed Rhodes in his team's red, white, and blue.

Corbin and Guy would undergo preliminary discussions without legal counsel, team management, or coaches. Though they were as competitive as any two people could be, the exes had remained cordial. Guy would wine and dine Corbin as any man would a beautiful woman. They would reminisce.

Over brandy, they'd get down to business. Corbin held her own in a man's world. Despite the head butting and teeth grinding each had done, respect remained foremost between them as they battled toward the pennant.

It was a quarter past eight by the time the Cessna touched down at Richmond International Airport. Valet parking delivered Brek's SUV curbside at the terminal. He then pressed the speed limit on his way to Richmond General.

Traffic was light as he reached for his cell phone to dial Hilary's home number. He hadn't planned to see her on his return. He only wanted to check in, hear how she was doing and how her father's campaign was progressing. He'd missed two fund-raisers while on the road, and a further donation was expected.

Her home phone rang a dozen times. No answer.

He next tried her cell phone. "Hello," she answered, low and breathy. Sexy.

"It's Brek."

"You're . . . home?"

"Just landed," he informed her. "You're where?"

A moment's hesitation. "Campaign headquarters. Stuart and I were writing Daddy's speech for the Kiwanis Club tomorrow."

Brek heard rustling in the background, as if she were straightening something, but it didn't sound like papers. He also heard a male grunt, which had to have come from Stu.

"Kiwanians participate in many school activities." Hilary continued. "My father wants their votes as well as educator support."

Wayne Talbott was covering all his bases. "Didn't know you'd taken up speech writing," he teased Hilary. Wasn't that Stuart Tate's job?

"I offered to help." Her tone was slightly defensive. "You were out of town, I had nothing better to do. We've been going at it since early afternoon. We're almost ready to call it a night."

*Going at it?* Strange phrase for speech writing.

"Do you need a ride home?" Brek knew Hilary wasn't big on driving. She preferred to carpool or catch a cab. "I can pick you up after I make a quick stop at the hospital." He prided himself on his honesty, so he admitted, "Taylor Hannah had knee surgery today. I wanted to check on her. Hope you don't mind."

"Don't mind at all." Her voice held more relief than jealousy. "Visit Taylor tonight, and I'll see you tomorrow. Stuart will drive me home." A short pause. "Can I count on you to attend the Kiwanis luncheon?"

Why not? He had a team meeting in the morning, but was free for lunch. When he agreed, she gave him the time and place, then sweetly instructed before she hung up that he bring his checkbook.

Stryke disconnected, then massaged his brow. His life seemed disjointed. Ever since Taylor had returned to Richmond, his thoughts had strayed to her instead of to the woman he was to marry. He felt unfaithful.

Had Taylor not destroyed her knee, she'd have been long gone, desert hiking across the Sahara. And his life would have returned to normal.

Normal and Hilary fit together nicely.

Hilary didn't need thrills to be happy.

Stryke had no problem living low-key.

He needed to concentrate on his fiancée, give her the attention she deserved. Be loyal.

*Hilary crosses your mind out of duty, not love,* a small voice whispered. *She can't replace what you lost with Taylor.*

The words unnerved him. Sweat broke out on his brow, and his palms grew damp. What the hell was his problem? He cared for Hilary Talbott. No one could tell him otherwise.

He slowed to well below the speed limit until his mind cleared. Maybe he shouldn't visit Taylor. If he had any sense, he'd take the next exit and turn around and go home instead of to the hospital.

He had no sense. Fifteen minutes later, he pulled into the hospital parking lot. It had rained in Richmond; small puddles glistened beneath the streetlights, his stride reflected in the pools.

A gift shop opened off the main entrance. Flowers, balloons, and stuffed animals were showcased in the window. A single white rose caught his eye.

*One rose says as much as a dozen,* Taylor had once told him. *Unless you plan to make love on the petals.*

He made a quick detour into the shop and bought the rose in the cobalt blue bud vase, as well as a box of gourmet jelly beans. Cherry was the dominant flavor.

By the time he reached reception, a soft gong signaled that visiting hours were over. Elevator doors opened, and family and friends filed out, leaving for the night.

Stryke never used his status as a Rogue to gain favors, but he did so tonight. He bartered tickets for the team's next series against the Cleveland Indians in order to see Taylor Hannah for five full minutes.

He signed autographs at the nurses' station on the fifth floor before being directed to Taylor's room—a private room, he was glad to note—at the far end of the hallway. The light from the call button cast a dozen bouquets and clusters of balloons in shadow.

"You just missed her grandmother and sister." A matronly nurse had followed him down the hall. "Ms. Hannah refused her pain medication. Call the station if she should change her mind."

Brek shook his head. Typical Taylor, forgoing drugs to mentally dominate the pain. Inside the room, he quietly approached her bed—a bed with the foot elevated. Her toes poked from beneath the blanket.

Taylor lay still, as white as the sheet pulled beneath her chin. He set the single rose and box of jelly beans on her nightstand, then edged a chair toward her bed. Once seated beside her, he focused on her paleness, the stubbornness of her chin, even in sleep, and her slightly parted lips.

Her left hand lay uncovered beside her hip. Stryke lowered the bedside bar and covered her hand with his. Her fingers were cold, twitchy. His contact soon warmed her, and she held his hand tightly.

In time, her eyelids fluttered and she blinked awake. Her pupils were dilated, her lips pinched in pain. "Brek?" Her voice came out dry, throaty.

He poured her a glass of water, stuck in a bendable straw, then held the glass while she took two long sips.

She settled back on her pillow and brokenly forced out, "Surgery today."

"So I heard."

"Who told you?" she asked, as if she'd expected to keep her surgery a secret.

"I overheard Sloan talking to Addie in the locker room after the game."

She tried to give him a small smile, but wasn't successful. "One-hitter." Her hoarse praise meant more than any congratulations at the park. "Eve told me."

Taylor's condition was far more important than his win. "How are you feeling?"

"Drowsy." Her eyes remained dilated, her words some-what slurred. "My head feels stuffed with cotton. Hard to think."

"No need to think, Taylor. Just rest."

"Rest? I hate lying here." She pushed up on her elbow and tried to roll onto her side. The exertion caused a spasm in her shoulder, and a deep moan. She dropped back, looking as tired as she was frustrated by her lack of strength.

Stryke hurt for her. "You're four hours out of postop. Cut yourself some slack."

She closed her eyes and sighed. "I won't be skiing for a few days."

"Maybe not for several weeks."

She clenched her jaw. "I will ski again."

"I'm sure you will."

"Ski La Grave."

"Is that where you damaged your knee?" They had yet to discuss the accident. This was as good a time as any. The darkened room gave them privacy. They might never be this isolated again.

She yawned, her body going soft beneath the blanket.

He sat tense, wide-awake, on the edge of his chair.

Her eyelids drooped. "Wedding . . . announcement." Her tone was raw, as if the words were torn from her soul. "Mind . . . wandered. Misjudged . . . dogleg."

And she slept.

Stryke strung her words together a dozen times. She'd mentioned a marriage announcement. Had his engage-ment thrown off her timing on a treacherous dogleg that needed her full attention?

He might never have those answers. Fuzzy headed and vulnerable, she'd given him a couple of leads. Fully awake, she'd never divulge the actual details of the accident.

They were no longer a couple. Taylor kept her business to herself.

Five minutes became fifteen. Almost an hour passed. He held her hand for a long, long time. He just couldn't let go.

At eleven, a nurse arrived to take Taylor's temperature and blood pressure, and to check her IV. Taylor stirred, coughed, rubbed her throat. Stryke poured more water, and Taylor sipped.

He waited for the nurse to toss him out, and was surprised when she handed him a pillow and told him the chair reclined.

With their hands still joined, Brek Stryker kicked back and closed his eyes. He had a team meeting in the morning. He'd stay with Taylor for a while longer, then leave. . . .

He never left. His internal alarm went off at seven. The window blinds had been cracked, and sunlight sliced across his eyelids, the warmth spreading over his face.

He stretched, rotating his ankle to regain circulation in one foot. Then he opened his eyes. He found Taylor's gaze on him. Not on *him* exactly, but on his groin.

He sported a morning erection.

Fully blown and wickedly painful.

To make matters even more uncomfortable, they still held hands. He'd drawn her hand across his thigh, and her fingertips rested a nail's length from his balls.

"Morning." He released her hand.

She drew back. "You're still here?"

"I spent the night."

His words made Taylor Hannah shiver. She'd thought him no more than a dream. She'd expected only nurses in her room this morning.

Yet there sat Brek Stryker, reclined, still dressed in yesterday's clothes. His brown hair was mussed, his jaw stubbled, his slate blue eyes dark with concern.

His hard-on surprised her. The bulge made a solid crease beneath the wrinkled fabric of his slacks.

Heat rose to her face, and she dipped her head. The man had an incredible body. She'd once worked *every* muscle. Having him turned on in the morning had been a great way to start her day. They'd both walked out the door happy.

Stryke leaned forward and brought the chair to its upright position. "How's your knee?" he asked.

"Hurts, but I'm ready for therapy."

"Physical therapy begins today." Dr. Ralph Harper, the most aggressive orthopedist in Richmond, entered the room, clipboard in hand. "But you'll be taking it slow, Taylor."

Noticing her frown, Harper continued, "You're not going to like what I have to say, but you need to listen. Your ACL reconstruction went well. Yet even when everything goes perfectly, the replaced ACL isn't as good as the old one. You've lost muscle, nerve fibers, and cartilage. You're also at increased risk for arthritis."

Taylor stared at the doctor, trying to take in his words. He'd told her all this yesterday, yet she hadn't absorbed the full ramifications of her surgery until now.

"You're looking at a knee brace as well as either a cane or crutches for ten days. Toe tapping, but no weight on your foot. Twelve weeks of therapy. And four to six months for a full recovery."

"That long?" Had her heart stopped?

"You're the type of patient used to being active," the doctor continued. "You'll push your limits."

"No, I won't."

"Yes, she will," Stryke put in.

Harper looked from Brek to Taylor. "You're under hospital care for a week. Your physical therapy will be closely monitored. But once you're an outpatient, you'll need someone to moderate your excess."

"A keeper?" Air locked in her lungs, and she found it difficult to breathe. She'd never relied on anyone in her life. She wasn't about to start now—injury or not. "I can do this on my own."

Stryke's hand came to rest on her shoulder. His touch was solid, strong, reassuring. "Taylor won't overexert. Her grandmother and sister will keep an eye on her. I'll check on her too, when time allows."

Harper tapped his pen against his clipboard and nodded. "I'll see you after therapy. Limit yourself to ankle pumps and circles and straight leg raises. Don't give my therapist a hard time." And he was gone.

Totally deflated, Taylor looked at the ceiling. She remembered the facts about her surgery, yet had pushed the recovery period to some far corner of her mind. She'd believed she'd be up and walking, if not running, in a very short time. *Short* was not four to six months.

She blew out a breath. "I'm sorry, Stryke."

"Sorry for what?"

"For remaining in Richmond longer than you'd like."

"Definitely my primary concern right now."

She cut her gaze toward Stryke, and caught him curving his hands over the bedside bar. His hold was tight, his knuckles white, as he openly stared at her knee. She sighed. "My life is going to revolve around therapy and recuperating at Addie's. I promise our paths won't cross. No Jacy's Java, no—"

"I want to help get you back on your feet." His voice

was low, yet his tone held an intensity that surprised her.

Her heart stuttered. He wanted to help her. No one knew her better. He was the only person she'd ever listened to concerning the direction of her life.

Her first inclination was to accept.

Her second to decline.

She didn't deserve Brek Stryker in her life. He had a fiancée, and Taylor could never settle for being his friend.

An ache centered in her chest, then spread throughout her body. It killed her to push him away. "You're engaged. Your responsibility's to Hilary, not me."

His eyes narrowed and his nostrils flared. Yet before he could argue, she offered a white lie. "Sloan McCaffrey's already offered aftercare once I leave the hospital."

"Sloan, aftercare?" He shook his head, unable to fit the two together. "The man couldn't tweeze glass from your foot. You'll need someone to support you when you exercise, someone to count and stop you so you don't overdo."

"Sloan can count—"

"To seven. He goes as high as four balls and three strikes."

"He'll see that I don't press my luck," she stated. "He's scheduled La Grave for December. He'll want his guide healthy and strong."

Brek stepped back, his gaze surprisingly sharp. "I know how important this recovery is to you, Taylor. You're going to feel as vulnerable as you will angry, and you'll scream at the four walls. If you scream loud enough, I'll hear you. And I'll be back."

He then turned toward the door and was gone.

She trembled at his leaving, so much so that her whole body shook. No matter their history, Stryke would be there if she needed him. Yet his closeness would cost her dearly. She couldn't bear for him to come and go throughout her day, knowing he'd return to Hilary at night.

It was far better to go it alone.

The pain and misery would pass.

Or she'd learn to live with them.

# CHAPTER EIGHT

"What time are you checking on Taylor today?" Brek Stryker entered the elevator behind Sloan McCaffrey.

The team meeting had broken up early. As the players split in twenty different directions, Brek had purposely tracked down Sloan. He now faced the reliever as they descended from the clubhouse to the ground-floor level.

Sloan looked at him strangely. "I've no plans to see Taylor. I called around nine; the floor nurse answered and said she was in therapy. I ordered flowers."

"Taylor said you'd handle her aftercare."

"She did, did she?" Sloan gave a cocky smile. "If the lady wants me, I'm there. I'm happy to handle her."

Sloan was talking sex, not rehabilitation. Stryke had the sudden urge to slam him against the elevator wall. Instead he clenched his fists and expelled a sharp breath. "She said you'd be there for her."

"She told you this when?"

"This morning."

Sloan shook his head. "Sorry, pal, but Taylor's low on my priority list. I've got a shitload of community-service hours today. I'm bouncing from Toys for Tots to Just Lose It, the new fitness club for overweight kids. After that, I'm picking up Addie, Eve, and seven seniors for an

129

early-bird dinner and shopping. I won't see Taylor until after our game tomorrow night."

"Taylor can't wait," Brek insisted. "She'll be coming out of therapy shortly and will need a friend."

"I'm not interested in being her buddy."

The man had sex on his brain. Stryke's muscles went tight. The elevator opened on the ground floor, and both men stepped out. Few cars were left in the parking lot, the majority of players having scattered to enjoy their day off.

Sloan McCaffrey crossed to his Vincent Black Shadow and straddled the bike. His T-shirt read, *Ride It Like You Stole It.* Stryke watched as Sloan put on his helmet. Sloan stared at Brek through the visor.

"Don't have a meltdown." Sloan keyed the engine. "If you're so damn worried about Taylor, go check on her yourself." He snapped his fingers. "Sorry, I forgot you're engaged and no doubt have plans with your fiancée."

He then gunned the bike, the deep rumble resonating between the men as Sloan edged the motorcycle around Stryke, then shot across the parking lot.

Frustration gripped Brek, immobilizing him. He stood staring out over the lot for several minutes. Addie and Eve would be with Taylor during much of her recovery. But neither woman could override Taylor's determination and stubbornness. They'd feel sympathy for Taylor. And Taylor would ruin her rehabilitation by doing more than she was capable of doing.

He pinched the bridge of his nose between his thumb and forefinger and mentally planned out his day. He'd promised to meet Hilary at the Kiwanis luncheon. His loyalty should lie with his fiancée.

Then why did his body ache with a need to see Taylor? She'd pushed him from her hospital room with the assurance that McCaffrey would see to her care.

Yet Sloan had prior commitments.

And Taylor, left alone, would go crazy over her slow recovery. She needed a stabilizing force and a voice of reason.

He shook his head. He had no obligation to Taylor.

Yet he felt torn in two. He might be engaged, but he was still held in the past by another woman.

His feelings for Taylor were buried deep, but undeniable. She came with no guarantees. At the end of her rehabilitation, he'd only have made her strong enough to leave him once again.

Was that a chance he wanted to take?

And what about Hilary? Soft, shy, sweet Hilary. Breaking off their engagement would crush her. Stryke didn't want to hurt her. He'd known the pain of being dumped. He'd never wanted to inflict such pain on anyone, ever.

He had choices to make. His mental debate was giving him a headache. He dragged his ass to his SUV.

He'd secured his seat belt when his cell phone rang. It was Mayor Talbott, looking for his daughter. Hilary was late for the luncheon, and Wayne was concerned. Stuart Tate should have picked her up an hour ago. Neither had made an appearance at the Kiwanis Club.

Stryke offered to swing by her condominium and see what had delayed her.

The drive was short and traffic was light. Stryke pulled into her driveway in under twenty minutes. He parked beside Stuart Tate's new red Mustang. The muscle car struck him as being out of character with the wiry little man who drove it.

Stryke headed up the walkway. Salsa music reverberated through the front door, played so loud that whoever was inside couldn't hear the doorbell. The curtains were drawn, no lights visible.

In contrast with his last visit, Hilary's green thumb was no longer in evidence. Neglect had allowed weeds to sprout in the window planters, once bright with spring flowers. And the low bushes beneath the window needed trimming.

Stryke skirted the front and went to the side entrance. He looked through the narrow pane of glass beside the door. Ebony and ivory, her kitchen displayed white cupboards, black granite countertops, and checkerboard tiles.

Sunshine shot through the skylight, showcasing shelves of glass holding ceramic roosters. A prism suncatcher cast rainbows across the sink. The small appliances were neatly covered.

Two large suitcases had been shoved beneath the café-style table. Pamphlets and papers were strewn across the tabletop.

He tapped on the window, then pounded the wood of the door with his fist. No one came to answer.

Concern pushed him to try the door. It opened easily. He hated to trespass, but Hilary was his fiancée, and he was beginning to be concerned. He had every right to check on her.

He entered, listening. The music from the living room blared loud and obtrusive. He would have moved toward the noise had the passports and bank statements on the café table not caught his eye.

Curiosity slowed him, and he quickly flipped through the documents. What he saw made his eyes burn and his stomach turn. It didn't take an accountant to certify that two sets of books had been kept during the mayoral campaign. Only one showed the actual disbursement of funds—to a foreign account.

A Costa Rican account with a whole lot of zeroes.

One entry remained to be filled in. Brek's name appeared in the left column, a question mark beside the dollar sign. He'd been expected to make a further donation at the Kiwanis luncheon—a donation to be siphoned off to Central America.

Beneath the documents, a real estate portfolio held the paperwork on the closing of a luxury beachfront condo—a paid-in-full cash transaction.

"What the hell?" he muttered when he discovered Hilary's engagement ring tucked between two one-way plane tickets and a set of passports. He flipped open the first passport and found it in Stuart Tate's name. The second pictured Hilary Talbott as Hilary Talbott-Tate.

Talbott-Tate, as in hyphenated—and married.

A lot had happened in the two weeks he'd been on the road. He needed to locate Hilary. His fiancée owed him an explanation.

His anger grew as he moved down the hallway. His stomach twisted when he discovered a trail of discarded clothing. He kicked aside a pair of men's dress slacks and a woman's tailored blazer. He scuffed across a white pair of jockeys and stepped on a pink satin bra.

A hallway mirror across from the living room entrance reflected activity near the media center. Stryke leaned against the opposite wall, taking in the commentary from a Latin dance video being played on the television. It was so loud, his ears buzzed. The instructors on the DVD were vividly costumed and engaged in demonstrating the steps.

Across the room, the mirror captured Hilary and Stuart in nothing but skin. They were engaged in much more than dancing. Stu was gangly and dangly and fish-belly white. He was as hairy as Hilary was waxed. She looked like a store mannequin.

The sight jolted Stryke like a swift kick to his balls.

In their attempt to master the salsa, the couple had lost track of time. The Kiwanis would now be well into their luncheon.

Brek stood still and stared into the mirror, momentarily unnoticed as the hot, sultry music pounded in his ears. Half-hidden by a red leather recliner, Hilary swayed toward Stuart. Their bare bellies brushed, and Stu missed a step.

"My foot!" hissed an aggravated and unforgiving Hilary. "The salsa is seductive. You're not seducing me, Stu. Pay better attention or be punished." She spanked Stuart's ass.

Brek blinked, as stunned as Tate. Hilary's slap left a red imprint on the man's butt cheek.

Stuart rubbed his buttock and whined, "The salsa's not my dance."

"Neither was the calypso or the merengue." Hilary's words cut sharply. "These are the dances of Central America. Learn one of the three, Stu."

To Stuart's credit, he tried. However, the man had two left feet. With each misstep, Hilary disciplined him further; she smacked him with the flat of her hand. The pop was as loud as the commentary on the DVD. Stu openly flinched.

Some men weren't meant to dance.

No man was meant to dance naked.

It was not a pretty sight.

Utterly disgusted, Brek left the hallway and returned to the kitchen. He pocketed Hilary's engagement ring, then quickly gathered up the documents and passports from the table. All evidence would be presented to Mayor Talbott.

He'd let Wayne sort it out. Stryke would request that his personal donations be used in a more productive manner than Hilary had planned. And that the Boys and Girls Clubs remain a valid issue on the mayor's agenda. Otherwise he'd withdraw his support.

Folding a blank piece of paper in half, Stryke left Hilary a note: *The salsa is not Stuart Tate's dance. Brek.*

He then slipped through the side door.

Once in his SUV, Brek headed to the Kiwanis Club. His life had done a one-eighty in less than two weeks. He didn't know if he should throw back his head and laugh with relief or let his temper rage.

In the end, he managed a smile. He'd escaped a woman he'd never really known or loved.

Hilary Talbott had used him. And in his own way, he'd used her as well. In his attempt to forget Taylor Hannah, he'd sought Taylor's opposite. He'd believed Hilary sweet and stable. The joke was on him. The woman had a criminal mind and spanked like a dominatrix.

How blind could he have been?

Pretty damn blind, he had to admit.

He ran one hand down his face. His history with women sucked—big-time. One fiancée had left him at the altar. The second embezzled his money.

Hilary Talbott he could live without.

Taylor Hannah still lived in his heart.

He was a goner where Taylor was concerned.

Would he be twice the fool to return to his past love?

Yet if he didn't go back, he'd never have his long-overdue talk with Taylor. She'd wanted to explain her reason for leaving him. Today she'd get her chance. Perhaps then he could move beyond the pain that kept them apart.

Stryke made two stops on his way to the hospital. The first took him to the Kiwanis Club, where he joined Mayor Talbott in a private meeting room. There, Brek handed over the documents and passports, and briefly explained the embezzlement.

As long as Brek lived, he would never forget the incumbent's shocked expression when informed of Hilary and Stuart's betrayal. Talbott had been unable to speak, and at moments unable to breathe. The man aged ten years in the thirty minutes he and Brek spent together.

Talbott's gratitude to Stryke for bringing the misappropriation of funds to his attention prompted his guarantee that the Boys and Girls Clubs would remain a priority.

That was all Brek needed to hear. He'd left the mayor, knowing the hand of justice would soon slap Hilary and Stuart, and not on the ass.

Stryke's second stop landed him at the Mercedes dealership. He traded in his family SUV for a sporty SLR McLaren. The showroom model was sleek and silver, and as sophisticated as a street-legal racer could be.

He requested that his Escalade be delivered to the Westside Boys and Girls Club, a donation to the dedicated administrator who kept law and order among the street kids.

It was after three by the time he reached the hospital. The main parking lot was full. Fortunately, the attendant recognized him. An autograph got Brek into the employees' lot, a short walk from the entrance.

He stopped in the gift shop and purchased another box of gourmet jelly beans. Bribery was good. Jelly beans had always made Taylor talk. He wanted to hear her side of the story.

Taylor was not in her hospital room. Brek checked

with the nurses' station, only to be told she was still in physical therapy. His gut tightened. Eight hours in therapy was not what the doctor had ordered.

He wove through the maze of hallways until he reached the adult therapy rooms. The lights were off, no sign of Taylor. He heard voices and tracked them to the children's area.

Pushing through the swinging doors, he located her across the room, balanced on a low-slung swing, clapping and encouraging three children through their exercises. She'd acquired a pair of green hospital scrubs; her feet were bare. One pant leg had been ripped to her knee and revealed her brace.

She had her back to him, so he stood quietly inside the door. What he saw both enlightened him and did strange things to his heart. Before him now, two boys and one girl struggled and healed under Taylor's coaching. She was a woman who couldn't sit idly in her hospital bed and watch the day go by. She needed to be active.

Working along with the physical therapist, Taylor inspired hope, gently nudging the little girl through her exercises when she became tearful and wanted to sit down and feel sorry for herself.

"Cassie"—Taylor's voice was strong, but gentle— "we've got the same injury, and I'm depending on you to show me the ropes. You're four weeks ahead of me in rehab. I watched you do your wall squats and leg presses. You're a phenom," she praised. "Now show me what you can do on the stationary bike."

Cassie, who appeared to be seven or eight, rubbed her knee and sniffed. "It hurts too much."

"The bike *is* the worst." Taylor looked sympathetic. "You have to remember that pain leaves the body once you've healed. A couple rotations on the bicycle and your knee will be more flexible."

Cassie looked at Taylor as if she wanted to believe her. "You sure?"

Taylor nodded toward the physical therapist. "That's what Bryan told me. And I trust him with my rehab."

"I'll ride if you tell me another story," Cassie bargained. "Maybe a bike adventure?"

Taylor nodded. "I've got a mountain bike tale that will curl your hair."

Cassie giggled. "My hair's already curly."

"Then it'll make your hair stand on end," Taylor teased her.

Cassie's green eyes went wide. "It's that scary?"

Taylor flattened her palm to her chest. "Made my heart pound."

Stryke had lived the story Taylor was about to tell. He'd traveled with her to Bolivia, had biked alongside her. His own heart had raced down the mountain road that snaked from the Andes to the Amazon Basin.

He crossed his arms over his chest and relived the adventure with her.

Taylor waited until Bryan had positioned Cassie on the stationary bike and the little girl had started her slow rotations before she began her story. Behind Cassie, Bryan flashed ten fingers, telling Taylor how many minutes Cassie needed to ride. Taylor could easily hold Cassie's attention for that length of time.

Using her good heel to push back and forth and gently swing, Taylor recounted her adventure with Brek Stryker. "Five years ago, a friend and I traveled to South America."

"A girl- or boyfriend?" Cassie immediately questioned.

"Boy," Taylor told her. "My best friend."

"What was his name?" asked Dalton, one of the boys in

the room. He and his twin brother, Dillon, had suffered a collision at a skateboard park. Dalton had broken his shoulder, Dillon his ankle. Under the therapist's watchful eye, Dalton now huffed and puffed as he lifted light weights, while Dillon worked his way through parallel bars.

"The man's name was Brek." Taylor said his name slowly. "We'd signed up for a bike ride on the world's most dangerous road."

"You like danger, don't you?" Dillon asked.

"Thrill seeking is in my blood," Taylor said without hesitation. "It makes me feel alive."

"I felt alive when I popped an ollie off the hip ramp," Dillon stated. "I had plenty of speed when I pulled my board into the air, but—"

"You didn't bend your knees when you landed," his brother finished for him. "You wiped out and took me with you."

"We do everything together." Dillon grinned.

"Mom says everything comes in twos," added Dalton.

The boys were definitely live wires, perhaps ten years of age, with spiky dark hair and daredevil grins. They were boys Taylor would have loved to raise.

"Your story," Cassie nudged.

"Keep pedaling," Taylor reminded her when the little girl slowed. Relaxing into the memory, Taylor let her mind wander back to La Cumbria, to the top of the mountain pass.

"A rickety old bus, all rusty and dented, drove a group of six thrill seekers high into the mountains. It was freezing up there," Taylor began.

"Did you have a warm jacket? Were you wearing socks?" Cassie sounded like a little mother.

"We dressed in layers to accommodate the extremes in

temperature," Taylor told her. "We rode Iron Horse bikes—"

"Awesome ride," Dalton cut in. "Suspension soaks up the bumps."

"Not all the bumps," Taylor said. She'd had several bruises from the trip.

"We headed downhill on a single-lane gravel road that hugged the side of the mountain. There were no guardrails. There was a thousand-foot drop just a few feet from the tire tracks."

Dalton whistled. "Damn dangerous."

"Mom hates it when you swear," Dillon put in. "You owe the curse jar fifty cents."

"I don't owe if you don't tell Mom."

"You can pay me instead," said Dillon.

Dalton pulled a face.

And Taylor continued. "We saw snow on the peaks off in the distance as we descended from the chilly mountain air, past waterfalls, through rain, and fog, until we hit the steamy jungle."

"Fog? How could you see?" asked Dillon.

"We couldn't see well," Taylor admitted. "We had to be very careful, but we also had to keep up with the downhill traffic. The group was passed twice by work trucks. It was a tight squeeze. We were nearly flattened against the mountain wall. If you misjudged a curve, you smacked into rock or went over the side. I almost took a nosedive."

The twins' jaws dropped.

Cassie went wide-eyed. "What happened?"

Taylor paused to let anticipation build as she drew the children deeper into the story. "Just outside the vacation village of Coroico, we heard a loud rumbling. The road shook. Within seconds, dirt and rocks were falling all around us."

"A landslide!" Dillon pumped one arm into the air.

"Were you scared?" Cassie's speed on the stationary bike had increased.

"A little scared," Taylor admitted. "I was on the lead bike when it skidded and the front tire blew. I could barely steer."

"Did you swerve?" Dillon stopped in the middle of the parallel bars.

"Swerved right to the edge of the road." The kids had gone silent, holding their collective breath. "I was lucky"—*damn lucky*—"my friend Brek was riding behind me. He went into action and saved my life."

"What did he do?" Dillon pressed.

"Talk faster," Dalton demanded.

Taylor smiled. "My slide felt like slow motion, like a movie frame. I started to go down, but instead of meeting the edge of the road, I slammed into Brek. He'd ridden up beside me and took the impact of my fall. Brek's a very strong man. He withstood my weight as well as the force of the bike. He saved me from falling off the cliff. When it was all over, we both stood six inches from the edge."

Cassie blinked. "Brek sounds like Superman."

Brek Stryker was as much like an action figure as any human could be. He'd remained Taylor's rock. He'd enfolded her in his arms, holding her so tightly she'd been unable to breathe. She hadn't minded. She'd clung to him in an adrenaline overload, fear and gratitude surging through her body.

Had anyone but Brek been at her back, she wouldn't have lived to tell her story.

"Were you hurt?" Dalton asked. "Do you have scars?"

Taylor pushed up the sleeve of her top to show them the white scar that ran down her inner arm from the curve of her elbow to her wrist. "Gravel burn. I was lucky."

"How'd you get around the landslide?" Dillon asked.

"The landslide stopped all traffic. Brek carried both our bikes over the rubble. We ended up staying in Coroico until the road was cleared. It took two days."

Cassie tilted her head, looking very thoughtful for one so young. "Did you marry Brek? I'd have married him."

The little girl was smarter than Taylor. "It's hard for a thrill seeker to settle down," she said slowly. "You can't marry unless you're ready."

"Are you ready now?" Cassie was persistent.

"Getting closer."

Cassie giggled and rubbed her arms. "Your story gave me goose bumps."

"Another adventure?" Dalton requested.

Bryan tapped his watch. "Taylor can tell another story tomorrow. We're done with your therapy sessions for today. Your parents should be waiting in the outer lobby."

The kids waved to Taylor as they left the therapy room. Reaching for her crutches, Taylor followed them out. She did no more than touch her toes to the floor, as the doctor had ordered.

At the swinging exit door, she came face-to-face with Brek Stryker. Tall, broad shouldered, and intense, he stood there wearing a blue-and-cream rugby shirt, jeans, and leather loafers without socks. He looked sturdy and self-sufficient.

A man's man and a woman's dream come true.

Taylor's heart went a little crazy.

She gripped her crutches tightly.

Tilting her head, she met his gaze and softly managed, "You came back."

"I spoke to Sloan after the team meeting. He had a list of obligations today, so I figured someone needed to check on you. I had time." A muscle flexed along his jaw-line. "When you weren't in your hospital room, I thought you might be in therapy—"

"Overexerting myself?" She forced back a smile. Stryke knew her better than anyone.

He nodded. "You always pushed your limits."

*You always tried to save me from myself.*

The realization was an eye-opener. She went breathlessly still, looking into the face of the man who'd so often requested that she exhale, that she become fully recharged before taking off on her next adventure.

Brek had never tried to hold her back, as she'd once thought.

He'd only loved her enough to let her go.

"You're pale." Concern pulled at the corners of his mouth. "You need to get off your feet." He stepped back and let her pass.

Taylor hobbled down the hallway with Brek at her side.

A nurse entered her room on her return. Taylor was helped back into bed and her vitals taken. "You've over-done it," the nurse stated. "Your pulse is fast, your blood pressure high. You're confined to your bed for the rest of the day."

Taylor blamed her quickening pulse on Stryke, not on the exercises. He'd come back to check on her—one of the biggest surprises of her life. One look at the man and her heartbeat kicked up.

She should be more hardened to him. He was engaged and would be leaving her soon. Yet she couldn't fight her attraction. Love had a mind of its own.

She licked her lips and had to ask, "Does Hilary mind that you're here?"

Brek took a moment to answer. He pulled a chair up to her bed, then dropped onto the cushion. He stared first at the wall, then at her, suddenly contemplative, as if he needed to tell her something, yet in the end changed his mind. "No, I can honestly say Hilary doesn't mind."

No jealousy from Hilary? The woman must be secure that Brek loved her. *Lucky lady*, Taylor thought. Hilary and Brek would soon marry and start a family. And Taylor would go it alone.

Emotion swelled her heart, and loneliness swept her inside. She'd never felt sorry for herself. Yet at that moment she faced a head-on collision with her grief.

"I miss my parents." She'd never said the words out loud, but they slipped out today on a sad sigh. She felt vulnerable and incredibly tired. Alone and lost.

From deep inside her soul, Liv's and Stephan's memories embraced her, bringing both happiness and sorrow. She'd never cried over their untimely deaths. Never shown any emotion whatsoever. She'd once been afraid that if she leaned on Brek, if she let him ease her pain, she'd lose herself.

She'd held on to the hurt as tightly as their memories. She'd kept everything so bottled up inside her, at times she couldn't breathe. She was having trouble breathing now.

White-hot pain jammed her chest. She shut her eyes to keep in the tears, yet emotion rose and choked her. She finally admitted that at the end of every day, she'd missed Brek as much as she did her mother and father.

"Taylor . . ." Brek must have sensed her need for him. "You don't always have to be strong. I'm here for you."

He'd always been there for her. She'd been too blind running away from him to see how solidly he'd stood and awaited her return. No matter how wild her escape, he'd always welcomed her home.

He'd loved her more than she deserved to be loved.

She opened her eyes and looked at him then, finding his expression gentle and kind and knowing. His slate blue gaze held understanding. The anguish in his soul mirrored her own.

He understood her pain.

She felt her heart break; the fracturing sadness of her parents' deaths was finally released. Years ago she'd held Stryke at arm's length. Today she reached for him.

"Hold me. I hurt."

Brek eased onto the edge of the bed and held her. He kissed her forehead and let her cry.

She cried her eyes out. Her body shook, and Brek absorbed her sadness. Strong. Sensitive. Vital. He lent her his strength.

"My parents died so unexpectedly." Her voice was watery. "I felt betrayed and left behind."

He smoothed back her hair and rubbed her back when she hiccupped and couldn't catch her breath. He gently patted her shoulder.

"My adventures kept me close to them." She sniffed, sighed, then broke down again. "You wanted me to stay home, and I felt trapped. I needed the wildness of nature to hold on to their spirits."

"I never knew how to make it better for you," he told her. "I watched you withdraw and leave me farther behind with each adventure."

"I didn't want you to heal me then, but I need to heal now."

He held her tightly, handing her tissue after tissue until she'd gone through the entire box. He offered her water when her throat turned scratchy.

"I'm sorry I left you at the altar." Her voice was soft. "I was hurting so badly, I couldn't see straight. But I never meant to take you down with me."

Long after her tears had dried, Brek remained a solid wall to lean on, offering soft words and comfort.

She pressed her cheek to his chest, to the one dry spot on his rugby shirt. The steady rhythm of his heart calmed her. She felt protected and safe.

Brek had shared her pain. He'd helped her heal.

"I loved you, Stryke. Never doubt that."

She wished with all her heart that she could have a second chance with this man. Yet in a very short time he'd be returning to Hilary. His fiancée. His future.

Taylor shifted and lifted her chin—just as Stryke turned his head.

Their mouths were separated by nothing but breath.

She inhaled.

And he exhaled.

The air warmed and stirred with their need to taste. Their bodies heated from closeness and familiarity. The slightest move—

Would be wrong. Taylor wanted Stryke as much as she'd wanted anything in her life. But he was engaged, and no matter their history, he'd moved on.

She pulled back and let him go.

Brek slid off the bed. He stretched, then looked down at her. "Better?" he asked.

"Less lost," she admitted.

"Glad you found yourself."

They stared at each other, the stare of two people who connected and communicated even in silence.

For the second time since his arrival, he appeared to want to tell her something, yet he let it slide. She had no right to push him to reveal what he didn't wish to share.

"Hungry, Ms. Hannah?" A food server entered the room, tray in hand. He set it on Taylor's nightstand and departed.

She checked out the food. "Salad. Turkey and mashed potatoes. Lime Jell-O."

"Guess that's my cue to leave."

She'd prefer for him to stay, yet found no reason to hold him. He'd soon be having dinner with Hilary. "Thanks, Brek—for everything."

He nodded, understanding. "It was a long time coming, Taylor."

Too long. And too late.

He smiled at her then, a smile that warmed her from head to toe and made her hot in the middle. "See you tomorrow. After the game."

"I'll be here or in therapy."

"I'll find you." And he was gone.

Gone to Hilary.

Which left Taylor alone with her dinner. She looked at her nightstand and saw the box of jelly beans Brek had left. She lifted the lid, picking out a cherry-flavored piece.

It tasted of sweetness and memories.

She ate her dessert first.

# CHAPTER NINE

"You ready for dinner and some shopping?" Sloan McCaffrey asked Eve Hannah when he arrived at Addie's condominium.

"You have a razor? A clean shirt?" she retorted, her nose in the air.

He scrubbed his knuckles along his jaw. A week's worth of stubble shouldn't offend her. Only if he kissed her would he leave whisker burn. His lips certainly weren't going to touch the pinched line of her mouth.

Just because she looked all tailored and tight-assed, that didn't mean he had to be equally stuffy. So what if his gray T-shirt had a few wrinkles? It was the cleanest one he had just now. There were no tears or sweat stains. He'd showered, put on deodorant. It was as good as it was going to get before he did some laundry.

Eye-to-eye with Eve on the front stoop, he wished he hadn't bought her a gift. He now regretted the impulse buy. His last image of Eve at Addie's birthday party had been of her doing the Bunny Hop. She'd been in the lead, and a blind man couldn't have missed the soft bounce of her breasts.

She'd been one hot bunny.

His afternoon at Toys for Tots had inspired him to buy

her a stuffed animal. What he'd thought might be humorous then didn't seem so funny now. When he produced the yellow duck from behind his back and teasingly quacked, Eve's mood turned foul.

"Childish," she said coolly as she set it on a plant stand just inside the door.

"It's good to feel like a kid on occasion," Sloan returned. "It's hell playing grown-up all the time."

"Especially when you don't play it well."

She was hostile. "Loosen up a little. It's our second date."

"We never had a first."

"Addie's birthday marked us as a couple."

She rolled her eyes. "In your dreams."

He *had* dreamed about Eve. Twice. Both times she'd crawled into his bed, buck naked and wild. Sadly, the real Eve was nothing like his dream lover. She didn't know how to have fun.

He'd wanted to show her a good time. "You're an artist and like paint. There's an indoor paintball park at Riverside Mall—Master Blasters. While Addie and her friends shop, I thought we'd go a round."

He'd like nothing better than to blast her with a paintball gun. Get down and dirty and chase her around the course.

"I paint with oils, using a palette and sable brushes," she said stiffly. "I don't blast a canvas with a splatter gun."

"If you win, no more dates. If I win, we go on a third."

She was slow to nod. "Fair enough. You're on."

He was suddenly charged. Hunting down Eve held real appeal.

"Hello, Sloan." Addie greeted him warmly as she and her seven friends came down the condo's hallway—six women and one man. After the introductions, the group filed out to the van.

At the curb, Addie suggested Eve ride up front beside Sloan. Her suggestion was met with a negative shake of Eve's head. Eve climbed to the rear of the van, ending up on the backseat beside Edwin Sweeney, Mr. Horseshoe.

The older man slid his arm along the back of the seat. Sloan wondered if that was a deliberate move on Edwin's part or if the man was merely stretching.

Sloan kept a close eye on them through the rearview mirror during the twenty-minute drive to Riverside Mall. Edwin would dip his head and whisper near her ear, and Eve would flash her dimple and braces. Damn if the man wasn't flirting with her.

"Where does everyone want to eat?" Sloan asked the group as he made his second pass through the parking lot looking for just the right spot. The Sprinter with the extended frame drove like a bus. He needed plenty of room to park between cars.

"The food court?" Addie tossed out. She'd been all smiles since they'd left her condominium, excited about a night out with her friends.

"There's also Belissaro Americano for burgers and steaks," Sloan suggested. "My teammate Romeo owns it. Or we can try Noodles, lots of pasta dishes."

Zeta Freed nodded from the third-row seat. "I could go for a bowl of buttered shells."

Sloan smiled at Zeta in the rearview mirror. The lady was tall and thin, her eyes framed with designer glasses— pink frames decorated with crystals. Tiny rainbows danced off her cheeks when the sun caught her just right. Zeta was quick to make decisions. He liked a woman who could make up her mind.

"Let's vote." Addie went democratic. "Who's for Noodles?" She took a hand count. "It's pasta," she told Sloan.

The restaurant was dark and intimate, geared for couples on a date. Seated between Addie and Zeta, and across from Eve and Edwin Sweeney, Sloan blinked in the candlelight. He listened rather than joining in on the conversation around him. He was not well versed in hemorrhoids, acid reflux, or hip replacements.

"Would you like my garlic?" Zeta held up a spoonful of the finely chopped garlic. "It gives me heartburn."

Sloan accepted the garlic and sprinkled it over his tomato linguini. He'd no plans for kissing tonight.

Across the table, he heard Eve giggle. He looked up and found her and Edwin sharing a large plate of spaghetti and meatballs. If they sucked a noodle like in *Lady and the Tramp*, Sloan would be sick. The older man seemed to have a healthy appetite. He took two bites to Eve's one.

Eve appeared to enjoy Edwin's company.

Which was beyond Sloan. What could they possibly have in common? There was a two-generation gap between them. The man could be her grandfather.

Addie leaned toward Sloan and whispered, "Edwin's such a nice man. Not many men his age have a full head of hair. He's quite lonely. A widower for twenty years now."

Sloan squinted across the table. The candlelight held Eve within its flame, casting her face in highlights and shadows. Her eyes looked greener. Her cheeks warmed with color. Her smile was brighter. He chomped down on a sesame bread stick. "Looks like Edwin's into younger women."

Addie's smile was soft. "I hope so."

His fork halfway to his mouth, Sloan stopped eating. Addie couldn't possibly consider Eve and Edwin a good match. The age difference between them was downright ludicrous. The man had one foot in the grave.

The conversation turned to pacemakers and cataract surgery, then on to dentures—more topics to which Sloan couldn't relate. Slouched in his chair, he gazed across the table at Eve. He stared until she stared back.

She looked flushed and happy until their eyes locked; then she closed down on him. Her eyes flitted over his T-shirt and she bit her bottom lip. "You're wearing your linguini."

To Sloan's way of thinking, tomato stains showed a man's pleasure in his food. He'd eaten with gusto. Screw Eve for pointing out that he should have tucked a napkin at his neck.

Beside him, Zeta clucked like a mother hen as she dampened a corner of her linen napkin with water from her glass and went to work on the stains. Her knobby elbow jabbed Sloan in the side, her arthritic fingers scrubbing away at the cotton fabric. Her fashion ring snagged the T-shirt and left a tiny hole.

A minute passed, and Zeta tossed her napkin on the table. "Much better, son."

Zeta's idea of *much better* and Sloan's own ran a dining room apart. She'd squished the stains fully into his shirt. Smeared pink, the top half stuck to his chest, and he now smelled like a tomato.

To make matters worse, Eve smiled.

And Addie chuckled. "It's club soda, not water, that removes stains," she reminded Zeta.

Zeta threw up her hands. "Too much to remember at my age."

Sloan patted her bony shoulder. "It all comes out in the wash."

"Go light on the bleach," Zeta said.

Sloan understood. He'd added way too much Clorox to

his clothes the last time he did laundry. A dozen T-shirts had disintegrated into nothing but thread.

"Dessert, anyone?" Addie asked of those at the table.

Eve and Edwin split a chocolate-raspberry cannoli. Zeta passed, claiming she was ready to pop. Everyone else had tiramisu.

"Can I sample?" Zeta reached across Sloan and scooped a bite of his dessert. "Just one little taste."

"Taste all you want." Sloan pushed the dessert plate between them.

And she did. Zeta's one small bite turned into her eating half his tiramisu. Sloan didn't mind. The Italian confection was thick and rich. A bowl of vanilla ice cream would have suited him better.

When the server delivered Edwin Sweeney the bill, Sloan reached across the table, nearly burning the underside of his arm on the candle. He lifted it out of Sweeney's hand before his shirtsleeve caught on fire.

"My treat," he told Mr. Horseshoe.

"I'll leave the tip," Edwin offered.

"Fine." Sloan nodded his acceptance.

"Let's do a little shopping." Addie rose from the table. "I need a new pair of shoes, and Zeta wants to browse the Happy Booker."

"I need a new mystery to read," Zeta explained.

"A stop at the drugstore for me," Edwin stated.

The remaining five women headed for the shops, handbags, hosiery, and a hair salon at the top of their lists.

Before going their separate ways, everyone agreed to meet at the main entrance in two hours.

"Sloan and I will be at the paintball center," Eve told her grandmother. "I have my cell phone if you need to reach me."

Addie waved them on. "Enjoy yourselves."

Sloan and Eve cut through Foss's Pharmacy, each taking a separate aisle. At the back of the store, Sloan caught Edwin Sweeney talking to a young female cashier. The girl looked confused. Sweeney also appeared out of his element.

"Prophylactics," Sloan heard the older man say.

The girl shook her head. "What are they? Wrist or ankle braces? Foot insoles?"

"Condoms." Sloan came up behind Sweeney.

The girl's eyes widened. "Two aisles down on the right."

Sloan led Sweeney to the Trojans. "Thank you, son." Edwin released a breath when they stood before the display.

Latex or lambskin? Magnum or snug? Sloan watched Sweeney read the labels.

"It's been a while," the older man admitted.

Yet Edwin planned to get lucky tonight. Sloan wondered if Eve knew Sweeney was making this monumental purchase.

He tapped his favorite brand. "Easy slide and glide."

Edwin thanked him.

Sloan nodded toward the pharmacy. "Need any enhancement? The little blue pill?"

"Desire works best, even with a man my age." He moved on to pay for his condoms.

Mr. Horseshoe could still get it up. Whom he would stick bothered Sloan most.

Eve came up behind him. She glanced from Sloan to the Trojans and frowned. "Thought we were playing paintball."

"I helped Edwin Sweeney make a selection."

"Edwin bought condoms?" She dimpled, her braces flashing.

"Yeah, appears he likes younger women."

"Addie hopes so."

He was suddenly lost. "Addie?" He'd thought Edwin was about to make a move on Eve.

"My grandmother is eight years younger than Edwin. They've been dancing around each other for a year now. Edwin's wanted approval from me and Taylor before he courted Addie. Taylor gave him the go-ahead last week. I told him tonight to go for it. It would be a second chance at love for both of them. No one wants to grow old alone."

Edwin and Addie. Relief filled him, and Sloan relaxed. He shouldn't have cared if the older man and snippy Eve were going to get it on. But he damn sure had. It had bothered him so much it had tied his stomach in knots.

He exhaled and motioned toward the door. "Let's go. Master Blasters is across the parking lot. I'm going to shoot you blue."

"You're already tomato pink." She eyed his shirt. "Guess I'll have to go with red."

Sloan snagged a tin of Altoids on his way out. He tossed an Andrew Jackson on the counter, but didn't wait for his change. He popped two breath mints as he followed Eve across the lot. Obviously she wasn't going to wait for him.

He enjoyed the severe set of her shoulders, the stiffness of her spine, down to her tight ass. She power walked with a righteous sense of purpose.

Sloan couldn't wait to splatter her with paint.

"Quiet night, Mr. McCaffrey," the manager said as he greeted them at the door to the large indoor facility where

Sloan was a regular. He frequently brought groups of underprivileged kids to Master Blasters. They played war games for hours.

"There's one group ahead of you," Gus informed him. "They should be finished in twenty minutes."

"I want a private hour. We'll play Black Ops." Sloan wanted to torment Eve Hannah in the war-zone maze.

"Rental package, or did you bring your own equipment?" Gus inquired.

"We rent tonight."

Gus showed them to the rental room, where they could select jumpsuits, boots, goggles, and paintball guns. Sloan took his time making just the right selections.

Eve Hannah cut a look at Sloan as she climbed into her black jumpsuit. She tugged it up and over her mauve knit top and white slacks. It fit loosely, with a dozen pockets for paintball accessories. She kept on her white Keds with their rubber soles. There'd be no slipping.

She topped her outfit off with a black baseball cap. She didn't want her blond hair standing out in the darkness.

She contained her smile as Sloan evaluated every gun on the racks. He tested the weight of a Squadbuster grenade, which contained enough paint to splatter a dozen players.

She had a gut feeling Sloan was out to get her.

"Tommy gun or Tippmann X7 Sniper?" he asked her.

"One-pop marker pistol."

He laughed at her. "It's going to take more than one shot to hit me."

"The pistol," she repeated. "Red loader."

She adjusted her goggles as Sloan pulled on his black face mask. He then slid his hands into paintball gloves.

He stood tall and well armed in his jumpsuit and traction shoes, packing two paintball guns and the grenade. He looked like a mercenary, ready to start a mission and take out his mark—with bright blue paint.

Eve was surprised he hadn't rented the double-barreled clip-fed air cannon or the miniature tank.

"You know the rules?" The manager nodded toward the list posted on the wall. "No blind shooting or construction of booby traps. No climbing the fences or cell phone use."

Gus looked from Eve's pistol to Sloan's arsenal. "No *over*shooting." He spoke directly to Sloan. "Go easy on the tommy gun. It packs a punch."

The manager finished with, "Players eliminate each other from the game by hitting their opponent with a paintball. You get shot, you're out."

Gus then led them to the narrow entrance to the park. "Once you cross the white line in Black Ops, the game begins."

Eve looked down. "Where's the white line?"

"Up here." Sloan moved ahead of her.

She followed him closely.

He crossed the line and turned his head, pointing down to be sure she saw the white stripe.

She pressed up behind him, her toes nudging his heels.

He turned, looking down at her questioningly.

Holding her breath, she slid her one-pop marker pistol between them—and popped him right over the heart.

Red paint splattered, covering his chest.

"Gotcha." She blew on the end of her pistol.

"*Got* me? What the hell?" Sloan stepped back and swore a blue streak. "That's not how paintball is played."

"We'd both crossed the white line," she reminded him. "Game on."

"Ah, she's right, Mr. McCaffrey." Gus came up behind them. "Technically you're out."

"Technically, my ass." Sloan stood over her, menacingly tall. His anger came at her, hot and pulsing. "The game's not over."

Eve could see that Sloan didn't take to losing. She caught the stormy narrowing of his gray eyes and the wide flare of his nostrils through the holes in his mask. He looked ready to shoot her with both paintball guns. The impact would send her into the wall.

She held up her hands. "Maybe we could—"

"Run." His word came deadly soft. "Run, Eve Hannah."

She blinked. "You're joking, right?"

The flex of his finger on the trigger of the tommy gun told her otherwise.

Sloan was the Rambo of Master Blasters.

He was ready to blow a hole in her.

She wasn't afraid of him. She instinctively knew he wouldn't hurt her. Yet a part of her wanted to see whether he could outrun her. Or whether she could outsmart him.

A shiver ran down her spine. And her heart tripped.

The challenge had been issued.

Winner take all.

"Take this." Gus shoved a freshly loaded pistol into her hand. "Just in case you get a second shot."

The manager jumped out of their way.

Eve backed away from Sloan. One step, then two.

"I'm counting to ten." Sloan's lips barely moved. "Then I'm coming after you."

"It's only a game," Eve reminded him.

"You cheated."

"I got you first."

"I'll get you last."

*Getting her* sounded sexual.

"One, two . . . ten." The man cheated at numbers.

He was now after her.

Eve dove into the maze. She could outsmart him here, just as she had at the white line. The man smelled of tomato paste and paint. She'd catch a whiff of him before he closed in on her.

She took the right hallway to Black Ops, then sprinted through a maze of fences and down a side path. The cement floor was uneven. Some walkways slanted sharply.

The shifting ceiling panels portrayed a nighttime sky. Clouds covered stars, then parted for the moon.

Torchlight flared on wooden posts throughout the playing field. Shadows confused her at every corner. Competitiveness was new to her. The adrenaline high from being chased kept her moving as fast as she could maneuver the maze. She could hear her heartbeat in her ears.

Signs for Skull Hill and the Swamp led her in a circle. She ducked behind a bunker to catch her breath, then softly moved down a trench. Mist fans blew moist jungle air.

A wooden fort stood dead ahead. If she could get onto the upper deck, she could peer out over the course and locate Sloan.

Crouched, holding her breath, Eve eased open the door to the fort and prayed it wouldn't creak. It didn't. Stairs led to the top deck. She took them quickly.

Her heart had never beat so fast.

Wanting to remain hidden, she crawled on her belly until she found a low slat that looked out over the field. Utter stillness settled around her. She set her pistol down, then removed her goggles for a better look.

A scream escaped her as the wide toe of a boot came down on her fingers. *Sloan.* He applied enough pressure so she couldn't wiggle her fingers free.

He'd captured her on hands and knees, a most undignified position for a warrior woman.

"Gotcha." His voice was winner fierce.

Eve closed her eyes, awaiting the unloading of his tommy gun. To her surprise, he gripped the back collar of her jumpsuit and hauled her to her feet. Still behind her, he pressed her to the wooden wall. She was his hostage.

He kicked her pistol and goggles aside.

"You have a second weapon?" he asked.

"You know I don't."

"That's what all snipers say." His breath heated her ear.

The heat didn't stop there; it stroked her neck, slid between her cleavage, fanned low into her belly.

She was high from the game, flushed hot for this man.

"Hands up," he ordered. "I'm going to pat you down."

She flattened her palms on the wall.

"Spread 'em." He inserted his knee between her thighs and shoved her legs apart.

Even in two layers of clothing, Eve felt vulnerable. When Sloan began his search, she nearly came out of her skin. His hands were big, his touch slow, as if he'd waited a long time to feel her.

He felt her up and he felt her down.

Her knees nearly gave out when he cupped her butt and slid his hand between her legs.

He then turned her toward him. Eve's breathing came short and shallow. Sloan sounded winded. They were both charged from the chase and capture.

He slipped off his mask. His hair was mussed, his gaze narrowed on her. "You're my prisoner," he stated.

"That's not part of the game."

"I play outside the rules. My win. Your consequences."

Her heart pounded and anticipation took hold, as raw and restless as the man who moved in on her.

Eve backed straight into the wooden wall.

They faced each other then, so close their zippers aligned. Eve felt the man, every flexing muscle, every inch of hardness—including the grenade in his jumpsuit pocket that poked her left breast.

Big and broad shouldered, Sloan blocked out the moon and stars on the ceiling. Darkness held them together.

She remained brave—far braver than she'd ever felt in her life, all because of a paintball game. She'd come alive during the challenge, and didn't want to come down.

When he tipped her chin up with his thumb, she knew Sloan was going to kiss her. He made his move, a slow, deliberate stalking of her lips.

Eve sank into him, sighing, as he nipped the corners of her mouth, then sealed his lips to hers. His need was evident, yet he waited for a sign that she accepted him.

She gave him that sign. Curving her arms about his neck, she welcomed the deepening of his kiss. Pleasure shivered through her body as he penetrated her with his tongue—a tongue that tentatively traced her teeth, as if he'd never kissed a metal-mouth. Once he was assured there were no rough edges, his kiss grew thorough.

The heat that ignited their bodies was as hot and explosive as the grenade in his pocket.

He controlled. Dominated.

And made her want him.

She wanted him badly. Her body had gone liquid. Her panties were damp.

Her dislike of Sloan was at odds with her desire. They had an insane attraction that neither could deny. Any involvement would prove short-lived. Their time together was limited. The man lived by a three-date rule. Sloan was not a man to go the distance in a relationship. She'd get a gift from his girlfriend closet as he walked out of her life—no doubt another duck. Sloan found humor in her childhood fear.

She felt no fear now, only a skin-hot deliciousness as he kissed her chin and neck and made her forget how quickly he'd leave her.

The slide of the zipper on her jumpsuit sounded loud in the stillness as he slid it down to her navel. He then unzipped his own suit to below his groin. His arousal strained against his button fly.

He worked his hand beneath her knit top, all the way to her bra. He brushed his thumb over the sheer satin, awakening her nipple. Then he exposed more of her skin as he kissed his way down her body like a man in need of a sexual fix only she could provide.

She came undone when he slid his hand over her belly and into the waistband of her white slacks. He slipped beneath the elastic of her panties, touched her with the roughened pads of his fingertips.

The sensation had Eve up on her toes. The man was rapidly bringing her to orgasm on the deck of the fort.

She moaned, squirmed, pressed into his palm.

"I won." Sloan's mouth moved against her hip bone. "You're my prize."

His prize? He thought he'd won her? He'd kissed her, not blasted her. There'd been no actual winner. The trophy was still up for grabs.

His grip on her ass forced her to shift her stance. Her hip brushed his tommy gun, now within her hand's grasp.

Desire left her, leaving her fully conscious and again ready for action. Conflicting impulses fought, both accepting and denying what she was about to do.

The warrior woman won.

Catching him off guard, she shoved Sloan back and snapped up the tommy gun. *Rat-a-tat-tat*, she blasted him blue.

Blue from his chin to his shins. The splatter was at close range, thick and messy, and could have covered six men. His jumpsuit would have repelled the mess had it been zipped. Instead the paint now soaked his street clothes and colored his skin.

Smurf blue.

# CHAPTER TEN

Sloan McCaffrey jumped to his feet and stared at Eve Hannah. What the hell had just happened? He'd been way into this woman when she'd suddenly shoved him back and blasted him with the tommy gun. His jaw worked, as much in anger as in disbelief.

"Why'd you go kamikaze on me?" he demanded.

She stood straight, her chin angled. "I wanted to win."

She sure as hell had. He rubbed a blue hand across the back of his blue neck, then looked down at his blue jeans, which were dripping with paint. "It's not very sportsman-like to get a man all worked up, then blast his balls blue. Major mood killer, Eve."

"The tommy gun got away from me."

"Freakin' understatement." He fought to control his temper. "I need a shower. If the paint sets, it stains."

She looked down at her own hands, spattered blue from the firing. "Water soluble?" she asked.

"Oil based." Which meant he'd need more than a hot shower to wash away the blue. He'd need paint thinner to remove the paint that now soaked through his clothes and onto his skin. *Shit fire.*

He snatched the tommy gun from her, then collected the Tippmann X7 Sniper. He thought about leaving her in the fort and tossing the grenade up over the side from the ground level, just to give her a taste of an explosion, something similar to the tommy gun, yet not quite so up close and personal.

The tommy gun had power. She'd killed his erection. His balls were blue and bruised. He needed an ice pack for his boys.

The descent from the fort proved slow, his hobble back through the maze even slower. Eve followed at a safe distance. As far as she was concerned, she'd won fair and square. He just wasn't ready to admit defeat.

The manager of Master Blasters went wide-eyed when he and Eve appeared in the rental room. "You're in need of paint thinner, Mr. McCaffrey," he said as he ducked into the storeroom and returned with a quart-size container, several clean cloths, and an industrial-size garbage bag. "The shower facility is down the hallway past the main office." Gus then offered a pair of navy sweats for Sloan to change into after he'd showered. "There's no one in the building to bother you."

Sloan returned the paintball guns and the grenade. He then grabbed Eve by the arm and walked her into the shower room. "You splattered me, and you're going to scrub me."

Eve resisted, digging in her heels.

Sloan outweighed her by a solid eighty pounds. One tug and she stumbled in behind him.

"No need to be so rough," she huffed.

He was feeling rough—and irritable. His skin itched and his balls ached. A man could turn mean when his nuts were cracked.

Inside the shower room, he rolled the jumpsuit off his shoulders, dragged it down his body, and deposited it into the garbage bag. He then started on his clothes.

"What are you doing?" Eve demanded as he struggled to get his T-shirt over his head without streaking his hair blue like some punk rocker.

"I'm stripping down so you can get to my skin."

He kicked off his boots and socks, then unbuttoned and dropped his jeans, down to his boxer briefs.

Eve looked horrified as she checked out his body: blue pecs and abs; even his navel sported color. Paint globbed his briefs. His thighs and calves were darkly smudged. Paint even creased his toes.

What a mess. He held out his arms and broadened his stance. "Cleanup on aisle five."

Eve didn't find him funny. "Paint thinner could irritate your skin."

"What's a few red blotches when I'm blue?"

Her hands shook as she wet the cloth to clean her own fingers. Her whole body trembled as she began wiping him down. A crease marred her forehead. Her lips were swollen from his kisses. Her jawline was rasped red.

She'd marked him with blue paint.

And he'd given her whisker burn.

Sloan's temper cooled. He'd been a damn poor loser. Eve had won fair and square. He'd been so into her, he hadn't noticed when her passion died and her pleasure turned to a desire to gun him down.

Somewhere between the paintball field and the shower room, she'd lost her fighting spirit. She'd become quiet and reserved. He wanted the fighter back.

"I played to win, Eve." He broke the silence. "I get mad at myself when I lose. I don't hit walls or women. So don't be scared of me."

"I don't fear you," she returned. "Not when you're covered with paint thinner and I have a cigarette lighter in my pocket."

He eyed her jumpsuit. No bulges. She'd turned him into a Smurf. A human torch held even less appeal.

He let her work silently. She concentrated on his shoulders, then drew the cloth down over his pecs. She dabbed at his blue nipple—and Sloan's testicles tightened.

He clenched his back teeth to stop a moan.

Damn if his dick didn't spring to life. It stuck straight up, trying to peek over the waistband of his underwear, painfully hard, and very, very blue.

Eve Hannah caught the stirring in Sloan's briefs. Her hand stilled on his six-pack. She wasn't sure if it was Sloan or the paint thinner that made her light-headed. Whichever one, she found his body thick, toned, and cut. She enjoyed cleaning him more than she'd ever admit.

Sloan's enjoyment didn't match her own. He'd shifted his stance a dozen times, seeming antsy and belligerent, wanting her to wrap it up.

She hurried. She scrubbed across his belly, a little harder, and a lot faster. . . .

Until he gripped her hand and pushed her away.

"I can take it from here," he gritted out as he turned his back on her.

He then snagged a towel and the sweats and headed for the shower.

Eve moved to the sink to splash cold water on her very hot face. She looked into the mirror and didn't recognize her own reflection. The bill on her baseball cap had flipped to the back, and her hair had escaped its braid. Her eyes were bright and a little wild. Her face was flushed. Her lips pouted, full and well kissed. Sloan's stubble had sandpapered her cheeks. Her jumpsuit remained unzipped to her navel.

She could still feel his big hands on her breasts. She vividly recalled the touch of his fingers inside her panties.

Her color deepened, and heat stole into her belly. She'd liked the way he kissed, had liked how he'd turned her on. She wished she'd gone a little farther with him. She hadn't touched him nearly enough. If she had it to do over, she'd have taken him out with her single-pop pistol, not fired the tommy gun.

The kick of the gun had been a kick to his balls. She knew Sloan was hurting.

Twenty minutes later, he approached her with blue shadows beneath his chin. His grim expression let her know much of his anatomy remained blue hued.

Without a word, he collected his discarded clothing and stuffed it in the garbage bag, along with the jumpsuit.

He then glanced at her. "You can return your jumpsuit to Gus. It can be cleaned and live to play another day."

Eve peeled the jumpsuit down her body. It caught on the heel of her tennis shoe, and she did a little hop before kicking it free.

Looking up, she caught Sloan's eyes on her breasts, narrowed and staring. He'd eyed her chest the same way during the Bunny Hop. Her breasts weren't overly large, but she filled a demi-B.

He knew her size. He'd felt her up less than forty minutes ago. He'd left her high on adrenaline, aroused and wanting more. More action. More man.

"I felt like Taylor today," she slowly confessed. "Silly, but true. I've never been chased, except by a duck, and that ended poorly."

Sloan looked surprised. "You had fun? With me?"

"Mm-hmm." She met his gaze. "I'd play again."

He crossed to her, openly curious. "What part of the game did you like best? Charging through the maze? Crawling on your belly? Getting caught? Kissing me?"

"Firing the tommy gun."

He looked pained. "You can't be serious."

"The blast was wicked, but I felt like a winner."

"I'm the loser with the blue balls."

"Still blue, huh?"

"And too bruised to scrub."

"I'm sorry, Sloan."

"Sorry enough to go on a third date with me?"

A third and final date. "What did you have in mind?"

"Adult go-karts."

"Sounds loud and low to the ground."

"It's not NASCAR, but it's fun and fast and makes your heart race."

The date sounded daring. "You're on."

"We'll go next week," he told her. "On Monday, my day off."

He then gathered up the garbage bag and motioned toward the door. "Time to get Addie and company."

Gus was locking up when they returned to the main entrance. Sloan sauntered over to the Black Ops Shop and bought her a souvenir: a small silver trophy with WINNER engraved on the stand.

She'd never won anything in her life.

She grinned. She felt strong and self-assured and a little kick-ass.


Back at the mall, Addie and her friends waited for Sloan and Eve just outside the entrance. The air was warm, the sky clear, and the stars helped light the parking lot.

Eve noted that Addie and Edwin were holding hands, a sweet gesture that had Eve believing love could come at any age.

Sloan drove them home safely. He took the time to walk everyone to the door—a rather slow walk, but the seniors weren't in any hurry.

"I'm on the road for a week," Eve overheard him tell Addie. "Out to San Diego, then to Chicago. Next week, the Rogues play at home, a four-game series with Louisville. I'll call you when I return."

"No hurry, son." She patted his arm. "Edwin and I will find plenty to do."

Addie offered her friends a cup of tea, and everyone followed her inside her condo. Everyone but Eve. Addie flipped on the porch light, and from just inside the door, Edwin shook Sloan's hand and Zeta kissed him on the cheek.

In less than a minute, Eve and Sloan were left alone outside.

"Thanks for the paintball," she began.

"You played hard."

"I'm not your usual date, am I?"

"No, you're definitely not," he said. "My first dates are flirty; my second heat the sheets."

Sex with Sloan McCaffrey. In the excitement of Master Blasters, they'd fooled around in the fort. She'd let herself go. Sloan wouldn't have stopped had she not tommy-gunned him down. They'd have done it in Black Ops.

Beneath the porch light, she looked at him, *really* looked at him, from his slicked-back hair to his dark gray eyes to the cut of his cheekbones. He had a mouth women wanted to kiss, and an athletic body that would perform to the max.

He was a Rogue, single, available, and never lacking for female companionship. Women came on to him every day of his life. They wanted his autograph and his body.

His arrogance grated on Eve's nerves. He acted grown-up around Addie and her friends, yet the boy inside the man came out in paintball.

Eve had watched Taylor and Stryke through their good times and bad. They were alike in so many ways; somehow they always matched.

Eve and Sloan had nothing in common.

They were oil and vinegar. Apples and oranges.

"You're looking serious," Sloan noted.

Eve forced a smile. "Just thinking."

"About me?"

"That's self-centered."

"I like when you look at me like you can't figure me out. You're considering getting to know me, but you're not sure I'm worth your time."

"Three dates will be enough," she assured him.

"So you tell yourself now."

Sloan McCaffrey slid one hand into her hair and eased her to him. His gaze lowered to her mouth, to those full, pink lips that now parted in surprise.

He went with one good-night kiss, deep and French to make her restless. Then he stepped back and left her breathless.

Her eyes were slow to open. When she looked at him again, her pupils were wide and dilated.

He'd teased her, and would leave her wanting more.

But his tease had backfired. With a touch of her lips, his heart had slammed and he'd gone spike hard. He was the one who'd been left aching.

"See you next week," he managed as he turned and carefully took the first of three steps to the sidewalk.

"Rat-a-tat-tat," Eve said to his back.

"Quack," he shot back at her.

Seven days streaked by. The Rogues lost the series to the Padres, but came back and kicked the Cubs' ass. Sloan had withstood a week of *blue* jokes. He was no longer sore, and his groin felt good to go, even though his butt, bat, and balls were still blue hued.

His teammates had razzed him, calling him everything from Bluebell and Blue Moon to Little Boy Blue. Another week and a touch more paint thinner, and his blue days would be at an end.

It was a Monday afternoon, and Sloan McCaffrey had the remainder of the day free. He'd put in his community hours that morning at Hollywood Harts, a sanctuary for retired animal film stars located outside Richmond. Its owner, Sophie Hart, had opened her gates to the School for the Deaf.

Lack of hearing had not been an obstacle when it came to watching the animals perform. Fancy, the square-dancing pig, Mocha, the acrobatic monkey, and the Frisbee-retrieving Sky Dog had kept the kids entertained for over an hour.

Rogues pitcher Chris Collier, temporarily on the disabled list, had tossed baseballs with the young boys. Chris was dating Sophie, and it had been rumored that he'd gotten between Fancy and her trough at mealtime, and the pink pig had taken out his knee. Fancy was a big, hungry girl, and when it came to feeding, nothing got in her way.

Chris had had surgery during the off-season. After a lengthy rehabilitation, he was scheduled to return to the team by the end of June.

After the animals performed, Sophie allowed the children to pet or hold each one. ZZ Paws, the American Curl, had purred and snuggled against more than one chest. And Oscar, the new ferret, had crawled over every child's shoulder and into their pockets. Oscar tickled, and made the kids laugh.

Ducks swam off in the distance in the man-made

pond—a pond dug and cemented by the Bat Pack. Romeo, Psycho, and Chase supported Sophie and her sanctuary. They were active in keeping the acreage cleared and the animals well fed.

Sloan wondered if he could ever get Eve Hannah near the pond, or if one quack would send her running back to town.

On his return to Richmond, he dropped the kids off at their school, then drove the van to Addie's to pick up Eve. He looked forward to seeing her.

She met him at the door wearing a white tailored blouse, pressed jeans, and a small smile. "You played well in Chicago," she said in welcome.

"You watched the game?" Somehow that surprised him.

"At Richmond General. Taylor was in therapy. A television was mounted on the wall. She exercised to Brek's pitches."

"Not to mine?"

"You relieved Brek after six innings. Taylor was worn out by then. She's not supposed to overdo, but with Brek out of town, she's pushed herself."

"Stryke's back now. He'll slow her down." Of that Sloan was certain. "You ready to race?" he asked.

Eve's chest rose and fell with two deep breaths. "How fast do the go-karts go?"

"Most Stratoses have a nine-horsepower Honda engine that runs at thirty-five miles per hour. Riding low to the ground, you feel like you're doing seventy."

He held out his hand, and she took it. "I won't let anything happen to you, Eve."

"I'd like to end our last date in one piece."

*Last date* . . . Sloan didn't like the sound of that.

KartWorld proved a noisy arena of adults acting like kids. Three oval tracks lapped the indoor facility. One straightaway held time trials for men wanting to beat their best time.

Sloan introduced Eve to Track Mac, one of the mechanics. He was pushing sixty, and had built or run go-karts his entire life.

"Let's get you geared up, little lady." Track Mac gave Eve the once-over. "You'll need a race suit, helmet, gloves, a neck collar, and a rib protector, if you want one."

"Rib protector?" Eve's eyes went wide.

Track Mac chuckled. "I've broken ribs and a knee racing. Blame it on brittle bones and questionable skills. I take too many chances for an old man."

"Eve won't be taking chances," Sloan told Track Mac. "We'll run a few laps, see how she likes it."

Sloan picked out a navy race suit with a white stripe across the chest. Eve selected one in cherry red to match her go-kart.

"Do all your sports require jumpsuits?" she asked as she fought with the long zipper.

Sloan pushed her hands aside and zipped her up in one smooth slide. "Sex I prefer naked."

She blushed.

And he grinned. He liked teasing Eve Hannah.

Fully geared, he helped her settle into her go-kart. She'd chosen number thirteen. Track Mac went over the rules. He requested that Eve go slow until she got the hang of the course, a one-mile racetrack Sloan rented on a regular basis.

Track Mac ducked into the mechanics' shed, and within seconds he pushed out a go-kart on steroids. "I just installed the Yamaha engine you requested," he said to Sloan. "Wicked fast. It'll hit sixty-five easy, turbocharged and nimble."

The engine rumbled in the muscle kart built to Sloan's

specifications. He'd wanted to show off for Eve. She, however, looked alarmed.

"Your go-kart looks like a bully," she shouted at him. "Don't run me off the track."

He had no intention of running her down. He wanted her to have fun. This was their third and final date. He planned to make the most of their time together.

They were the only two on the oval speedway. Sloan hung back, allowing Eve to get the feel of the track. She putt-putted along as if on a Sunday drive. He whipped up beside her and motioned her to go faster. If anything, she slowed down.

His racer begged to cut loose. Sloan gunned it. The kart shot forward, fishtailed around a turn, and left Eve in turbocharged exhaust.

He went eight laps before he slowed. Idling by Eve, he flipped up his visor and shouted, "Want to race?"

She lifted her helmet shield and rolled her eyes. "Race you so you can win?"

"You won at paintball; cut me some slack."

"How many laps?"

He flashed ten fingers.

"Ready, set, go!" she called.

Sloan had gone six laps flat-out when his engine sputtered. Spark plugs or out of gas? *Son of a bitch.*

He pressed the accelerator, only to glide to a stop. One of the workers between the tracks waved a white flag, telling Eve to slow down. She breezed past Sloan with a wiggle of her fingers.

He pushed his kart over to the side, stood beside it, hands on his hips, and shook his head. The tortoise and the hare. Eve would beat him again.

Track Mac came to his rescue. The older man jogged between the tire barriers, gas can in hand. He refilled the kart, and Sloan took off again. He made up a lap, but couldn't take Eve on the straightaway.

She passed the checkered flag two go-kart lengths ahead of him. She raised her arms, victorious, and nearly ran into the tire wall.

In the winner's circle, Eve hopped from the kart and removed her helmet, jazzed and glowing. Sloan begrudgingly handed her a trophy in the shape of a go-kart.

"I'm tired of awarding you trophies," he said.

Eve hugged the trophy, then embraced Sloan. She rose on tiptoe and kissed him full on the lips. He widened his mouth over hers and they touched tongues.

She had a way of sighing against his lips that made him want to strip down for go-kart sex. Unfortunately, the track was populated with racers and visitors, and privacy was at a minimum.

He reluctantly let her go. "We need to celebrate your win," he concluded, wanting to extend their time together.

She hesitated. "I thought—"

"Go-karts and we were over?" he asked, reading her mind. "I'd like to prolong our date. We could hit New Year's, an uptown club that celebrates December thirty-first every single night."

New Year's in May had appeal. Eve had heard of the club. It was a place to dress and be seen, to sip champagne, and to kiss wildly at midnight.

"I've never had a date on New Year's," she admitted.

That seemed to bother Sloan. "Never?"

She shook her head. "Taylor tried to set me up, but I've never been fond of blind dates."

"You know who you're getting tonight. Me."

Sloan was just fine by Eve.

He took her hand, and they departed KartWorld.

He dropped her off at her studio apartment, located above Thrill Seekers. "I'll pick you up at nine," he told her. "Let your hair down, and wear something sexy."

Eight thirty came and went, and Eve was still debating what to wear. Sloan was due to pick her up shortly, and the most she'd done was brush out her hair. It hung long and straight and almost to her waist.

She'd laid out three possible dresses for the evening, little cocktail numbers that Taylor had insisted she buy over the years, yet she'd never worn. All were low-cut; two were slit to her thigh, and one skimmed her like a second skin.

She stood before her mirror, holding each one up for the sixth time. She was unsure which dress would bring magic to the night. She definitely wanted magic.

"Go with the black."

*Sloan.* She'd recognize his voice in a crowd of one thousand. Eve turned slowly and found him leaning negligently against the door, which she'd left unlocked.

"You're early," she managed.

"I wanted to see where you lived."

"You're seeing more than my loft." She looked down at her black bra and short slip.

He came toward her then, devastatingly handsome in a dark gray suit that matched his eyes. A dressed-up Sloan McCaffrey was a shock to her system. He'd gotten a haircut and shaved, and the pine scent of his bath soap lingered on his skin.

He looked tamed, but she sensed his restlessness. The man could be confined in a suit for only so long. She hoped he'd make it to midnight.

"Mind if I look around?" he asked.

"The loft is one big open space. Art studio, kitchen, bedroom, and bath shoved inside four walls."

"I like it." He moved to her studio corner, where a painting stood nearly completed. "James River Stadium?" he asked.

"Risk Kincaid asked for the painting," she replied as she slipped into her little black dress. "The Rogues hold a silent auction each year to raise money for Animal Rescue. The painting of the ballpark is my donation."

"It'll draw a lot of bidders."

"I hope so. Last year I donated a lighthouse. It went to Romeo Bellisaro and his wife, Emerson, on a pity bid."

"No one will pity—"

The hitch in Sloan's voice drew Eve's gaze.

He was staring openly at her.

And Eve looked down at herself. Her slinky black dress cupped her breasts and stroked her hips like a man's hands. She showed a lot of leg between the flirty hem and the straps on her stilettos. She'd forgone nylons. The heat from his gaze indicated that he liked her legs bare.

He came slowly toward her. "Lady, you look hot."

Maybe not hot, but good enough to be seen with Sloan. Eve suspected that the man traveled in the company of the sexy and the slender. Calendar and *Sports Illustrated* women. Eve couldn't claim to be either.

"Let's celebrate New Year's." He ushered her out the door.

He'd rented a limo, black and stretch, with room for a dozen people. There was a bar, a television, and room for a double bed.

"Glen is our designated driver." Sloan nodded to the man behind the wheel. "We want to welcome the New Year in style."

*In style* meant Sloan got his ass kissed from the moment he entered the club. Always in demand, he got the

VIP treatment. Everyone knew his name and that he drank Johnnie Walker Gold. He and Eve were given the best table in the house. The deejay asked for a list of his music requests.

A waiter brought a broad selection of hors d'oeuvres, and female revelers crowded their table as if it were open season on the Rogue reliever.

The women were sleek, their makeup perfect. They smiled as often as they touched Sloan. They walked their fingers up his chest and down his arm. When he suddenly twitched and shifted on his seat, Eve swore they were stroking him under the table.

The partiers donned hats, blew on horns, and threw confetti long before the midnight hour.

"Excuse me." A dark-haired, almond-eyed woman adorned in emerald sequins squeezed in between Eve and a leggy brunette. Eve had started the evening next to Sloan, but by eleven thirty she was six women down the table from where he sat.

And he hadn't seemed to notice.

Sloan was caught up in himself. He believed his own press. He seemed fascinated by his own statistics when they were enumerated by glossy and puckered pink lips.

"Another piña colada?" the cocktail waitress asked Eve.

She lifted the one before her. The ice had melted and the paper umbrella had torn. Her drink had been neglected, and so had she. She shook her head. "I'll pass."

"How about you, Kendra?" The waitress turned to the new arrival.

"Tangerine mojito," Kendra requested. "And get Sloan another Johnnie Walker Gold. Be sure to tell him it's from me."

Sloan saluted Kendra when the cocktail waitress delivered his drink. His gaze lit on Eve and he smiled—the same smile he shared with the dozen other women at the table.

There was nothing special about their date. The man was playing to a table of thirteen.

Kendra bumped Eve's thigh as she crossed her legs. "I plan to take Sloan home tonight. Once Brooke goes to the restroom, I'm making my move."

"Brooke?" Eve looked down the table.

"The bleached blonde in the red dress slit to her crotch. Bet she's not wearing panties."

Eve wasn't taking that bet.

She recognized Brooke. The woman had nearly sat on her lap to get to Sloan. "What if he already has a date?" she asked.

The woman openly laughed at her. "Sloan doesn't date." She made air quotes around the word *date*. "He shows up with one woman, but leaves with another. The man has a number three tattooed on his groin. We're all aware our time's short-lived."

Eve was confused. "Then why bother?"

"Same reason you're sitting here, sweetie," Kendra said. "McCaffrey's the best game in town."

He was definitely a major player. Sloan hadn't looked her way for a very long time. His tie had lost its knot, and he'd shrugged off his suit coat. Lipstick smudged the corners of his mouth. One of the women had run her fingers through his hair. A dark lock now fell onto his forehead. He looked very roguish.

Kicked back, relaxed, and eating up the attention, he'd forgotten they had a limo waiting.

This was his world.

"Damn, he's handsome." Kendra smacked her lips. "Athletes make the best lovers."

Eve's stomach tightened. "It's all about sex, then?"

"What else is there?" Kendra sipped her mojito.

There was paintball, go-karts, and driving senior citizens to the mall. There was getting to know someone beyond three dates. There was putting in time and seeing if it paid off.

She didn't know the man at the end of the table.

She had no plans to figure him out.

Feeling invisible, Eve excused herself. "I'm calling it a night."

Kendra raised a brow. "Before midnight?"

"Once you get close to Sloan, tell him Eve said, 'Happy New Year.'"

"Eve is you, I gather?"

"I'm the one he came with. You're the one taking him home."

Kendra sent her a pitying look.

Eve made her escape when Brooke got up to powder her nose. The entire table shifted, and the remaining women scrunched closer to Sloan. Kendra rose and made her move. She and her sequins made a beeline for the man of the hour.

Amid the lighting of sparklers and the sound of horns blowing, Eve made it to the door. The doorman hailed her a cab—a cab that smelled strongly of pastrami, perfume, and feet. She returned to her loft in less style than she'd left.

New Year's clubbing with Sloan had proved the most eye-opening and disappointing night of her life. She'd thought they were friends. There had been a strong possibility that they could have been lovers. But not after tonight.

Third date, and the party was over.

She'd slipped off her dress when a sharp knock turned her toward the door. She clutched her dress to her chest.

"Eve?" Sloan's voice stole between the cracks.

She stood quietly, unable to move.

"Eve, I'm sorry. Honest-to-God sorry. I got into the celebration and forgot—"

"—you had a date?" She hated the fact that she sounded jealous.

"You moved down the table."

"Your women squeezed me out."

"They tend to play musical chairs."

"The music stopped and you didn't miss me." She bit down on her bottom lip. "Go home, Sloan."

He smacked the door with his hand. "We need to talk."

"Our talking days are over. Three dates and I'm breaking it off."

"You can't do that."

"I can, Sloan, and I am." She closed her eyes and sighed. "Go play paintball, ride go-karts, and be the center of attention at any club in town. That's your life, not mine. I like being an adult."

There was silence on the other side of her door, long and restrained. Several minutes passed before the dull thud of footsteps retreated down her staircase.

Eve's heart felt sad as she hummed "Auld Lang Syne."
*Happy New Year, Sloan McCaffrey.*

# CHAPTER ELEVEN

*Happy Memorial Day weekend.*

It was Monday, and the Rogues reported to James River Stadium, ready to take on the Louisville Colonels.

The game went three scoreless innings until Psycho McMillan powered the ball out of the park with two men on base. The Rogues had a three-run lead in the bottom of the fourth.

Top of the fifth, the Colonels battled back. Louisville scored two runs to keep the fans on the edge of their seats. The Rogues' second-base man was charged with an error when the ball hung up in his glove.

Brek Stryker was playing his all-time best. His fastballs drew strikes, and the home plate umpire's calls came quickly, without hesitation—a good sign of a good game.

Top of the sixth, and the Colonels best base stealer managed to make it to third as a result of a high hopper over the shortstop's head. The player was known as Greyhound. He could make it from third to home in 3.6 seconds. The man would score, even on a bunt.

The crowd collectively hissed as Kason Rhodes moved from the on-deck circle to the batter's box. Rhodes wasn't fazed. He was hated in every major-league park except his own. And he played to his reputation. The man was on a tear, going after Barry Bonds's home-run record.

*Take him down a second time.* Brek had thrown Rhodes out on strikes in the third inning. The batter had glared at him all the way to the dugout—one of those next-time looks that forecast a home run.

Brek shook out his arm, then faced the top power hitter in the American League. He knew Rhodes's hot zone, and threw just outside.

Rhodes laid his shoulder into it. His raw muscle whipped the air for a swing and a miss.

Strike one.

Rhodes was crowding the plate.

Brek dusted him with a breaking ball, forcing Rhodes back a step. Ball one.

Rhodes spit and snarled.

Ball two came on Brek's splinter—a bad call by the home plate umpire. The ball had been perfectly placed.

Brek gave the umpire an extra-long look, then covered his face and said a few choice words into his glove.

Another fastball, and Rhodes slapped it toward the fair-foul pole. The ball resounded off the metal, bouncing left instead of right and flying into the stands.

Strike two.

One more strike, and Brek would retire Rhodes.

Kason extended his arms and dug in. He swung on a fastball, only to tip it toward the television crews. One of the cameramen picked it out of the air.

Rhodes continued at bat.

Forcing Brek to increase his pitch count.

Brek's last pitch would end their pissing contest. Kason Rhodes had come into James River Stadium with attitude and assurance. He'd planned to slam a ball down Brek's throat. Rhodes had disrupted Brek's no-hitter the month before. Brek wasn't letting Rhodes walk away with a hit this time around. He would exceed his human powers to send Rhodes back to the dugout.

All around him, the stadium rose to a screaming, foot-stomping high. Foam fingers poked the air, and signs and banners waved wildly. *Hit the Rhode* was printed on hundreds of signs.

Rally Ball led the cheers from atop the Rogues' dugout. Charlie Bradley pumped his arms and rolled his costume in circles. Brek's name was chanted like a mantra.

Fans brought an adrenaline high to the game. Brek Stryker was infused with their energy. The rush added fire to his pitches.

He caught the catcher's sign, then held Rhodes's stare for ten seconds. He inhaled and went through his windup. Rhodes wouldn't expect a changeup. The man was counting on another fastball.

Changeups were regulated by finger pressure. Brek tightened his hand to slow the ball down.

The pitch was right down the middle.

Rhodes swung with a deliberation that would send the ball into the parking lot, perhaps all the way to the mall.

His connection stunned fans into silence as his bat splintered and the baseball slammed low instead of high.

Slammed right for Brek.

Duck or dive? Brek did neither. He barehanded the ball just as the broken bat clipped his left shoulder.

He was hit so hard and fast he felt he'd been shot in the hand. The pain was immediate, a fire-hot burn.

All breath left him. His shoulders bunched as he shook out his hand, but he couldn't release the ball. His fingers curved crookedly over the cowhide. A bone in his thumb broke the skin. His little finger was bent at a right angle. What he could see of his palm had turned black.

Play was halted as the team manager, the pitching coach, the trainer, and the entire team gathered at the mound.

Risk Kincaid ordered the players back so Brek could breathe. Words were spoken from every direction, but nothing soaked in. He had no feeling in his hand, and his arm had gone numb. His shoulder now throbbed from being hit by the broken bat.

The crowd stood and solemnly applauded as he followed the trainer to the locker room. He passed home plate and Kason Rhodes, and Brek met the man's stare.

Rhodes was out. His jaw worked and his hands flexed. His expression remained hard. The men were now tied one-to-one in their competition.

"We're taking you to Richmond General," the team doctor told Brek when he wasn't able to pry the baseball from Brek's hand. "You need a specialist."

The baseball had drilled into his palm. His fingers had broken over the ball, and his nerves had spasmed. The team doctor wasn't able to take X-rays. Brek imagined that the removal of the ball would come through surgery.

He traveled by ambulance to the hospital, a first for him—and hopefully his last. The EMTs packed his hand in ice, as well as his shoulder.

To his surprise, Taylor Hannah met him at the emergency room door. She looked as shell-shocked as he felt. She hobbled toward him in her workout sweats as fast as her crutches would carry her. She was pale and frightened, her eyes wide. She'd bitten one corner of her lip raw.

Sunlight hit her as she maneuvered across the shadowed walkway on the emergency ramp. Haloed, she looked like an angel.

Brek was damn glad to see her.

Suddenly it seemed those three years apart no longer

separated them. Taylor stood before him now, blocking his way, yet wanting to help in some small measure.

"Ma'am, you need to step back," one of the EMTs ordered as a wheelchair was rolled out for Brek.

Taylor held her ground. She rested her hand lightly on Brek's arm. "I was in therapy, watching the game. I saw Rhodes hit and you go down. How bad is it?" she asked.

"That ball had bite."

"It's stuck in your hand?"

"For the moment."

"What can I do?" she asked.

He reached out. "Hold my good hand."

They were a sight, Brek realized, the walking wounded: he in his wheelchair and Taylor hopping alongside him. Yet she refused to leave.

*I'm here; deal with it,* her expression told anyone who might suggest she move on.

The emergency room doctor recognized her stubbornness and let her stay during the examination. Brek watched Taylor watch every move Dr. Anders made. She asked more questions than Brek would have thought to ask. All the while she held his left hand so tightly, he swore she'd break it, too.

"You'll need X-rays and an MRI on both your shoulder and hand," Dr. Anders concluded. "We'll work around the baseball. Removing it now could cause more damage in the long run. Hold on to it."

Brek couldn't release it if he tried.

A transporter arrived to take him for his X-ray.

"I'm going too," Taylor stated.

The transporter frowned. "You're on crutches."

"Call for a second wheelchair and I'll follow you down the hall," Taylor told the hospital employee.

The transporter shook his head. "Sorry, hospital policy—"

"Let her come," Brek said. Taylor had spirit and fight and refused to be left behind. The transporter would have to break Brek's good hand to remove Taylor's from it.

Her vigilance surprised him. She protected her own. And she was now protecting him.

A hospital volunteer was called to wheel Taylor to X-ray and the MRI. She laid her crutches across the armrests.

Wheeled through the hallways, Brek took comfort in having Taylor at his back. She'd reassured him over and over again that he'd be just fine. That his career was only temporarily on hold, and that he'd continue to break and set new records.

Brek believed her. No one reaffirmed the positive like Taylor Hannah. The lady had guts, drive, and faith.

Dr. Anders laid out the good news with the bad once he'd read the test results. "You've a bruised shoulder, nothing more. An inch to the right, and the bat could have fractured your collarbone."

He looked at Brek's chart and moved on. "You've broken twenty of the twenty-six bones in your hand. You'll need immediate surgery, which I've scheduled for four o'clock."

It was two thirty now.

"His rate of recovery?" Taylor asked for Brek.

"He's strong and healthy, and after six weeks in a cast and extensive rehab, he should regain eighty percent mobility."

Brek shook his head. "That's not enough." He needed a full hundred to climb back on the mound.

The doctor understood. "I'll do everything possible." He tapped his clipboard. "A few tests, and we'll move you upstairs."

Dr. Anders looked at Taylor over the rim of his glasses on his way out. His smile was understanding, fatherly. "No, Ms. Hannah, you cannot join me in surgery."

Taylor smiled. "Got my answer before I even asked."

Brek looked at Taylor. He liked having her close, but wasn't sure it was wise to draw her back into his life. He cared for her, but was damn cautious with his feelings. He didn't want to start what they couldn't finish.

"You don't have to stay," he said. "You were in therapy. You should get back to your exercises."

She bit down on her lower lip and blushed, suddenly self-conscious. "I've imposed on you." She rose from the wheelchair and reached for her crutches. "You need to call Hilary, need to have her here—"

"Taylor." He cut her off. This was as good a time as any to tell her. "There's no more Hilary."

She looked at him blankly. "I don't understand."

"I broke off the engagement."

Her lips parted. "Why?"

"Hilary is married to Stuart Tate."

She stared at him, looking hurt and concerned, as if she'd taken on his wounds as her own. "I'm so sorry."

"Don't be," he managed. "Better to know now than to be left at the altar a second time."

"You wouldn't want to go through that again."

"Never again, Taylor."

She leaned heavily on her crutches. "Sloan thought there was something between Hilary and Stuart at Addie's party. Sloan caught Stuart's hand on Hilary's butt."

"I caught them dancing a naked salsa."

Taylor fought her smile, but laughter won. She raised one hand and apologized. "Not funny, I know. But the visual hit me right between the eyes."

"Embezzlement brought Hilary and Stuart together, and will now separate them in jail." He laid out their story, detail by sordid detail.

Taylor listened, sympathetic, supportive, understanding. "How do you feel?" she asked.

"Relieved," he had to admit. "I'm glad it's over. It's time—"

"To draw your blood, Mr. Stryker." A nurse pulled back the curtain. She looked at his hand. "Still gripping that baseball, I see."

"I bring the game with me wherever I go."

"Ducking might have proved a better choice," the nurse said.

"Pure reflex," he replied. And the need to prove to Kason Rhodes that Brek controlled his home stadium.

"I'm off." Taylor took a few shuffling steps.

"You don't have to go." Brek didn't want her to leave.

"I'm not going far," she assured him. "I saw some board games in the children's therapy room. I'll pick up a few and meet you in your assigned room when they wheel you upstairs. I'll keep you company until you're prepped for surgery."

The nurse checked his chart. "Room seven-sixteen. Family only until after his surgery."

Brek caught Taylor's uncertainty. "I want you with me," he said. She looked relieved.

Taylor tried to stay positive. She'd never seen a hand as messed-up as Brek Stryker's. And she'd witnessed countless accidents throughout her thrill-seeking years.

She hobbled into the hospital chapel and hit her knees. She prayed as she'd never prayed before. Then she moved on to the therapy room, where she received the therapist's permission to select games to be played with one hand.

Somewhere between emergency and his private room, Brek was forced out of his Rogues uniform and into a hospital gown. His athletic shorts were visible at the back opening.

"Don't you look cute," Taylor teased him when they again met up in his room. Brek had great legs for a man, long, muscled, and dusted with dark hair.

Concern etched his brow. "I feel exposed. These gowns shift and bare my ass."

"I don't hear any nurses complaining."

The nurses didn't complain. Taylor counted thirty-one coming and going over the next ninety minutes. All professional, yet all checking to see if Brek needed anything—anything at all.

Taylor had forgotten how the Rogues attracted women. She was now seeing Brek as single and available. His smile made women blush. He always said the right words to make fans feel at ease.

Taylor grew apprehensive. She'd known Brek Stryker as both friend and lover, yet now she felt in limbo, unsure what direction their relationship would take.

"Let's catch sports highlights before we play checkers." Brek reached for the bedside television remote. "I need to know who won the game."

They soon learned Sloan McCaffrey had taken the mound, following Brek's departure. He'd struggled, and Louisville had tied the Rogues by the top of the eighth. Pitching coach Danny Young hadn't brought in a closer. He'd forced Sloan to go the distance.

Determination lined Sloan's face even as he threw more balls than strikes and walked two players.

"He'll mature, gain his mound presence." Brek showed

confidence in his backup. "Sloan will make defense work their asses off, but the team will make a decent showing."

The highlight reel showed the Colonels' leadoff batter smashing a ball to right field. Psycho McMillan ran, dove, slid across the grass on his belly, glove out, and made a run-saving catch. No player left the game more grass-stained than Psycho.

The game was still tied by the bottom of the ninth when the Rogues took their bat. The sports announcer documented Psycho's explosive line drive into center, which earned him a double. Romeo Bellisaro and Chase Tallan were called out on strikes. Risk Kincaid claimed the Rogues' victory by belting the ball out of the park.

"Glad they pulled it off," Brek said.

Taylor caught the relief on his face. "How's your hand?" she asked.

"Still numb."

She set up the checkerboard and they played for thirty minutes. They avoided talking about old times, and concentrated on jumping opponent checkers and crowning kings.

A transporter arrived at three forty-five to take Brek to surgery. Taylor didn't want him to go alone.

Her throat went dry and her stomach knotted. She took his good hand and held on tight.

Brek stared at her with absolute focus. "It's okay, Taylor. The sooner I have surgery, the sooner I'm back in the game."

"I'll be here when you return."

"I expect you to be."

And he was gone.

Taylor remained in his room for a long time. She stared at the checkerboard, realizing that Brek was in position to have captured her last two kings, but hadn't made his move.

He'd let the game go on as long as possible.

By seven o'clock she hobbled toward the nurses' station. She slowed outside the visitors' lounge and took in the scene. There were Rogues everywhere. The entire team roster packed the sitting area. Many of the players paced the hallway.

The men had drunk gallons of coffee and emptied the vending machines. Yet none of them thought to leave the hospital until they'd received word on Brek's condition.

He was their team captain, and the players were loyal.

"Taylor." Risk Kincaid broke from a group holding up the wall. "Any word on Stryke?"

"Nothing yet," she said. "Could be another hour."

"Come sit down." Risk directed her into the lounge.

Every player seated quickly stood and offered Taylor his chair. She took Romeo Bellisaro's, which placed her between Psycho McMillan and Sloan McCaffrey. She slumped low; her knee was sore and she'd grown tired.

Sloan took her crutches, then lifted her leg across his knees. He began rubbing her calf up to her brace. The ache soon diminished.

She brushed crumbs from one corner of his mouth.

"Vending machine cake," he told her.

"You shouldn't eat so much junk food."

"I arrived late. It was either cake or a prune muffin."

Psycho wrapped one arm about her shoulders. "Heard you met the ambulance."

The lounge and hallway had gone silent, the players all awaiting her answer.

"I was in therapy and had the game on," she told him. "When the announcer said Brek was being transported to Richmond General, I headed for the emergency entrance."

She bit down on her bottom lip. "His hand was swollen to the size of a catcher's mitt. They weren't able to remove the baseball before surgery."

The silence grew heavy with concern.

Sloan leaned in close, his voice low. "Where's Hilary?"

"With her husband, Stuart Tate."

"No shit?" He cut her a look. "I told you so."

"You were right," she whispered back.

"How's Stryke taking it?"

"She didn't destroy him."

"Not like you did."

"Low hit, McCaffrey. That was three years ago, and I'm trying to make amends." She turned, punched his arm. "Why did you invite Eve to New Year's only to hook up with your bimbos?"

"She told you?" Taylor nodded, and he blew out a breath. "I was a real shit."

"Yes, you were. If you treat my sister poorly again, I'll add black to your blue, Smurf boy."

"I've sent her flowers and stuffed animals, and called until I'm out of wireless minutes. Eve refuses to see me."

"I don't blame her."

"Harsh, Taylor. I could use some sisterly advice."

"Leave her alone."

"Not an option. I like Eve. When I looked down the table and saw her amid my groupies—"

"You felt more than you'd expected?" Taylor guessed.

"Yeah, something like that."

"*Exactly* like that, Sloan," she returned. "You're not smart enough to pick a soul mate over a Hooters chick. Until you recognize the difference, stay away from Eve. I don't want her hurt."

He scowled. "I'll keep my distance."

Movement in the hallway caught Taylor's attention. Seconds later, team owner Guy Powers entered the lounge, followed by power hitter Kason Rhodes.

"What the hell is he doing here?" Psycho jumped to his feet, blocking Rhodes at the door.

"This is a closed lounge, for team members only," Romeo Bellisaro announced.

Guy Powers shot both men a dark look, which they ignored. "Following today's game, Kason Rhodes is officially a Rogue. Management acquired him in a midseason trade with Louisville."

A stunned silence settled over the players. The looks they shot Rhodes were intimidating and dark, unwelcoming.

Eyes narrowed and jaws worked.

Only Psycho dared speak. "Why Rhodes?"

"Ryker Black pulled his hamstring during spring training and hasn't played a full week since," Powers stated. "We've brought up players from the minors, but no one's done the job. Rhodes solidifies our left."

"But can he bat?" Taylor quipped as she pushed through the testosterone-charged teammates.

Everyone knew Rhodes could bat the hell out of a ball. Taylor's outrageous question prompted snorts, dipped heads, and swallowed smiles.

Psycho took up where Taylor left off. "You top the American League in home runs," he said to Rhodes. "The National League separates the men from the boys. Can you cut it here?"

"Not only cut it, but will lead off in a month," Rhodes predicted, warning Psycho to guard his spot in the rotation.

"Game on," Psycho replied.

Guy Powers knew when to step between his men.

"Kason came with me to check on Brek. Any word?" he inquired.

The men deferred to Taylor. She turned to Powers, and the team owner embraced her with fondness. "Thanks for the flowers," she said in greeting. Powers had sent her an enormous bouquet of raspberry pink roses shortly after her knee surgery. "We've no word as yet. Hopefully soon."

She then looked to Kason Rhodes, tall, dark, and a loner. He was surrounded by men who hated his guts, yet he remained cool and unfazed.

*Hard-core* and *badass* struck her as appropriate descriptions. He met life head-on and never blinked. He stared men down and won at chicken. He walked in harm's way, and would put his ass on the line during every game.

She couldn't blame him for the broken bat or the hit that had landed Brek in surgery. Accidents came with baseball. Brek was a competitor. So was Kason Rhodes.

Rhodes's integration into the team would be slow, despite his batting power and outfield performance.

It was how the game was played.

The Rogues took care of their own. At the moment, their team captain was foremost on their minds.

"Ms. Hannah?" Dr. Anders stood at the door in his scrubs, his expression somber. "Can we talk?"

She looked around the room at the fraternity of players that stood as tight as brothers. "Talk to all of us," she requested. "In layman's terms." She wanted his explanation easily understood by everyone.

Anders handed Taylor the baseball he'd removed during surgery. "It's not the World Series ball, but it's a moment in time Mr. Stryker will never forget."

He crossed his arms over his chest and continued. "The surgery went well. The deep calluses from his years of pitching took much of the impact when he caught the ball. I had to set a lot of broken bones. His hand's in a cast. Six weeks is on the light side for his recovery. It could run to eight. Then there's rehab. In the very best scenario, he'll be back for the playoffs."

"The worst?" Taylor needed to know.

"The bones in the hand are small. Fragile, even in a man's hand. Flexibility is my primary concern. He will be able to grip and throw a baseball, but his release may be slow."

"Visitation?" Taylor asked.

"Three people, no more than five minutes. A nurse will monitor your visit. My patient's groggy and needs to sleep."

"Three people?" Psycho's jaw shifted, along with his stance. "Doesn't work for me."

"Pick your three, Taylor." Risk Kincaid made it her decision.

She looked around the room. Forty men had waited three hours for news of their team captain. Brek carried their respect. They needed his leadership. Each one deserved to see him, even if only for a second.

"We're all going in," she told them. "You can pass by his bed like a parade. I want Brek to see you. Your support will bring him back to life faster than Rhodes hit that baseball."

Taylor led them down the hall and stopped just outside Brek's room. She stood guard as his teammates filed in, and heard each man's encouraging words.

Three minutes later, a horrified nurse shot toward Taylor, her expression argumentative. "Too many visitors." She blocked the doorway.

It was Sloan McCaffrey who came up behind the woman and whispered something in her ear. The nurse blinked, blushed, and slowly nodded. She took a step back and allowed the men to pass.

"What did you say to her?" Taylor asked when the nurse returned to her station.

"I told her I'd line her up with Brek once he'd recovered enough to date."

Taylor swung her crutch at his crotch.

Sloan dodged left. "The Hannah sisters and their need to unman me. First Eve and the tommy gun, now you and your crutch."

"You need to be put out of commission."

Sloan nodded over his shoulder to where the lanky closer, Cooper Smith, leaned against the wall across from the nurses' station. "Coop's been checking out the nurse, and she's liked his eyes on her. I offered to set them up."

"You're quite observant."

"If I don't make it in baseball, I'll turn to matchmaking."

"You played well today," she complimented him.

"I kept waiting for Coop to come in and close. There was never any action in the bullpen."

"You brought it home. The Rogues won."

"But we've lost a key man to injury." Sloan looked at Kason Rhodes, now headed for the elevator. "Powers put a bullet in the cartridge when he brought him aboard."

Taylor didn't want Rhodes to leave. Not yet, anyway. "Kason," she called out.

Rhodes stopped in the act of pressing the elevator button.

She hobbled toward him. "You haven't visited Brek."

He raised one brow, a devil's arch.

"He needs to see you."

He looked unconvinced. "You trying to give the man a coronary?"

Taylor swallowed hard. "It's important that he comes out of surgery fighting. Seeing you will bring him to his feet faster than anything else."

Rhodes didn't seem so sure. He studied her, his gaze dark, fathomless, unreadable. "You belong to him?" he finally asked.

"Once, but not anymore."

"You will again."

His words lingered in her mind long after he'd brushed past her and taken his place at the end of the line.

Looking at the hard set of his shoulders, the sharp jut of his chin, Taylor decided she'd better be in the room with Brek when he laid eyes on Kason.

Just in case his heart monitor spiked.

# CHAPTER TWELVE

Life moved in a slow-motion haze. Brek Stryker sensed more than saw his teammates as they passed through his hospital room. He heard their mumblings of, "Get well soon," and, "Hell of a game," yet was too damn tired to fully acknowledge the players' presence.

The scent of Amber Nude told him Taylor stood beside his bed. With his good hand he reached for hers. Her soft warmth took hold immediately.

The shadow of a man stood off to the side. Brek forced himself to focus. Dark hair, hard face, an evident smirk.

Kason Rhodes.

Brek's knee-jerk reaction sat him up in bed. His heart thumped, and his vision cleared. What the hell was Rhodes doing in his hospital room?

"Hell of a catch," Rhodes said as he jammed his hands in the pockets of his jeans.

"Hell of a hit," Stryke returned, his mouth full of cotton.

Taylor released his hand and poured a glass of water.

Stryke took a short sip.

"Kason became a Rogue today," Taylor explained softly. "Guy Powers made a midseason trade."

Her announcement jolted Brek like a royal kick to his groin. Powers had hinted at the proposed trade. "Guy traded four minor leaguers—"

"Five," Rhodes corrected him.

"Along with Ryker Black to get you?"

"And a top draft pick."

Brek narrowed his eyes. "Powers thinks you're that good?"

"I am that good." Rhodes wore his conceit like a second skin.

The short conversation tired Brek out. He yawned. The surgery had taken its toll.

Without a word, Kason Rhodes departed.

Taylor again took Brek's hand and lightly squeezed. "Rhodes is not an easy man to like."

Brek closed his eyes. "Yet you brought him in to see me."

"I thought he'd put some fight in you."

"I have fight; it's just not going to be easy."

"Nothing worthwhile is ever easy."

"Does that include us, Taylor?" The words escaped on a tired sigh.

"You're worthwhile, and I'm easy," she whispered. "Rest now. I'll be here in the morning."


Taylor was as good as her word. Morning found her slouched in a chair, her leg elevated on the foot of his bed. Her hand still held his in the morning light.

They'd traded places, Brek realized. Three weeks ago he'd been in the chair and she'd been on the bed. Life had a way of flip-flopping things. He'd helped Taylor get on her feet, and she was back to help with his hand.

He rubbed his thumb over her wrist and across her pulse point. He felt it thump. He turned his head and found her eyes on him. She had bed-head, and a sleepy flush left her cheeks pink. Taylor looked beautiful to him.

"How's your hand?" she immediately asked.

He looked down at the cast. "Numb."

"The feeling will return," she assured him.

His jaw locked. "Damn, this sucks."

"You played to win and were rewarded with a broken hand. Life's not always fair."

"I had to make the catch." His stadium. His turf. He'd had no other choice.

"A great catch, one for the record books."

"That catch could end my career."

"But it won't." She spoke so positively, he believed her. "Mind over matter, Stryke. You have a strong will. You'll throw another hundred-mile-an-hour fastball."

He damn sure hoped so. "How's your rehab?" he asked, glancing at her knee.

She scrunched up her nose. "I'm tired of driving to the hospital every day for therapy. I'm going to invest in a home gym and set it up on Addie's back porch. I haven't yet overdone—"

"But you will if someone's not watching."

"Addie's got an eagle eye."

"I have an idea," he slowly suggested. "Why not use my equipment? I have a workout room with a multistation gym, rowing machine, stair climber, stationary bike, weight bench, and dumbbells. The works."

She ran a hand over her knee brace, looking uncertain. "Rehab with you?"

"Unless you have a better offer."

She looked thoughtful. "I'd be driving half the distance."

"Or not driving at all." His words slowed even more. "You could move into my guesthouse, which would save on gas altogether."

She stared at him, stunned by his offer.

"The invitation stands," he said. "You could come and go as you please. I'll be around some, but not often. I still have team commitments, public endorsements, and community-service hours. My days are full."

Taylor pushed to her feet and limped the width of the hospital room and back, contemplating out loud. "Addie and Edwin deserve their privacy. I've camped out at my grandmother's far too often. I could use a change of scenery."

Brek's heart kicked. His offer would ease Taylor back into his life. It was time to see if their future could survive their past. As his guesthouse neighbor, she'd cross his path daily. They'd work out, maybe share a meal. Afterward, she could escape to her own space.

He'd let Taylor be Taylor.

No pressure. No commitment.

Only freedom—to stay or to go.

In the end, she agreed to stay.

With his release from the hospital, Brek helped Taylor move. She still limped, and he could lift with only one hand, yet within six hours, she was fully settled in the guesthouse.

"Tired?" he asked when she dropped onto an over-stuffed sofa done in blue and white stripes.

"A little." She slipped off her tennis shoe, gingerly stretched out her leg, then loosened her brace. "No swelling." She rubbed her knee and breathed easier. "I was concerned, being on my feet all day."

"You were pretty active."

"We both were. How's the hand?"

He shrugged. "Still numb."

"Give it time."

He crossed his arms over his chest, looking down at her. "Hungry?"

She traced circles on the arm of the couch. "I'm here to work out. You don't have to feed me."

"Look, Taylor . . ." He thought it best to lay out the ground rules now, so they didn't debate every single issue. "I'm being neighborly when I offer dinner or a movie or something in between. You're under no obligation. Accept or reject, whatever suits your mood."

"My mood says pizza. Hawaiian, triple cheese."

He flipped open his cell phone. "Delivered here or to the main house?"

The main house was a two-story estate with five bedrooms, four baths, a kitchen the size of a small diner, a den worthy of a boardroom, a sunroom with a cathedral ceiling, a library, and formal living and dining areas, topped by turrets with big bay windows and circular window seats.

Brek had bought the house for her. Taylor had lived in it less than a month. She wasn't ready to face her past. When she did, she'd do so alone.

"Let's eat here," she suggested.

Brek ordered, and Rochichio's delivered.

Taylor kept the evening casual. She pointed to the coffee table and said, "Pizza tastes the same on a plate or right out of the box."

Brek took the opposite end of the couch. He set a six-pack of Pepsi between them and a handful of napkins. Then he dug in.

Taylor watched him eat. Big man, big bites.

He'd eaten three pieces to her one by the time he came up for air. She smiled at him. And he smiled back.

He went for a fork, scraped the pineapple off his next slice, and slipped it to Taylor.

She returned the favor, but with the ham.

Pizza had never tasted so good.

At the end of an hour, Brek folded the pizza box, collected the empty Pepsi cans and napkins, and got to his feet. "I plan to work out twice a day," he told her. "Dawn and dusk. Use the equipment whenever you like. Gym's set up on the first floor, between the garage and my den."

He reached into his pocket and removed a key from the ring. "You'll need this to get in. A cleaning service comes twice a week, Mondays and Thursdays. It takes them a full day to work through the house. Groceries are delivered on Tuesday."

"Thank you," didn't seem adequate to express her appreciation.

"I'm glad you're here, Taylor."

"Yeah, me too."

He went on to dump the garbage, then took off.

Taylor sat alone, wishing Brek had stayed, yet knowing neither of them was ready to share more than pizza.

The next day, she slept later than planned. She'd exerted muscles and energy in her move to the guesthouse, and her knee hurt. A long, hot shower helped. Then she took off for Thrill Seekers.

She found Eve adjusting clients and trips, postponing adventures until Taylor could downhill, white-water raft, and trek the Sahara once again.

Eve caught sight of Taylor from the corner of her eye and smiled. "Good to see you."

"Good to be seen." Taylor limped over to the counter. "How's business?"

Eve flipped through the calendar. "You're booked two years out."

"Maybe it's time to expand." Taylor proposed what

had been on her mind ever since her surgery. "Maybe we should hire a few experienced guides."

Eve's eyes grew round. "You've never trusted anyone to do your job. You've always been hands-on."

Taylor blew out a breath. "It's time to let go. Just a little."

"All this stems from . . . ?"

"I've moved out of Addie's and now live in Brek's guesthouse."

"His guesthouse?"

"A safe distance from the main house," said Taylor. "Brek's been solid and decent, and given me space. I want him to make a move, *any* move, so I know where we stand."

"When he moves, you'd better be ready. Don't lose this man a second time."

"You're giving me advice?" Taylor teased Eve. "A woman who won't return Sloan McCaffrey's calls? Who ducks out the back door when he appears on the sidewalk?"

Eve pulled a face. "I'll talk to Sloan eventually. Just not today. Or tomorrow."

"Don't let too many days pass," Taylor told her. "It's hard to recapture the time you've lost."

She then headed toward her office, located beneath the stairs that led to Eve's studio apartment. "I'll be on the computer most of the day. I've got people to contact, guides to hire. Knock on the door if you go out for coffee. I could use a hazelnut latte and a raspberry scone."

Over the course of the day, Taylor sipped three lattes and ate four scones. She'd been diligent in her searches, and was pleased with the outcome.

She'd screened and hired two American men and one European woman to guide Thrill Seekers. They were elite adventurers with *daredevil* tattooed on their souls.

It was six thirty by the time she returned to the guesthouse. She changed into a willow green tank top and black athletic shorts and decided to work out.

She braved the front entrance, then stood in the foyer for what seemed a lifetime. The cleaning crew had left the house immaculate, a showcase of high-end furniture and Oriental rugs.

It was the house of a man who'd walked through life, but never really lived it. Had Taylor not left Brek at the altar, the echo of their teasing and laughter would be as much a part of this home as the stillness that now claimed it.

She walked through the house room by room, a slow exploration of what she'd lost. Even after three years, Brek's hurt lingered in the hallways. She caught his deep pain reflected in the decorative mirrors. Her betrayal remained in the master suite she'd once designed.

She felt no other woman in his bedroom. He'd spent his nights alone. She dropped down on the oak bench at the foot of his bed, crossed her arms over her chest, and held her own pain inside.

She hurt for Brek, hurt for herself. Hurt for the mistakes she'd made. She needed to fix all that she'd damaged, beginning with Brek Stryker.

The sound of his McLaren drew her from his bedroom.

He entered the house as she came down the wide center staircase. Their gazes locked, and heat crept into her cheeks.

He stood before her in a gray shirt and black slacks, tall, formidable, and all business. His expression was unreadable.

She tightened her grip on the banister. "I came to work out." Her excuse was lame; they both knew the exercise equipment was on the first floor.

"Thought you might be going through my sock drawer."

"That . . . too."

To her relief, Brek shook his head and ruefully replied, "I gave you a key. You're welcome to look around. The place hasn't changed much over the years."

"You've added more books to your library," she noted. "I like the new redwood deck over the sunroom."

"The deck allows me to breathe. I often sit outside, have a beer, and release the stress of the day."

She descended the remainder of the stairs. "Time to exercise."

"I'll join you shortly," he said.

Brek soon appeared. He'd changed into a Rogues jersey and sweatpants. The man looked relaxed—and very hot.

Taylor sneaked look after look. His closeness distracted her. The metallic, rhythmic sound of the lat machine broke her concentration while she walked on the treadmill. She nearly fell on her face.

Stryke's body resonated with strength and testosterone. His workout was a kick-ass release of adrenaline, while her body knotted with each consecutive step. She'd need a masseuse to ease the kinks from her shoulders if the stress of watching Brek lift weights pinched any more of her muscles.

In the days that followed, Taylor managed to relax. She and Brek fell into a pattern of rehab, training twice a day. They often ordered takeout. They spent more time at the guesthouse than the main one. The atmosphere was less stressful there, and new memories were made.

The politeness and contemplative silences in June led to familiarity in July. They'd grown accustomed to each other, yet neither broached the subject foremost on their minds: Did they have a future together?

Taylor took each day as it came. She embraced her time with Brek. He had yet to touch her, yet to kiss her, yet to take her to his bed. The anticipation made her skin itch.

When Brek's cast came off, she decided to celebrate with a candlelight dinner. Feeling daring, she set up the catered meal in the formal dining room of the main house.

A manicure, pedicure, and a hot little red dress brought the evening together. If Brek didn't make a move on her tonight, she'd make a move on him.

His bare-chested workouts had gotten to her—badly. She wanted to trace his abs, blow on his belly, and make him hard.

Frenzied, burning, carnal hard.

She knew he wasn't immune to her either. She'd caught him checking out her butt when she walked miles on the treadmill and did her deep knee bends.

Their bodies wanted contact, even if their minds hadn't fully accepted the fact.

Brek's arrival put Taylor's romantic thoughts on hold. He slammed through the door, looking tense and annoyed. He threw a gray rubber ball against the wall, the resounding bounce an echo of his frustration. Bending, he placed his hands on his knees and breathed deeply.

Taylor froze. She'd never seen him so mad. She took her cue from his mood. Dinner could wait.

"Stryke?" she called.

Surprise hit Brek as he looked up and spotted Taylor. He'd thought himself alone in the foyer. More often than not, he came home, changed clothes, and met her in the gym. She seldom ventured beyond her treadmill.

Yet tonight she stood before him in a sexy red number, wearing Amber Nude, and looking concerned.

"Sorry, Taylor." His apology hissed through his teeth. "I didn't mean to take my doctor's visit out on you."

She picked up the rubber ball and approached him. She gently touched his arm. "How's your hand?"

He straightened, admitting, "Not as good as I'd hoped. I've got feeling in my fingers, but no flexibility. I couldn't knead the damn ball."

Taylor dropped the gray ball onto his palm. "Try again," she encouraged.

He trapped it within his fingers, then put every effort into the squeeze. His shoulders rolled and his muscles strained. A knuckle cracked. His hand shook.

No pressure. No imprint.

"Shit," he growled.

Taylor took the ball from him. "Highly compressed rubber. You need to start with something softer. Maybe a tennis ball. There's one in the gym."

Brek followed her down the hallway. The brisk, seductive sway of her hips and the soft click of her low-heeled sandals on the brown marble foyer drew his mind off his hand and onto her body.

She was one prime distraction.

The light scratch of her nails across his palm as she handed him the tennis ball tightened his stomach. He liked red polish, and Taylor's fingers and toes were painted ready-for-sex red.

Brek had given her time. He'd waited patiently, allowing her to call the shots. He'd take control tonight.

"Squeeze," Taylor prompted him.

Brek tried, unsuccessfully.

He clenched his jaw, refusing to give up.

Taylor looked around and located a rosin bag he often used to chalk his hands before lifting weights.

She switched the bag for the tennis ball. It was light, like a beanbag. "Try this," she suggested.

Still nothing.

"Foam, a pillow, a sponge, a . . ." She looked around.

Brek sensed her urgency; her concern was as deep as his own. He didn't want her panicking, so he calmed her.

Catching her arm with his good hand, he eased her toward him. "Slow down, Taylor." He steadied her.

They'd touched on occasion, lightly, yet hadn't come together as man and woman. Now, as he held her close, they fit perfectly, an intimate pairing of hard planes and soft curves.

Time had not diminished their heat and need. Desire pulsed, surged south, and stretched him hard.

Taylor released a breath on his neck, warm and moist, as his erection pressed her belly. "I want you, Stryke."

He wanted her too. He kissed her then, remembering the past, creating the future. He ran his hands down her spine, cupping her bottom.

He'd give his left nut to be able to squeeze her butt.

Taylor Hannah turned him on, and he wanted to return the favor. They kissed until his lips went numb, until his chest heaved, and his breath came rough and ragged.

It was Taylor who remained sane through their insane kisses. Taylor who drew his hand to her breast, a supple, soft, C-cup breast. Taylor who curved her hand over his and urged his fingers to squeeze. Taylor who moaned when he soon kneaded her on his own, slowly, awkwardly, yet with enough pressure to pucker her nipple.

His hand spasmed when she touched him in turn.

She unbuttoned, then spread open his shirt, baring his chest. Her nails scraped and her gaze admired. Her mouth made love to his pecs and abs.

Lower still, she blew on his belly. His erection strained against his zipper. He caught her soft smile. His response pleased her.

He wanted her so badly, the pain in his groin hurt worse than his hand. And his hand was throbbing.

Air jammed in his chest when she shimmied out of her dress. She stood before him in a scarlet strapless bra with a rhinestone clasp and matching bikini panties.

"Rehab, Stryke." She inhaled and her breasts lifted. "Release the front hook."

Six tries and a grinding of teeth, and he freed her breasts. There was little dexterity in his fingers, but what there was, he used to undress her.

He wanted her naked.

In the soft evening light he took her in, his beautiful Taylor. Several new scars were visible to him—scars he found sexy.

"What happened?" He traced a thin white line on her breastbone.

"Deep-sea diving, Tasman Sea. Barracuda, black coral, my wet suit caught and ripped." Her words were murmured against his chest.

"How about this one?" He skimmed his thumb across a red slash on her left hip bone.

"Rock climbing, Edinburgh, Scotland."

"And here?" His fingers worked down her body, now at her inner thigh, where he skimmed just above her knee.

"Downhill at La Grave," she told him. "I misjudged a turn."

"The skiing accident that brought you home."

"You brought me home, Stryke," she admitted. "Eve sent me your wedding announcement. My mind was on you and not the dogleg when I went down."

He gently kissed her forehead. "I'm sorry you got hurt."

"I got to rehab with you." She returned his hand to her breast and said, "Work your fingers; knead me."

He kneaded until her knees gave out and her thoughts went horizontal.

"There's a bed in the master suite." Brek's gaze was hot, knowing.

Taylor swallowed and looked at him. His hand was weak. No way could he lift her. She made a split-second decision and leaped into his arms. She clasped him around the neck; her legs wrapped around his waist. She clung with her inner thighs.

The rub of her bare breasts against his silk shirt aroused him with each of his steps. His good hand slipped between her thighs and found her sweet spot. She was so wet and aroused, she nearly came halfway up the staircase.

They reached his bedroom and found the bed freshly turned down, thanks to the cleaning ladies. One window was cracked, and the summer breeze sifted through, lingered, seduced.

He made it to the edge of the bed, and she slid down his body, a slow slide, where their planes and angles meshed together.

Taylor took her time with Brek—with this man who'd waited three years for her return. She used her tongue as much as her touch. Their scents mingled. Their desire was a mixture of memories and new sensations.

Flushed, her heart racing, she rolled Brek's shirt off his shoulders. And he dropped his pants.

She removed his boxers.

He took her panties.

They were naked, hot, and starved for each other.

Time and tenderness gave way to lust.

"Protection." His deep voice blew moist in her ear.

A condom, now, before they both went mindless.

His nightstand provided one, and she sheathed him.

They dropped onto the bed, rolled about, then faced each other. Taylor cupped his face, admiring the strength of his brow, the slate-blue heat in his eyes, the hard line of his mouth that softened in sex.

It was a face with character, she realized, and one she'd never tire of looking at over morning coffee or during midnight sex.

His body seemed larger than life, all muscled and cut, and sporting a major-league hard-on, an erection she began to pump in her palm.

Brek worked her as well. His hand stroked from her breast to the hollow of her hip, where his fingers fanned out over her pelvic bone. Two fingers dipped between her legs on his way to her toes. His touch was slow and reverent as he savored the contours of her thighs and the slope of her calves. He made her feel beautiful.

The return of his fingers sought her readiness. He found her wet and slick and open to him.

Their breathing changed, became deeper, rougher, and foreplay became total turn-on.

She bit his lip, and his dick bumped her belly.

He thumbed her nipple, and hot little currents shot straight to her groin.

Overheated, her pulse rampant, Taylor rocked against him. She needed him inside her—right now.

Brek understood *now*. Splaying her leg over his hip, he penetrated her. A slide all the way to his hilt, a torrent of pleasure.

Taylor sighed, the deep sigh of being taken.

He gave a preliminary roll of his hips, and she mirrored the rotation. He withdrew, thrust, then intensified the rhythm.

Their bodies rubbed in a slick, sparking friction.

They were breast-to-chest. The smooth and the hair-roughened. She was sleek, and he all rippling muscle.

Gasping, crazed, they climbed and climaxed.

Time spun away as their souls touched.

In the afterburn, they lay twined and content. Her shoulder was tucked into his chest; the swell of her hip fit against the narrowness of his waist.

She kissed his bare shoulder, smiling at him. "You look as satisfied as I feel."

He nuzzled her neck. "Best therapy I've ever had."

Eventually they paused for dinner, both wrapped in silk robes.

They ate barbecued ribs with their fingers, sipped a rich red wine, then agreed dessert was best served in bed.

They loved long into the night.

Brek Stryker woke early, Taylor still beside him. The morning sun hit her skin from her nipples to just below her navel. He watched her breathe, and peace settled in his soul. His heart warmed with her presence.

She hadn't escaped to the guesthouse. She'd spent the entire night in his bed, a bed she was hogging with her diagonal position. The lady was a cover thief.

He reached over, running his hands over the sleek lines of her body. His hand curved beneath her, and he cupped her bottom. Squeezed.

His fingers dug into her tight little ass with significant pressure, enough to wake her.

"Copping a feel?" her husky voice teased him.

She felt warm. Her scent was all woman. "I like touching you."

"Then touch me for the next hour before I go to work."

He touched her all over—twice for good measure.

From that day on, pleasure and purpose claimed their lives. Their days separated them, yet the nights brought them together.

Thrill Seekers thrived, even with Taylor remaining in Richmond. Placed on the disabled list, Brek couldn't travel with the team, but he attended every home game— games viewed with Taylor from the team owner's box.

Through it all, they reminisced and made new memories. He loved this woman, yet hadn't told her. The right opportunity had yet to arise.

As the days passed, he noticed that she'd begun to study the Weather Channel, watching for reports of fresh powder.

His heart clutched.

A collection of skiing magazines now stood on the living room coffee table. The European locations were dog-eared.

The magazines made his stomach hurt.

She spent a lot of time on her cell phone talking with Miles Pardeaux, her most recent hire in La Grave.

The delight in her voice left his throat tight.

She'd nearly healed, and a restlessness now claimed her. She wanted to test her knee. The slopes in France beckoned, a challenge as big and tall as the mountain of Le Meije.

Needing to distract her, Brek requested Taylor's assistance in planning Dog Days of Summer. It was a yearly Rogues' event, open to the public and always well attended. Held at the Carlton House, the silent art auction benefited Animal Rescue. Pets could be adopted at the event, too, and many found good homes.

All the while they worked together, she grew more distant. Her mind was often elsewhere, far away from him.

It killed him to think she might leave him again.

So he watched and awaited her decision.

And hoped her heart would remain with him.

# CHAPTER THIRTEEN

Dog Days of Summer. Eve Hannah strolled the south lawn of the Carlton House. An outdoor art gallery welcomed the guests. Worked in both oils and pastels, the paintings were portraits, landscapes, abstracts, and all that was baseball.

A sunset palette tinted the wraparound veranda in pink and gold. Hollyhocks and wild roses scented the air.

Professional dog walkers circled among the guests, relaying information on each dog's age, breed, and rescue history. Those wanting to adopt would fill out paperwork and be screened by a committee.

Eve shook her head, still chuckling over Psycho McMillan's entrance. The Rogues' right fielder already had two Newfoundlands, yet wanted to add a third pup to his family.

He'd stepped onto the veranda and howled, as if he'd been raised by wolves. A hair-raising silence had followed. Guests turned their heads and stared, and every dog's ears flickered. Several canines hid behind their handlers.

The first animal to return Psycho's howl would go home with him and his pretty wife, Keely.

Psycho didn't want any sissified 'fraidy-cat. His howl told all those present that only a muscle dog would survive in his household. He'd looked at the Burmese and Saint Bernard nearby, certain one of the big boys would respond.

His call of the wild gained only one response. The return yip dropped Psycho's jaw. It came shrill and excited from a miniature red dachshund named Gretchen, who nearly wiggled out of her skin to reach him.

Psycho picked Gretchen up and eyed her suspiciously. "You're a stick of pepperoni. My Newfoundlands have tug toys bigger than you." The dach licked his chin.

He and Keely began to argue over who should hold the pup. Gretchen seemed happiest in Psycho's arms.

Eve had watched Jacy and Risk Kincaid pick out a dog as well. They went with a two-year-old golden retriever named Gunner. Jacy stood out in the crowd with her purple hair. She wore a violet knit dress and a wide red patent-leather belt slung low on her hips. She'd immediately collared her new pet in matching patent leather. Risk raised a brow, claiming the collar was too girlie. He preferred brown leather.

Jacy told Risk *she'd* wear a leather collar if he left patent leather on the dog. A wicked smile split his face, and Risk agreed.

Eve stood back from the crowd, enjoying the shade from a weeping willow. A faint breeze swayed her white linen skirt. She slapped at an ant that crossed over the peep toe on her cork wedgies, then secured a loose strand of hair in her ballerina bun.

Off to her right, a fancy lemonade-and-iced-tea stand was set up beside a buffet of decadent desserts. She'd sampled a slice of mint cherry cheesecake earlier and now debated going back for a deep-dish hot-fudge brownie.

She was nervous about seeing Sloan McCaffrey. Taylor had warned her that he'd be attending Dog Days. Eve hoped eating would distract her from noticing his arrival.

"You look like a Pekingese or poodle person."

The deep male voice startled her. She turned slightly and found a tall man in a brown button-down and khakis, sipping a Coke. He had a hard face, and his gaze hit her with an intensity that made her jump.

"You look like the type to own a Doberman," she returned.

"I had two as a kid."

Eve took a second glance and couldn't imagine him as a child. The man looked as if he'd been born grown-up. He packed an edginess that steered people clear of him.

"You hiding?" he asked.

Eve shook her head. "Merely people watching."

"More like avoiding someone."

She clutched her hands before her. "I don't want a confrontation."

He nodded his head as if he understood.

"Eve Hannah," she said politely, introducing herself.

"Kason Rhodes."

Taylor had told her about Rhodes. She'd described him as tough and antisocial. Eve looked him over with an artist's eye. Dangerous. Fallen. Alone. Beyond his sharp features and athletic build, she sensed a depth to the man that she wished neither to explore nor analyze, yet instinctively knew was there.

He'd be a difficult man to paint. She'd have to peel away layers of his past to get to his soul. She was certain he'd be wounded.

"Who's your adversary?" Rhodes scanned the crowd.

She hesitated. She didn't know Rhodes, yet he stood solidly beside her, as if protecting her.

"A man whose apology I refuse to accept," she finally told him.

"He must have done something pretty damn bad to upset you."

"He treated me like a groupie."

He looked down and shook his head. "There's nothing groupie about you, sweetheart."

"I'm not ready to talk to him. Not yet, anyway."

Rhodes rubbed his jaw. "He'll go white-hot if he sees us talking and thinks I'm hitting on you."

"You're not hitting on me, are you?"

"No, Eve Hannah, I'm not." One corner of his mouth tipped a fraction. "You're too sweet for my tastes."

Rhodes preferred women on the darker side of midnight. Women who partied late, slept over, and never sought commitment. He and Sloan traveled a similar path.

A dog walker approached them with a Jack Russell leashed at her side. The animal was shy, skittish, and rib-skinny. "Her name is Juliet," the handler told them. "She's three, sweet tempered, and has a slight overbite."

"Here comes her Romeo," Kason noted as an English bulldog tugged his walker toward Juliet. Two good sniffs, and the bowlegged boy sat on command beside the Jack Russell.

"His name is Dozier," the handler said. "He's five, and prefers a harness over a choke chain."

Kason went down on one knee and scratched Dozier's ears. Eve followed suit, letting Juliet lick her hand.

"Juliet likes you," Kason said as the Jack Russell tried to wedge herself between Eve's knees.

"Dozier likes Juliet," she noted. The bulldog butted close, wanting to clean the Jack Russell's ears.

"Who do you like, Eve?"

Sloan McCaffrey's voice hit her like a clip to the chin. Her head jerked back, and her gaze skimmed up his gray slacks to the collar on his cobalt blue knit shirt. His eyes were narrowed and sharp as he studied her crouched beside Rhodes. A hint of uncertainty creased his brow.

"I don't like you," she said, and hated the fact that her voice broke. "Go away."

"The face-off." Rhodes got to his feet, then drew Eve up beside him. He stood close enough that their hips brushed.

"Get lost, Rhodes." Sloan's hands were now fisted, his stance threateningly wide.

Rhodes flexed his own hands. "I'll leave when I'm ready."

"Ready is *now*," Sloan stated.

Rhodes took his time departing. "I need to place a bid on the painting of James River Stadium. It would look good on the living room wall of my trailer. A double-wide."

*A double-wide?* Eve blinked. Rhodes made millions of dollars, yet his roof could detach and his trailer roll in a storm.

The man was an enigma.

The teammates stared at each other for another full minute before Rhodes and the dog walkers moved on.

"Asshole," Sloan muttered under his breath. "The man comes into the Rogues organization and moves to the top of the batting order. Now he's trying to steal our women."

"I'm not your woman."

Sloan looked battle-weary. "We need to talk, Eve. Give me five minutes. That's all I'm asking."

Still she hesitated. She'd heard from Taylor that Sloan had matured. As a starting pitcher, he was taking his new responsibilities seriously. When he wasn't playing, he was practicing. On his occasional night off, he took Addie and her friends to the mall or to a movie.

Both Taylor and Addie favored him with a compliment whenever they brought up his name. Eve had closed her ears to their praise.

She fingered a pearl button on her swing jacket. The white skirt suit had clean-cut lines and made her feel feminine.

Sloan looked very masculine. Even though she was wearing wedge heels, he topped her by six inches. The width of his shoulders blocked all that was going on behind him. The laughter and barking indicated many of those gathered were finding the perfect pet to take home.

Sloan held his ground, looking determined. "Five minutes," he repeated.

She wasn't sure if she could handle sixty seconds with this man. Standing close, surrounded by his body heat, she wanted nothing more than to lean into him and remember how their bodies fit.

But physical fit wasn't good enough. He lived life by his three-date rule. And they'd hit the three mark months ago.

She was close to agreeing to talk when two women in tight tops and short skirts bracketed Sloan. The redhead carried a Chihuahua in a mesh satchel; the brunette talked baby talk to the tiny dog.

Both women greeted him with the look of having seen him naked. The brunette playfully ran her fingers across his shoulders. The redhead touched his arm.

All the color drained from Sloan's face. "Bad timing, ladies. I'm trying to make up with my . . . my . . ." He blanked on the right word.

"Your girlfriend?" The redhead tossed her hair.

"Your fiancée?" questioned the brunette.

Sloan gritted his teeth. "Yet to be established."

The redhead stuck out her bottom lip, pouting. "If things don't work out, you've got our number."

Eve had their number too. She watched the slow twitch-twitch of their hips as they moved on, both tall and slinky, and absolute head-turners.

"Your time's been cut to two minutes." She looked at her watch. "Starting now."

He didn't waste a second. "I've missed you, Eve."

She'd missed him too. Only her heart knew how much.

"I was a jerk," he admitted. "I should never have taken you to New Year's and subjected you to—"

"Your rotation squad?"

"I've enjoyed most of them once, some of them twice," he admitted. "But I haven't taken anyone to bed since the night we went to the club."

Hard to believe. But she hoped his words were true.

"I'm not a bad guy. I may not get things right the first time out, but I'm worth a second chance."

"What comes with a second chance?" she asked.

"Starting over."

"Another three dates?"

"Why not?"

"What happens when those dates end?" She needed to know. "Do I hold my breath for a third renewal?"

His jaw worked. "You're complicating a simple issue."

"There's nothing simple about us," she said.

"I have fun with you, Eve. I want us to be friends."

Friends played paintball and rode go-karts. Friends caught a movie. Maybe he meant friends with benefits.

She'd wanted more, and Sloan had offered less. Disappointment almost choked her. It was time to move her life along.

She released her breath. "Friends . . . I'll give it some thought."

"How much time do you need? Twenty, thirty minutes?"

"A lot longer than that."

She eased around him while her knees still held up.

Her steps were as heavy as her heart as she crossed the lawn to examine a painting of a sun-warmed brick street and an outdoor café in the historic district. The rich golden hues depicted summer in Richmond. She placed her bid. The painting would brighten Thrill Seekers.

She bumped into Kason Rhodes on the north side of the lawn. He was hunkered down beside a black-and-rust Doberman puppy. "This is Cimarron," he said.

Eve watched as the little gator mouth sawed on Kason's hand, leaving teeth marks. Rhodes didn't seem to mind. "I bid on your painting," he said as he scratched Cim's ears.

Eve felt relieved. "Glad someone did."

"I wasn't the only one, sweet Eve. I cheated and looked at the auction slips in the envelope beside your painting. You had twenty solid bids, one as high as fifty thousand."

Eve's eyes went wide. "It's not worth—"

"That's the value Sloan McCaffrey's put on your painting. I added ten grand."

She stiffened. "Why would you do that?"

"To see if he'd fight for you."

"Sloan won't."

"I'm betting he will."

"I don't want him to have the painting. He can keep his money—"

"The money goes to Animal Rescue," Rhodes reminded her. "Let Sloan win you."

At eight o'clock, Brek Stryker stood behind a podium on the veranda and announced the winners of the silent auction. He looked clean-cut and all business in a white button-down and navy slacks. Taylor stood beside him in a sky blue sundress. They made a handsome couple.

Brek went down the list of paintings and announced the winners. Eve's bid won the outdoor café in the historic district. Brek held her painting of James River Stadium until the very end.

She scanned the crowd and found Kason Rhodes on the outskirts of the bidders, alone, his face hard—but not as hard as Sloan McCaffrey's expression as he worked his way toward the veranda. He stood before Brek, his gaze locked on the painting.

Taylor slipped the bids from the envelope and quickly sorted through them. She then handed two slips of paper to Brek. "There's been a tie." Brek's deep voice carried on the night air. "Sloan McCaffrey and Kason Rhodes have both bid sixty thousand for Eve Hannah's painting. Does either man wish to go higher?"

Eve stood perfectly still. Sloan had sneaked in and upped his bid, matching Rhodes's own.

"Sixty-five," Rhodes called out.

Everyone's gaze shifted to the Rogues' latest acquisition. Kason's eyes connected with Eve's. He was waiting for her to signal that she preferred Sloan to get her painting.

"Seventy." Sloan was not to be outbid.

"Eighty." Rhodes kicked it up a notch.

"One hundred." Sloan's voice was tight.

Eve cut the air with her hand, backing Rhodes off. Sloan had bid an enormous amount of money. He deserved to win. Kason Rhodes nodded—and Sloan was awarded her painting.

Eve had thrown her heart into that project. Sloan would take half her heart home with him.

Brek went on to announce all those who'd adopted pets. He mentioned Psycho McMillan and Risk Kincaid, then noted that shortstop Zen Driscoll and his wife Stevie had chosen a Boxer named Gibson.

Sophie Hart from the animal sanctuary had selected a swaybacked black Lab to keep Sky Dog company.

Twenty additional rescued dogs were placed with good homes. At the end of the night, three dogs remained: the Jack Russell, Juliet; the English bulldog, Dozier; and the Dobie pup, Cimarron.

An odd couple at best, Juliet and Dozier lay side by side on the veranda. The Jack Russell's head rested on the bulldog's paws. Cimarron tugged on his leash, full of puppy energy and wanting to play. The Dobie would prove a handful for his owner.

"Let's make the evening an all-out success," Brek Stryker encouraged from the podium. "Juliet and Dozier appear to be soul mates. I'd like to see them go together."

So would Eve. She crossed her fingers and bounced on her toes, anxious for someone to bid on both. Her studio apartment was too small for the twosome; otherwise she'd have taken them in a heartbeat.

"Five thousand for the pair," Sloan McCaffrey called out.

He looked at Eve as if he'd known she wanted Juliet and Dozier to go to a good home. Her lungs filled with air she couldn't expel. She was utterly stunned by Sloan's generosity. He'd proved he'd do anything for her.

The crowd applauded McCaffrey as he climbed onto the veranda and claimed Eve's painting as well as the two dogs.

Dozier's and Juliet's souls matched. The dogs needed each other. Only Cimarron now remained.

Holding the two leashes, Sloan led the dogs down the steps. He looked at Eve and cocked his head, requesting help.

The man knew she couldn't resist lending a hand.

"Thank you," she managed.

"These are *our* dogs," he told her straight-out. "Make time for us, Eve. I want you involved in their care. We'll set up a schedule for walks and playtime. Deal?"

She nodded. She'd make time for the dogs, and maybe even for Sloan. She'd never seen him more sincere. They'd go slowly. Maybe friends could be lovers—someday.

Cimarron's whine turned Eve around. The Dobie was tugging and gnawing on his leash, lunging and trying to capture someone's attention. He wanted a home too.

Eve knew whom Cim needed. She touched Sloan's arm. "Buy Cimarron," she requested.

Sloan lifted a brow, skeptical. "*Three* dogs?" He blew out a breath. "Guess I could extend my backyard fence."

"Only two for us," she quickly explained. "I'm giving one away."

He poked his tongue into his cheek, narrowing his eyes. "Giving it away to who?"

"You won't like my choice."

Sloan shifted the painting to Eve, along with both dogs. "I can guess, and I'm already hating it."

He caught Brek Stryker's attention and raised his checkbook for Cimarron. The crowd whooped and howled, clapping their hands red. Sloan was their hero.

In his race down the verandah steps, Cimarron tripped Sloan. The man caught himself before he went head over ass. "This pup is trouble," he told Eve.

"So is his owner." Eve took Cim's leash, then looked over the crowd. People were dispersing fast, and it took her a full minute to locate her man.

He'd turned and was already heading for the parking lot.

"I'll be right back," she told Sloan.

She took off at a fast walk, only to be pulled into a jog by Cimarron. The dog sensed her direction, and was off to the races.

"Kason!" she shouted.

Rhodes looked over his shoulder, then turned slowly. His expression remained hard, even when he saw Cimarron.

"What's up, sweet Eve?" he asked when she approached.

"I have a puppy who needs a home," she said.

Rhodes's lips compressed. "You thought of me?"

His lack of enthusiasm set her back a step.

Cim ignored Rhodes's indifference. The dog jerked Eve off her feet in order to reach the man.

Cim pawed Rhodes's leg, whining obnoxiously, and bit at his knee. All the while Kason looked down at the Dobie, unmoved.

For a split second Eve thought she'd made a mistake. Rhodes could easily refuse Cimarron. Maybe her instincts had been off. Maybe Kason truly was a loner.

"I'm sorry," she blurted out. "I thought—"

"I needed a friend?"

She slowly nodded.

"I'm my own man. I do alone just fine." Rhodes looked from her to Cimarron. "Puppies are needy."

"It's okay to need."

"Do your attentions come with the dog?" he asked.

"I'm too sweet for you, remember?"

"Way too sweet." His gaze dropped to Cimarron. The pup now lay at his feet, his head resting on the toe of Rhodes's boot.

"I'm making Cim a gift." Eve made one last-ditch effort to convince Rhodes to take the pup. "One you can't return."

An indecisive silence ensued. In the end, Rhodes surprised her. "We'll give it a trial run, no promises."

Eve's hand shook as she handed him the leash.

She knew when he took Cim that he wouldn't be giving

him back. The pup got his second wind. The only way to calm him was for Rhodes to pick him up.

One last look at man and Dobie, and Eve knew Kason belonged to Cimarron. The pup had claimed him and would dominate his life—in a very good way.

Rhodes gave her no more than a brief nod as he departed.

Eve didn't expect more. The *swoosh-swoosh* of the dog's tail against Kason's side brought the day to a positive close.

It was time to find Sloan.

She turned and nearly slammed into him. The painting shifted beneath his arm and he caught it. The dogs stood poised, Dozier protecting his Juliet. *Family* crossed Eve's mind. All waiting for her.

Sloan had stood back and allowed her time with Rhodes. He'd no doubt hated every second, yet he'd allowed her to do what she'd needed to do.

He shot a dark look at Kason's back. "I can't believe you gave him a dog."

"Cimarron needed a home. The pup will be a second heartbeat in Kason's double-wide."

"I've heard Rhodes lives deep in the woods."

"Where do you live, Sloan McCaffrey?"

"Thirty minutes south."

"Maybe I'll follow you home."

He looked at Juliet and Dozier, then back at her. "We'd like that."

In the middle of the parking lot, Eve went up on tiptoe and kissed Sloan full on the mouth. She appreciated this man—appreciated him so much they stopped traffic.

It was Kason Rhodes, leaning on the horn of his battered Hummer, who broke them apart. Eve cut a look at driver and dog as they passed. Cimarron had taken a seat on Rhodes's lap; she wasn't sure who was driving.

She took Juliet's leash from Sloan's outstretched hand, and together they crossed the lot to his gray Silverado.

"I'm right behind you," she told Sloan once the dogs were loaded. She'd driven her Saturn to Dog Days, and didn't want to leave her car in the hotel parking lot.

After the drive across town, Sloan McCaffrey held the door for Eve to enter his home, a two-story Chesapeake brick house, newly constructed and recently purchased.

Set on an acre and surrounded by trees, the four-bedroom house opened into a wide foyer with a curved staircase on the west side. Skylights throughout welcomed sunshine and moonbeams. Rich rosewood floors lent a polished veneer.

Sloan watched Eve take it all in. She'd unleashed the dogs, and Juliet and Dozier now ran free. He opened the back door, and the twosome took off to explore the perimeters of the fence.

"I'd like to hang your painting here." He pointed to a blank wall in the living room to the right of the fireplace. He considered it a place of honor next to his entertainment center.

"How long have you lived here?" She breathed in the new-house smell.

The scent of fresh paint and lemon-polished wood still lingered from the builders and cleanup crew. Even his furniture hinted of showroom decorators.

"The house came on the market three weeks ago," he told her. Right after their New Year's club breakup. "You're my first houseguest."

A houseguest whom he wanted to stay. He'd house hunted off and on for the past year. No house had felt right until this one. The moment the Realtor had walked him through the four-bedroom, he'd felt an immediate sense of homecoming.

He'd wanted Eve to see the house as he saw it: a place to raise kids and dogs, and grow old. Yet she withheld judgment as she moved into the kitchen.

The island caught her attention. She ran her hands over the brown marble top, which held a small sink and a butcher block center. Her eyes widened over an expensive set of kitchen knives. Those knives could chop, dice, and skin a deer.

"Stainless-steal appliances should last a long time," he said, hoping for a response.

She merely nodded.

The kitchen opened to a sunken sunroom with a rear staircase. Starlight flickered through the French windows, as bright and twinkling as strands of tiny Christmas lights.

Overstuffed furniture in natural wood crowded together in intimate closeness—his furniture from his old apartment. A short bookshelf housed his favorite espionage and psychological thrillers.

"I like this room." She smiled at him for the first time. "It's cozy."

Sloan wanted Eve cozy. He wanted her to feel warm and protected and into him.

"Your girlfriend closet?" Her gaze searched out several closed doors.

"Not at this house," he said. "I tossed the teddies, but kept the sex toys."

Her eyes rounded, and she blushed.

"Care to see the upstairs?" he asked.

The sound of dogs barking delayed her decision. These weren't playful yips. They were protect-the-property barks.

"We should check on Juliet and Dozier," she said.

They moved to the back door. There, Sloan flipped on floodlights that illuminated bright circles in the yard.

Eve squinted into the darkness, then touched Sloan's arm. "There's something moving outside the fence."

Definitely moving. And Sloan took a deep breath.

The only downside to the house had arrived. He'd hoped the trespasser would have stayed at lake's edge until morning, yet his invasion came tonight. Amidst Juliet's woofs and Dozier's howls rose a distinctive quack.

A quack so loud, Eve jerked back, her eyes wide. "A duck?"

"Quackers," he said, giving the name of the neighborhood duck.

A mallard weighing in at twelve pounds, with a whole lot of attitude.

# CHAPTER FOURTEEN

"Call the dogs and close the door." Eve's voice shook as she sought protection behind Sloan.

"The duck is *outside* the fence," he quickly assured her. "Quackers lives on the lake."

She'd gone sheet white.

"He's a nice duck, Eve," Sloan went on to say. "He's come into the garage when I've left the door up. I toss him day-old bread on occasion."

Totally annoyed by the dogs, the duck gave one final quack, then waddled back toward the lake.

Sloan whistled, and Juliet and Dozier charged the house. "I'll get dog food, bones, beds, and toys tomorrow. Tonight you feast on leftover roast beef," he told them.

He flipped off the lights, locked the back door, and went as far as hooking the chain. He didn't want Eve to fear a duck invasion later that night.

They all moved to the kitchen. Retrieving the roast from the refrigerator, he sliced off several generous chunks and delivered them in two soup bowls, with a side of water.

"Do you cook?" Eve eyed the side of rare beef.

He ducked his head as he returned the roast to the refrigerator. "Not well."

"A neighbor took pity on you?"

She read the situation well. He could lie, tell her he'd bought the meat at the deli. Yet lies always came around and bit him in the ass. He'd lose her trust. Truth mattered most to Eve.

"Kallie Ward, two doors east, cooked dinner for me last night. She delivered the meal in a tight little red sundress. When I didn't invite her in, she left. Kallie's going through a divorce. Her kids are grown. Her husband of twenty-five years moved out. She's still cooking for two. I got her husband's portion."

Eve leaned against the back of the sunroom couch. "That's a lot of information."

"I want everything out in the open. No secrets."

She nodded.

And Dozier burped, a doggy belch from eating too fast. Juliet finished shortly thereafter.

Eve glanced at her watch. "It's late." She straightened and took her first step to leave.

Juliet sensed her departure and whined.

"The dogs would probably sleep better with you in the house," suggested Sloan. "Your presence would give them a sense of security."

"Security, huh? Me, who dives behind you, afraid of a duck?"

"Stay, and I'll protect you."

Still she hesitated. "Where would I sleep?"

"Your choice of the four bedrooms," he offered. "Although only one has a bed."

To sleep or not to sleep with Sloan McCaffrey; that was the question of the night. Eve craved him with an intensity that made her body ache.

She'd tried to act blasé as Sloan had shown off his home—an incredible house that made her feel safe, despite the sudden appearance of the duck.

235

She wanted to walk up those stairs with all the confidence of a woman in charge of her sexuality, yet shyness overtook her.

"Eve?" Sloan looked as uncertain as she felt.

"I'm willing, but my feet won't move."

He came to her then, tall and broad shouldered, his gray gaze hot as gunmetal, his body already showing his need for her.

He caught her beneath the knees and lifted her high against his chest. The dogs barked, believing this was a new game, and they wanted to play too.

Sloan carried her up the curved staircase. He stopped several times and kissed her, deep and French and with the promise of spectacular sex.

Dozier darted ahead of them into the master bedroom.

Juliet made a daintier entrance.

"The dogs need pillows," Eve breathed against his chest once Sloan set her on her feet.

Sloan whipped two seat cushions from a short contemporary sofa that sat beneath the wide arc of the bedroom windows. He dropped them on the floor and patted each. "Good night, sleep tight," he told the dogs.

Juliet settled sweetly onto one cushion.

Dozier eyed the bed.

"No way, pal," Sloan told him.

With a snort, the bulldog tucked himself beside the Jack Russell.

Eve also looked at the bed. A bronze-and-brown comforter covered the king-size mattress. Dark chocolate satin pillowcases rested against the headboard.

Sloan dimmed the lights, then moved in behind her. He curved his arms about her waist and pulled her back against him. His broad body framed her own. The prominent ridge of his sex pressed the small of her back. His strength dominated. His desire titillated

He held her for a long, long time.

The conjunction of man and shadowed bed was as potent as foreplay. Eve drew his hands to the buttons on her linen jacket, ready for him to undress her.

He took his time with her.

The slide of the pearl buttons through the fabric slits was smooth and sensuous.

The roll of the linen off her shoulders was seductive.

A cream camisole lay between his palm and her skin. When he rested his hand on her breast, her nipple rose to meet him—a nipple that puckered with the faint brush of his thumb.

Pleasure shot low, dampening her panties. A flick of his wrist, and her lace cami vanished. She stood naked to the waist.

Eve didn't care how many women had come before her; she lived only in the moment, reveling in the heat and rapid pulse of Sloan McCaffrey.

The man made her moan, squirm, want him.

He concentrated fully on her breasts, dedicating himself to making her shudder. Taut and tingly, she rose on tiptoe, her back arched, as he drew her out of herself and into him.

She needed his kiss.

Turning in his arms, she sought his mouth. He kissed her with penetrating thoroughness.

Her hands worked off his shirt.

He was all tight skin and straining muscle.

She kissed his collarbone, his male nipples, and straight down his happy trail. She unbuttoned his slacks and took down his zipper. She tucked her fingers into his waistband, gave one tug, and his slacks and boxer briefs soon circled his calves.

He heel-toed his boots, then sidestepped. Fully naked, he epitomized pure male beauty. She could paint this man, Eve realized. He was symmetrically perfect.

She bent to kiss his belly, which was flat and cut.

Then she dropped to one knee to nip his hip bone.

He was fully erect, long and substantial.

She licked his length, flicked the tip with her tongue.

Sloan's knees gave out. Curving his hands over her shoulders, he drew her to her feet. "Too much too soon, sweetheart. You're killing me."

He then went on to kill her.

Off came her skirt; her panties followed. Her nerves skittered as he stripped her to the skin. His touch was deliberate, sensitive, knowing. Her body pressed against his, soft with desire. He reflected her need with white-hot arousal, shared silky, dark whispers, anticipation and wild heartbeats. Eve blushed at her own boldness—and Sloan encouraged her fantasies. He soon pulled her down on his bed. She spread herself over him.

"You want to ride like the rodeo." There was a smile in his kiss as he stroked his big hands down her spine. He cupped her bottom, ran his thumbs along the crease. Then, squeezing her hips, he lifted her until she straddled his thighs. "Forward or reverse, cowgirl?" he asked.

Eve's heart skipped, and her breath caught. Her hands flattened on his chest. Heat steamed between their thighs. "Forward . . . first."

His chest rose and fell. "Reverse makes great seconds."

She bit her bottom lip. "You don't mind my experimenting?" She felt safe and daring with this man— uninhibited and unafraid.

"Have your way with me."

Yet before he let her ride, he withdrew a condom from the top drawer of his bedside stand. He ripped the foil with his teeth, and Eve rolled it on.

He then relinquished control.

She rose onto her knees, positioning herself to take him. Inch by deliberate inch, she settled back until he was fully embedded. He filled her, thick and throbbing. A rock of his hips told her to ride.

She dominated the movement: slow, then fast, then slow again, until his breathing jerked and his muscles went taut.

The slight rolling of her hips made him sweat. His jaw clenched and his eyes glazed over. He squeezed her thighs, a plea for action.

Her own thighs tightened as she rose until she was barely holding him inside her. She squeezed her inner muscles, then lowered herself with a satisfying little twist.

She swore Sloan's eyes rolled back in his head.

"I'm dying here," he gasped from deep in his throat.

She let herself go. Her increased rhythm buried him completely.

Sloan whispered, coaxed, helped direct her hips with his hands. His moan of heightened pleasure shot through her, driving her higher.

They were both suddenly there.

Both stiffening.

Both shattering.

Both mindless, boneless, replete.

She collapsed on his chest.

Their breathing was heavy in the stillness.

Her cheek rested over his heart. She could hear its loud beating. She'd worked Sloan McCaffrey's body to satisfy her own. The man looked very much taken.

He lazily stroked her back. "Lady, you can rodeo."

Eve felt the heat of a full-body blush.

"Don't be embarrassed." He squeezed her arm. "Experiment all you want in my bed. Here's where you can let go and get your buzz on."

*Buzz on* came with the reverse cowgirl.

Her back was to him when she heard a drawer open. The flick of the switch got her full attention. The sound alone took her to the edge. The touch of the vibrator sent her over.

Eve played with Sloan and his sex toys long into the night. They laughed, moaned, did each other dirty.

She wakened to Dozier's whimper. The dogs needed to go out. Eve quickly slipped on her panties, then snagged Sloan's cobalt blue shirt from the floor. The knit held his scent, pine and male, and stretched almost to her knees.

As quietly as possible, Juliet, Dozier, and Eve sneaked out of the bedroom. The click of the dogs' nails sounded homey on the hardwood floors. When Juliet hesitated at the top of the stairs, Eve carried her down.

She unlocked the back door and let the dogs out. The chain-link fence ran wide and long, bordering the lake. She stood in the doorway and scouted for Quackers.

The duck was nowhere to be seen.

Her childhood fear was silly. Yet she had no desire to face off with the mallard.

While the dogs sniffed and wandered, Eve moved to the kitchen. In little time she'd made coffee. A cinnamon bun caught her eye in the bread box.

A mug of coffee and the sweet roll in hand, she walked into the living room. There she sneaked a peek from the front windows. Sheers and sandstone-colored cotton covered the French-cut glass. The street was quiet, the neighborhood not yet awake. Several new homes still sat empty.

A rolled newspaper caught her eye. Thrown, it had landed near the front tire of her Saturn. Surely she could crack the door, run out, grab the paper, and return without anyone seeing her. She decided to risk it.

Her decision was a poor one, Eve soon realized. She should have set down her coffee and roll and had both hands free when she went for the paper. Instead, both were full when Quackers stormed the driveway.

He came at her with wings spread and an earsplitting quack.

Eve went so light-headed, she saw dots before her eyes. Fear froze her feet. The duck was going to bite her. . . .

Sloan McCaffrey stretched his arms across the bed. Eve's scent lingered, soft, sweet, sexy as hell. A smile broke behind his yawn. The woman had fantasies. Last night they'd been played out to the fullest. She had ridden him dry.

He'd be hard-pressed to get it up until he'd had a protein shake and some scrambled eggs.

He pushed up and found himself alone. Surely Eve hadn't kissed him off and left. Rising naked, he scratched his belly, then moved toward the windows to see if her car remained in the driveway.

Car, Eve . . . *duck*. All three were in the drive.

Eve stood pale, barefoot and statue-still as the mallard circled close, seeming to want whatever she held in her hand. A sweet roll, Sloan realized. The duck wanted her breakfast.

*Shit fire!* He grabbed a pair of running shorts from a dresser drawer, tugging them on while taking the steps. He made it to the door just as Eve tore off a bite of cinnamon bun and tossed it to Quackers.

The mallard snapped it up and demanded more.

Eve took a step back, and the duck waddled forward.

She quickly tossed more roll.

Quackers stopped, ate, ruffled his feathers.

Sloan was about to shoo the duck from the driveway when Eve took charge of the situation. "A bite for you and a bite for me," she told the mallard.

Her hands shook as she split the last of the sweet roll with Quackers. She took a sip of her coffee and swallowed hard.

"You okay?" He came up behind her.

He heard her sniff and saw the tears that had collected in the corners of her eyes, yet she managed a nod.

Openly annoyed that there was no more food, Quackers took off for the sprinklers that had gone off in the neighbor's yard. Sloan and Eve watched as the duck cleaned himself and preened beneath the spray.

Eve sighed, and Sloan pulled her back against him.

"You were brave." He dropped a light kiss on the soft curve below her ear. He raised goose bumps on her neck, and fought a grin that he'd turned her on.

She leaned heavily against him. "I stood up to a duck."

"And lived to tell about it."

"You're making fun of me."

He nuzzled his jaw against the top of her head. "We all get scared for different reasons."

"What scares you, Sloan McCaffrey?"

"That you might leave and not come back."

She turned in his arms, facing him full on. "You gave good rodeo. You're worth another ride."

Relief ran bone-deep. He said what he'd been considering from the moment she'd entered his home. "Move in with me, Eve."

She blinked. "Live . . . here?"

"Would it be so bad?"

"I couldn't think of anything better."

Sloan relished the moment as he stood in the sunshine in the middle of the driveway with his barefoot Eve. His knit shirt touched her knees. He was certain she wore panties, but her breasts felt soft and free.

He wanted to feel her, yet waited until they returned to the house to do so. Behind closed doors, he touched and teased and took her against the entrance wall.

He liked breaking in different rooms with this woman. The house was big. There'd be a lot of sex.

Only after they'd sagged to the floor did Sloan realize Eve had forgotten her newspaper.

And he'd gone without a condom. It was time to marry this woman.

"You want to marry me?" Eve stared at Sloan McCaffrey across the dining room table, uncertain whether she'd heard him correctly.

The Rogues had won their home series against the White Sox, and Sloan had celebrated with Chinese take out and a square velvet box.

Eve remained perfectly still. Chopsticks crossed her plate, and the fortune in her cookie went unread as the princess-cut solitaire winked at her.

Nerves gripped her. Three weeks had passed since she and the dogs had settled into Sloan's home. The move had been comfortable and easy, the sex phenomenal.

His proposal should have reassured and excited her, yet doubt made her cautious. She licked her lips. "Why now?"

"Why not now?" he returned. "Should I have waited for Christmas or your birthday?"

"Now works; just tell me why."

The *why* seemed to confuse him. She nudged just a little. "People marry because they're compatible . . ."

"We have plenty in common. We both like rodeo."

"For financial reasons. . . ."

"I don't need you as a tax write-off."

"They want to have kids."

"Are you pregnant?"

There was a little too much hesitancy in his tone. She now understood what had prompted his proposal. Sloan had taken her in the entryway that first morning without a condom. He wanted to be honorable.

Eve handed him his get-out-of-jail-free card. "I don't need a condom to protect me, Sloan. I'm on the pill."

He rolled his shoulders, reached across the table, and took her hand. "I want children. Lots of them. But I'd like time to spoil you first."

"Why me?" She needed the words.

"I'm into tight-ass blondes."

"More," she insisted.

He skimmed her wrist with his thumb. "I love the scent of your shower gel, the slick sweetness of your skin when the steam clears. You look good in my T-shirts. You stand up to ducks. You're an amazingly gifted artist. I enjoy watching you paint." He squeezed her hand. "Most of all, I love listening to the evenness of your breathing right before I fall asleep. You bring me peace."

She went soft inside.

He'd said all the right things; she owed him as much. "I love watching you play with the dogs. The way you get down on your hands and knees in the backyard and don't worry about grass stains. I love how you hand-wash my car instead of running it through the car wash. How you send me flowers from Cincinnati and Minneapolis when you're on the road."

She sighed. "You set my spirit free and let me be daring. Nothing compares to your tucking the comforter beneath my chin when you think I've fallen asleep, right before you lift Dozier and Juliet onto the bed."

"She knows," Sloan whispered to the dogs sprawled beneath the table. "Who spilled our secret?"

"I woke up one morning to Dozier's dog breath."

"Boy could use a Tic Tac." He edged his chair closer to hers, admitting, "I've wanted you from the moment I walked into Thrill Seekers. Eventually my heart got into the game."

"I thought you wanted Taylor."

"Taylor was a knee-jerk reaction. She belongs with Brek Stryker. You're the sister that I want for the rest of my life."

"What about your holiday trip? Do you still plan to ski La Grave?" From the moment she'd met him, she'd feared for his life. The mountain was dangerous. She wanted Sloan all in one piece.

"I could be persuaded to cancel my trip."

She convinced him three times before midnight.

The man would be home for the holidays.

He coaxed her into a Christmas wedding on her last orgasm. He hadn't let her come until she'd agreed.

They'd gone on to spoon, their sleep soon deep.

Morning stole into their bedroom much too early for Eve's liking. She'd turned during the night, and now faced Sloan. She delicately traced his features with a fingertip: wide forehead, dark brow, square chin. And gray eyes, now half-veiled, as he watched her watch him.

"You look serious," she said. "Mental preparation for today's game?"

"Today could be my last start," he told her. "Stryke comes off the disabled list tomorrow. The Rogues have a five-man rotation. Chances are good I'm back to being a reliever."

She massaged the strain from his temple. "Maybe Guy Powers will go to a sixth rotation."

"Maybe Dozier won't pass gas under the covers."

Eve couldn't help laughing. "There's always the off chance. You're good at what you do, Sloan. Prove yourself worthy."

Beneath a September sun, Sloan McCaffrey played his ass off against the Milwaukee Brewers. He wanted to start, and he needed Powers to know how badly. He tried to stay loose and shake off his doubts, but his body tightened with each pitch.

His shoulder felt metal-hinged by the third inning. And his elbow was cranky.

"Oil for your joints, Tin Man?" asked Psycho as he passed Sloan on the way to the dugout.

Sloan shot Psycho the bird from inside his glove.

He took his place at the end of the bench, away from the other players. Solitude was a pitcher's friend. Alone, he had time to think. He needed a plan of attack.

"Exhale, McCaffrey, or you'll turn blue. Blue isn't your color."

The words came from Brek Stryker as he dropped down beside Sloan. Brek had dressed out, and now watched the game from the dugout instead of the bullpen.

"Congrats on your engagement," Brek continued. "Taylor spoke with Eve before the game. Big ho-ho, man."

Christmas vows. An image of a very naked Eve at the moment of agreement colored Sloan's mind. He'd held her on the verge of climax, her face flushed, her breasts raised, her pelvis barely restrained, until she'd said yes.

Brek smiled. "Knew I could get you to relax."

"Eve does it for me."

"I know the feeling."

The frenzied sound of the crowd made Sloan crane his neck. Kason Rhodes now stood in the batter's box.

Sloan and Brek counted pitches.

Rhodes swung on two fastballs and got called on strikes. He dug in, gaze narrowed, nostrils flared.

"Three hundred twenty feet?" Sloan bet Rhodes would slam the baseball over the right-field wall.

"Four twenty-five," Brek countered. "He wants center field bad."

Rhodes got center. He smacked the shit out of the ball, then took the bases at an all-out run.

"The man plays for keeps," Sloan begrudgingly admitted.

"Take a page from his playbook," Brek stated as he pushed to his feet. "Loosen up, McCaffrey. Stop playing like you're afraid to make a mistake."

Sloan went seven innings, allowing only one run.

The Rogues led by four when he took to the locker room.

He iced his elbow, then watched the remainder of the game with the trainer, Jon Jamison.

Victory carried the team on an adrenaline high. The win ranked them first in the National League East. They were the team to beat. Their eye was on October.

Pitching coach Danny Young caught Sloan on his way out. According to Young, Brek Stryker had put in a good word on Sloan's behalf. The coach had listened. A six-man rotation started tomorrow.

Sloan threw back his head and roared his good fortune.

It was Christmas in August.

*Ho-frickin'-ho.*

# CHAPTER FIFTEEN

"Addie and Edwin Sweeney have announced their engagement. They're getting married at Thanksgiving," Taylor said as she clicked off her cell phone. She looked up at Brek, tall, solid, and all male. His power and strength never ceased to amaze her. "Followed by Eve and Sloan at Christmas."

Brek snagged a towel off the workout bench, where he'd been pressing weights. He yanked off his T-shirt and wiped sweat from his face, chest, and under the waistband of his athletic shorts. "Women and their holiday weddings."

"Valentine's is ready-made for a wedding," she suggested. "Hearts, flowers, chocolate, romance."

"Too much fuss. Big weddings take away from what's important," he countered. "You need no more than the bride and groom, a justice of the peace, and the intent to go the distance."

"Distance"—she met his gaze—"was never my strong suit."

He sent her a halfhearted smile. "You're telling me?"

Brek had known her at her worst.

She was a better person because of him.

They needed to talk. Now was as good a time as any.

Brek returned to the rotation today, his first outing since his injury. He'd broken his self-imposed silence, requesting that Taylor keep him company during his morning workout.

It was do or die today. Taylor needed to move beyond the gray area of their relationship. They'd lived together for three months now. They'd danced around their future, yet made love like there was no tomorrow.

Addie's phone call had pushed Taylor out of her comfort zone. Did Brek see them as a couple or as a man and a woman soon to part ways?

She straddled the stationary bike in a hot-pink belly shirt and low-rise jeans. Her shoulders were stiff, her spine straight. She'd always been blunt and bold, yet today fear claimed her. She had no control over Brek's feelings. He hadn't said he loved her. She couldn't predict the outcome of their conversation.

Maybe she should leave things alone.

Maybe she should let Brek make the first move.

Maybe—

"Talk to me, Fearless?" he asked, using her nickname. Dropping to the mat, he began a set of stomach crunches. "You've gone dead air on me."

Now or never. She went with now. "I ran us through my mind and found a lot of blanks."

He slowed his crunches. "What blanks do you need filled in?"

"Future blanks."

He tucked his head against his chest, deepening his curls. Two hundred later, he rolled to his feet. He was mildly sweaty, his muscles pumped.

He flexed his arm and fingers, waiting for the energy current that made his fingers tingle. He smiled at the rush of circulation.

He massaged his palm, then looked at her. She sensed him shutting down. "What future, Taylor?" he asked.

She played it light, but her heart was heavy. "We're both recovered from our injuries. I thought you might like your space back. You're neat. I'm messy. My undies drape the shower rod, my shoes and clothes live outside the closet, and I forget to make the bed." She sighed. "I'm not part of your lifestyle, Brek. Say the word, and I'll pack."

A hardness etched the corners of his eyes. "Is that what you want?"

"I want what's best for you."

He ran his hand through his hair and blew out a breath. "I'm stuck in the moment," he finally admitted. "I can't go back; yet forward brings me full circle."

Full circle meant loving her again.

His leap of faith stopped at the cliff's edge.

She understood his reservation. He wasn't ready for her. Might never be ready for her.

Restlessness stirred her soul.

She'd wanted his proposal.

He'd passed on their relationship.

Pain speared and split her in two.

How many times could a heart break and still beat? she wondered. Maybe this time she'd go completely numb. Feelings were overrated, she decided.

"We came together broken, and we're walking away healed," she managed. "Dr. Harper's released me to the bunny hills. There's fresh powder in Portillo."

"Chile . . ." His expression shifted; his game face was on. Indifference shadowed his eyes. "You're catching a flight, and I'm starting against the Raptors."

Their silence stretched into forever. Neither wanted to look away, yet they both knew their time had come to an end—a very sad, soul-numbing end.

It was Taylor who slapped her hands against her thighs, then hopped off the stationary bike. "I need to make plans, run my schedule by Eve."

Brek shook his head. "You've never adhered to a schedule in your life. You're free-spirited, Taylor. If it feels right, do it. Make yourself happy. It's the only way you'll survive."

She drew what seemed her last breath, licked dry lips. "You won't ask me to stay?"

He shook his head. "If I were to ask, you'd have to answer. Your last response came from New South Wales. Long-distance relationships never worked for me."

Tears pressed her eyelids. She blinked them back. "I love you, Stryke." She might not have another chance to tell him. "I hate the fact that I ever hurt you. But I hurt myself too. Leaving you was my biggest mistake. You're my only regret."

She clutched her hands behind her back to still their trembling. "You may not break records this year, but there's always the next. You're the most talented pitcher to come along in decades. There's no one better."

"You're the thrill seeker who makes hearts race," he replied. "No one downhills like you do. You white-water raft, mountain climb, dare incredible odds, and live to tell about it. You're a battery pack of energy. And utterly fearless."

She was scared spitless. She hated feeling alone and vulnerable. Hated being at this crossroads of her life without signs to direct her course.

Only after the silence grew oppressively long, and words failed them both, did Taylor approach Brek.

She stared at him, holding on to the moment.

He bent and kissed her.

She kissed him back as if it were the last kiss of her life.

251

Tears fell as she flicked her wrist in farewell, the saddest good-bye ever.

She remained alert to Brek's voice should he call her back. Disheartening silence followed her out the door.

Late-afternoon rain was forecast. Clouds gathered dark and gloomy, a mirror of Brek Stryker's mood as he warmed up in the bullpen prior to the game.

"Hand looks strong." Sloan McCaffrey stood against the fence. "Good surgeon. Dedicated rehab."

Rehab. The squeeze. Brek's frustration with the rubber ball, followed by the pleasure of Taylor Hannah's breast. She'd brought new meaning to recovery. Her breast had filled his palm, soft and pliant. He'd squeezed and kneaded, and his hand had healed.

He broke into a sweat.

And the baseball rolled out of his glove.

He gave his head a clearing shake.

"Thanks for getting me into the rotation." Sloan retrieved the ball and tossed it back to Brek.

Brek refused the credit. "You earned it."

Sloan shaded his eyes with his hand, scanning the third-base line. "Addie, Edwin, and Eve are in the stands today. They're supporting your comeback."

"Taylor?" he had to ask.

Sloan couldn't meet his eyes. "Eve mentioned snow and Andean slopes. Taylor pulled her skis, booked a flight."

She was gone. Again.

Brek knew the truth: Taylor needed her freedom. Had she opened her heart to him, she'd have found an eternity of space. His forever would have allowed her to travel, to seek thrills, to know where to find him when she tired of hotels and adventures.

She belonged with him.

Maybe he should have requested that she stay. Yet he'd wanted her to remain without his asking. That was the only way he'd ever know she truly loved him.

She was halfway around the world by now.

He was off his game.

An aimless emptiness settled deep. He felt gutted to the core.

Taylor continued to cross his mind at the most inopportune moments. Her memory was so alive, he could reach out and touch her.

His uneasy state of mind seemed to be echoed by his teammates'. His concentration lagged, and defense played in slow motion. The outfield made errors. The Ottawa Raptors loaded the bases with two line drives and a walk. Their top hitter now stood in the batter's box.

That was when catcher Chase Tallan called time and trotted toward Brek. Pitching coach Danny Young followed. A conference was held on the mound.

"How's your hand? Need relief?" Young asked, concerned.

Brek flexed his fingers.

His hand was in good shape.

It was his heart that hurt like hell.

"I'm in it for another inning," he told Young.

"You do know the bases are loaded?" Chase demanded.

Loaded, with no outs. Brek still had fight left in him. He had to dig deep and find it. He nodded to Chase, and the catcher jogged back to home plate. Danny Young returned to the dugout.

Brek Stryker inhaled. Exhaled. Focused.

He couldn't let real-life issues interfere with his concentration. The team had too much at stake.

He pulled it together. Found the strike zone.

He retired the next three batters. The fans roared and rocked the stadium.

In the dugout, Kason Rhodes challenged the Bat Pack. "Fifty down the line?"

Psycho's grunt entered him in Rhodes's contest. Whatever Rhodes hit from leadoff, the Bat Pack had to either match or beat. Usually Rhodes pocketed more than he paid out.

Rhodes slapped the first two pitches foul.

"Straighten the son of a bitch out," Brek heard Psycho growl from down the bench. Psycho didn't mind paying out when it benefited the team.

Rhodes straightened it out, all right. He airmailed the ball to the nearest post office, then rounded the bases at a dead run.

Rhodes jabbed a finger at Psycho on the on-deck circle. "Match it."

Brek shook his head. Rhodes stood on the outside looking in. He wasn't accepted, but nor was he ostracized. He just hadn't yet found his fit with the organization. He taunted Psycho. And Psycho went for Rhodes's throat.

Yet they played together to win. The Rogues led their division. They ranked first in the National League East. Winning was everything to these men. They wanted home-park advantage in the playoffs.

Brek watched as Psycho powered a hit deep into center. The ball hit the wall and gave him a triple.

Rhodes's smirk drove Romeo Bellisaro to bring Psycho home. Romeo jacked the ball into the upper deck in left field.

The Rogues led three to nothing.

Chase Tallan didn't fare as well. He went down on strikes, as did the next two batters.

Top of the fifth, Brek rolled his shoulders and stood, ready to return to the mound. He'd hit the first step when he heard Romeo say, "Mascot brawl. Rappy's the meanest mascot in the league. The bird's on the third-base line taunting Rally Ball again."

"Word got out that Charlie Bradley has the flu," Risk Kincaid said. "Rappy's making fun of Charlie's upset stomach and frequent trips to the john."

"Where's security?" asked shortstop Zen Driscoll. "The Raptor needs to be bounced."

Brek looked at the mascots. Rappy's long plastic bird toes now tromped Rally's oversize blue sneakers. There was pushing and shoving, and significant ball butting.

For a man not feeling well, Charlie was holding his own. He wasn't backing down. He was all steam and jab.

Rally Ball kicked out, connecting with the Raptor's shin. Rappy flapped his wings and hopped about on one big bird foot.

The Raptor then swiped his wing at Rally's knees.

Rally Ball jumped and cleared the feathered wingtip.

Risk lifted a brow. "Charlie can't jump. Man's got bad ankles."

"Bad ankles, girlie thighs," Psycho observed as he slipped on his sunglasses. "Bradley needs to bulk up."

*Girlie thighs.* Brek narrowed his gaze on Rally. His heart slammed so hard it jarred his entire chest.

Taylor Hannah had hopped a flight for Chile. No way could she be on the field, blocking punches, displaying fancy footwork, and going after Rappy with a vengeance. It just wasn't possible.

The mascot scuffle brought the crowd to its feet.

Rappy got in one good wing slap, and Rally Ball wobbled and nearly went down. The Rogues' mascot lost a sneaker. Rally's foot was narrow, the fuzz ball's toes painted red.

"Kinky, Charlie," Psycho commented.

Brek's entire body seized.

*Taylor.* Déjà vu pressed him to move and move fast. He cut through his teammates and charged to Rally Ball's defense.

Risk Kincaid had his back.

Taylor didn't need their help. By the time the men arrived, she'd belly-butted the Raptor and climbed onto his big, wide feet. Her momentum knocked the bird flat on his back.

The two mascots hit the ground rolling.

Taylor was first to rise. She placed one sneakered foot on the Raptor's wing and held the bird down. She raised her arms in victory.

The fans went ballistic.

Beer and soda sprayed. Popcorn hit the air like confetti. Whistles and war whoops shrieked like sirens.

"Way to go, champ," Risk congratulated her.

Security arrived, and Taylor released the Raptor.

"Charlie is not a puke face," she hissed as the bird was led away. "Brek Stryker does not throw like a girl."

"I'll leave you two alone." Risk stepped aside.

Alone amid a crowd of eighty thousand.

Brek tuned out the noise and focused on Taylor Hannah. The mascot's roundness pressed against him, sweet and intimate. And very fuzzy.

The eye slits revealed Taylor's sea green gaze, soft and hopeful. "I came back," she told him.

"So I see. You and Rappy put on quite a show."

He caught her smile. "I kicked Raptor butt. No one bad-mouths you or Charlie."

"You've always stood up for just causes."

"That's why I'm here, Stryke. To stand up for us."

His breath locked in his chest. *Us.* The word conjured up others: couple, family, permanence. "What about Chile?"

"I never made it to the airport," she confessed. "James River Stadium held more appeal than downhill. I called Charlie Bradley and asked if I could be Rally. He said he was sick and that I could take over as soon as I arrived at the park."

He leaned in and briefly captured Taylor's lips through the mouth slit, sealing her homecoming.

Cameras flashed—big, blinding flashes. His moment with Rally was captured for all time. He didn't care. He'd locate a reporter after the game and give an exclusive on himself and Taylor, his soon-to-be wife.

Risk Kincaid tapped his shoulder. "Home-plate umpire's called delay of game. Go be Rally, Fearless. Stryke's needed on the mound."

"Mascot love won't beat Ottawa." Kason Rhodes tossed Brek his glove as he headed for left field. "Can we have our pitcher back?"

Taylor touched Brek's arm. "Mascot lounge, seventh inning?"

Brek agreed. Quickly, he wrapped up the fifth inning: three men up, three men down. Consecutive outs followed in the sixth and seventh. He then retreated to the locker room.

He called to the trainer, indicating that he'd ice his shoulder and hand shortly. Within seconds he stood outside the mascot lounge, the place where he'd first confronted Taylor. It was now where he'd commit his life to her, this time for keeps.

He wanted her as much as he wanted a career in baseball. Scoring with her was as important as breaking National League records.

The records could wait.

Taylor could not.

He entered the lounge, only to find the room empty. The fuzz ball lay in a heap in the middle of the floor, the long-sleeved striped shirt, tights, and blue sneakers shed on the way to the shower. A discarded navy bra and matching boy shorts were visible through the crack of the bathroom door.

Brek secured the main lock, then stripped off his Rogues uniform.

The sound of running water drew him to Taylor.

He joined her in the shower. The water ran hot, a sauna for their bodies. The haze of steam played off her nipples and teased her hip bones as the water streamed over her breasts and slipped between her legs.

He wanted to do the same.

They came together, gifted with a fresh start. They planned to make every second count.

He shampooed her hair. She lathered shower gel all over his body. And sex became slippery.

They clung all the tighter.

Their hearts pulsed and their kisses reached.

Because he had no protection, Brek limited himself to a whole lot of touching. Their hands worked each other's bodies until both could barely stand.

The mounting tension drew Taylor up on tiptoe. She let herself go the exact instant Brek's hips pumped his release.

Shortly thereafter, they leaned against the shower wall, facing each other. The water remained as warm as their final pants of pleasure.

Brek looked at Taylor, a woman liquid from their love-making, a soft smile on her lips. A newfound peace surrounded her. She was exactly where she wanted to be—with him, right now, in the mascot shower.

They stared at each other for a good long while, until the spray ran cold and he turned the water off. He pulled back the shower curtain and snagged two white towels off a stand. He wrapped one about his waist, and Taylor took the second. She slipped it around herself, tucking the ends above her breasts.

Brek leaned against the sink and drew Taylor between his thighs. He took her hands, kissing each palm. "I'm very glad you're back."

She sighed. "So am I."

"I accept your adventures, Taylor," he conceded. "You can continue to guide tours; just call Richmond home."

"I'd like to run Thrill Seekers, but no longer as a guide," she said. "My next adventure comes in planning our wedding. Marry me, Brek Stryker. I want to wear my engagement ring again."

His relief settled bone-deep. "Valentine's Day?"

She kissed him lightly. "The end of this week. No fuss or fanfare. You, me, at the courthouse."

"You're sure?"

"Let me show you how sure."

Taylor Hannah put her adventuresome spirit into thrilling Brek Stryker—in that moment, and for the rest of their lives.